The Woods

John Simmons Short Fiction Award

The Woods

Stories

Janice Obuchowski

University of Iowa Press · Iowa City

University of Iowa Press, Iowa City 52242
Copyright © 2022 by Janice Obuchowski
uipress.uiowa.edu
Printed in the United States of America

Cover design by Derek Thornton, Notch Design
Text design and typesetting by Sara T. Sauers
Printed on acid-free paper

Library of Congress Cataloging-in-Publication Data
Names: Obuchowski, Janice, 1976– author.
Title: The Woods: Stories / Janice Obuchowski.
Description: Iowa City: University of Iowa Press, [2022] |
    Series: John Simmons Short Fiction Award
Identifiers: LCCN 2022010767 (print) |
    LCCN 2022010768 (ebook) |
    ISBN 9781609388751 (paperback; acid-free paper) |
    ISBN 9781609388768 (ebook)
Subjects: LCGFT: Short stories.
Classification: LCC PS3615.B83 W66 2022 (print) |
    LCC PS3615.B83 (ebook) | DDC 813/.6—dc23/eng/20220318
LC record available at https://lccn.loc.gov/2022010767
LC ebook record available at https://lccn.loc.gov/2022010768

Contents

To my parents

The Woods

The Cat

FOR ALMOST TWO YEARS, I've lived at the edge of the bucolic, where the land begins to shift into something untamed, in a tiny neighborhood in the woodsy outskirts of a New England college town. There's a gas station, a church, a tiny brick library, and one exquisitely quaint inn. When I first arrived, for a visiting professorship, a colleague explained that if in town is New York, then outside town—where I live—is Brooklyn. We laughed at this. Brooklyn, if Brooklyn were essentially the woods with a modicum of the suburban, if Brooklyn were populated by sheep farmers and art historians, if it were bordered by woods and, to the east, mountains.

Running down from one mountain is a sinuous, rough river that winds past my apartment, which is on the second floor of what once was, the locals tell me, the old general store. When the weather holds, I sit on my back porch and watch the water—wide and shallow and eddying around large rocks—create its constant cascade. On its far side, the land slopes down, greenery turning to small boulders. On my side, where houses have slivers of backyards, there runs a low concrete wall cracked and patched with moss.

Part of me wishes I could endlessly watch this river, could breathe in the quiet of the surrounding woods, which seems to offer its own watchful stance. The beauty here is dense, disordered, unruly. I almost find it claustrophobic—an encroaching pressure, a constant assertion of some other presence. There's something too in this constant mix of the highfalutin and the feral: it invites thought of the spectral. All experience feels as if on the cusp of some other experience.

Also, acutely, living here is not what I want, because it is purgatory —a job, if a job I'm hugely lucky to have, that runs only two years, that I took in service of the next job I will take, which also likely will be impermanent. This is, of course, a life of my own making. If I wrote more— and better—maybe I could already be settled. Regardless, I've moved four times in the last decade and always while casting my thoughts forward to some future in which I have tenure and live within the comforts of suburban sprawl, in which I have a house with a large yard, a family, and a slobbering dog, in which I have ease and space and security. This constant imagining renders my current life always interstitial, empty.

I am tired of thinking so much.

Soon after I moved, a poet who also teaches at the college and lives nearby invited me to meet her at the inn's pub for a drink. As we sat, surrounded by low light and dark wood and dark green walls, a moose head above the fireplace's mantle, she told me of the Blue Lady, a ghost who haunts the inn. No one knew her past—who she was, where she came from—but she would sit in the far back corner of the inn's dining room, which overlooks a patio. Or, in one of the inn's upstairs bedrooms, she would sit in an armchair by a window. The poet said people who've stayed at the inn have caught, in low light, a blue nimbus in the dim. This when the dining room had been empty and the dark should've been even. Or, upstairs, they've glanced in the mirror above the bureau and seen in the reflection that same subdued aura—the shade of gaslight. In the stories, the woman was drawn and still, her eyes directed always toward the window, as if what preoccupied her was far in the distance.

Occasionally, I go to the pub to grade. I sit in the warm dark, order a glass of wine, and go through a stack of papers. I drink slowly, grade slowly, and feel conscious of myself as alone. In fact, during the winter months, when everything is shadowed by four o'clock, the pub fills in the early evening, and the space is thick with conversation. People stamp their boots as they walk in, their cheeks ruddy from the cold. All sorts come—men with beards down to their bellies sit at the bar and order oysters and beer. Those cheerful after a day skiing, still in their snow pants, their turtlenecks, eat burgers and fries. The crackling fire is luxurious, smoky. It casts dappled shadows everywhere. There is no chance for the Blue Lady to sit, pensive, and stare out to the chilled white. We make no room for her.

But when I return home to my apartment—spacious, if thinly constructed—and I'm surrounded by my large old drafty windows, I reimagine her. On nights the wind rattles the window glass, and cold air picks up inside, gusting and then stilling as if defeated, I think of the Blue Lady flying in and then flitting out again into the night, tossed by winds, careening about, looking for excitement.

Walk far enough in any direction off the main road and the houses thin out, and the woods take over. Wandering the paths in the woods, I've found two small, abandoned quarries—craters with pits of sand that in spring hold thin, still ponds. Someone told me they'd been limestone quarries and that feral cats often live in them. I've yet to see anything there except tall grass and low brush reclaiming the sand. Still, I imagined these cats, light eyed as they prowled the woods, stalking mice through the trees. So when, last April, I came out of my apartment and saw a small gray-brown cat with a chipmunk half in its mouth, I thought it was a feral quarry cat come to hunt along the river.

I was on my way to class. The cat swiveled its head and stared spring-green eyes at me. It spat out the chipmunk and sat swishing its tail as the chipmunk, in a drunken lilt, scurried into a crevice in the crumbling concrete wall. "Cat," I said, not sure what else to say.

When I got back that evening, my downstairs neighbor, Anna, was pacing the sidewalk, talking scornfully into her phone—likely about her divorce—and smoking. Had she not been on the phone, I might've asked her about feral quarry cats. Our conversations are a mix of no information or too much. She's told me she wants to volunteer for the local fire department. I've told her the book I'm writing is going nowhere. We discuss the plum tree growing in our shared backyard.

I'd only met her—and her then husband—a few months before. I'd been washing dishes when the air seemed to crack and then something crashed outside. I'd hurried downstairs to find a huge tree limb, under the weight of new snow, had fallen just beside my car. My neighbor had also come out. She lit a cigarette, and we assessed the situation. No, we couldn't lift the tree limb; no, there was no damage to the car; yes, this was very good luck overall. Snow was everywhere, gray in the evening light. I couldn't place Anna's accent. She said she'd get her husband, a Vermont farm boy, big and strong, and he came out to good-naturedly lug aside the limb. She kissed his cheek, and we stood in the cold and talked a little. Below me, I learned, in essentially the same space I occupied by myself, lived Anna's children, aged twelve and four, Anna—originally from Romania—her husband, her mother, who spoke no English, and an epileptic German shepherd who I mustn't pet lest he get overexcited. I told them I taught writing and suggested we go get brunch one Sunday at the inn, which we all agreed to and then never did. A few months later, her husband was gone. I believe Anna kicked him out. She now had a new boyfriend, who occasionally came around.

I went upstairs. It wasn't warm enough to be out on the porch, but

I stayed in my coat and watched the river—sluggish with chunks of ice slow to thaw even though it was spring. The branches fanning out along the river's edges were stark, empty. The chilled air smelled of cigarette smoke. I wondered whether I'd saved that chipmunk from being eaten, and, if I had, whether I'd deprived that cat of essential sustenance.

A week later, I pulled into the gravel driveway at the side of my apartment. It was dark, and as I was grabbing a bag of groceries from the back seat, the cat emerged, crying, from the shadows of the river wall. Its eyes were neon, a green-white shine. I dropped the grocery bag, then reached down to pick up what had tumbled out—blueberry yogurt, a bottle of wine, brown rice—and the cat began winding between my feet, its fur brushing my calves. "Cat," I said. "You scared me." The cat leapt into the car. "Out, out," I said. "We can't have this." It meowed—a complaint, a protestation—but did jump out. I thought of lice, of fleas. It resumed twining through my ankles. I stepped over it to get to my small side porch—my door separate from the downstairs front entrance—but then put down the groceries to sit on the porch's top step. The cat joined me, sitting on the step below and leaning into my feet. I ran my hand over its head, flattening its ears. I knew nothing of cats. I'd grown up with dogs, who were my heart. It'd been a decade plus of grad school and then adjuncting, a quiet, exhausting hustle, but once I didn't have to move every few years, a dog it would be—one who'd bound across the grass, chasing endless tennis balls. My childhood had revolved around our golden retriever, Max, whose favorite game had been to race to the far corners of our lawn, almost tumbling over himself to snatch the tennis ball from the grass. Then he wouldn't give it back right away, instead prancing in my mother's tiger lilies or flopping briefly in the shade of a weeping willow before rushing once more to the patio, where we'd begin the game of getting him to drop the ball so we could do this all again. My mother has told me that when I was young, I'd play this game with Max for hours, that she'd watch me from the family room window. It made her think, she'd said, how love is a kind of constant patience.

The cat was sprawled on the porch step, rubbing its face against my shoes. I sat listening to the river until my fingers went numb with cold. "Okay!" I said, as if talking to bored students. "I'm going to go in now." I stood, and the cat again began to cry, but as I opened the door, it stopped mewling and lounged silently, its ears a small twitch as it stared toward the concrete wall. I hoped it would go away.

Spring progressed from a constant chill—the lingering sense that ice and snow could, at any moment, reappear—to a lacy branching of green, to white flowers in the woods and glossy, dark ivy running beneath last fall's rotting leaves. Finishing the semester strong preoccupied me—appearing poised among my students and colleagues. I was over prepping, practically memorizing my lecture notes, and spending hours typing up feedback for my students' creative and analytical work. I was writing very little of my own. This was always the problem, but I thought I'd make real progress during the summer. I'm irrationally hopeful about summers. I'll write so many pages, working with such diligence, once I have time.

The cat started appearing every few days. I'd get home, and it would emerge from the bushes or from the neighbor's garage. It might leap down from its sunbathing on the concrete wall. Always it would start meowing, thin and heartbreaking, and make a beeline for my side porch's steps. I'd sit with it awhile.

Early on, I thought to feed it. "Wait right here," I said and trotted upstairs to open a can of tuna. But when I set the fish in a Tupperware container before the cat, it only sniffed. "Better than chipmunk," I said. Eventually, it ate a few tiny bites—pink tongue, tiny, sharp teeth—then flopped at my side and nudged my elbow until I scratched its ears.

I left the tuna out, imagining the cat just wanted space or privacy to eat. But the next day, the tuna was still there, sun warmed and stinking of oceanic rot. I didn't offer the cat more food after that, even though it was thin and, many days, smelled like dirt and excrement. I did buy a big, old-fashioned hairbrush with wide bristles. This way I could scratch the cat's ears and sides without having to touch it. And, if the cat was flopped on its side, then it wouldn't try to crawl on my lap. Still, after the cat sessions, I'd go inside and obsessively wash my hands. I also always threw my clothes in the hamper. I kept meaning to buy a flea collar and then forgetting.

My side porch faces a small house—these neighbors and I are separated by a small patch of land. At the river wall, this couple had set up a rock garden—largely river boulders—that at center has small steps leading to a raised patio of slate tiling. When the weather is decent, they put out matching sky-blue Adirondack chairs. I'd see them coming and going, this husband and wife, but most often I'd notice the husband, Michael, out on his river deck, smoking. He has a thick beard and short-cropped dark hair, and I was seeing him more because I was sitting more often on my stoop, petting the cat with the hairbrush and murmuring to it about my day.

One night, Michael came out while I was telling the cat that in class, while teaching Stephanie Vaughn's "Dog Heaven," I'd become confused about what was my life and what was story. This is never a position you want to be in—much less while standing before a room of college sophomores.

In the story, a woman recalls when she was young, her father in the military and her family about to move from one base to another. Two days before the family moves, they leave their dog with a mess sergeant. This is to be temporary, just until they can send for him. The major uplift in the writing—a piece laden with death and the imagery of death—is when the dog, Duke, breaks free and runs fourteen miles home.

Teaching that day, I kept thinking of the opening image of Duke swimming in a river. The Vermont weather had finally tipped irrevocably toward summer, and people were coming to my river, so I was simultaneously thinking of a woman who'd let her yellow lab wade in up to its belly, panting, grinning, dipping its snout. And then I was thinking of Max, watching his silky sprint into the lawn's back reaches, his silly rustle into the drooping tangle of willow branches. It all blurred. This as I'd been holding a dry-erase marker and discussing foregrounding action.

As I was telling the cat this, I missed the moment Michael came out—I'd been too caught up in having earlier been too caught up. I stopped talking. The cat tried to climb on my lap. "Quit it!" I said and stood. The cat went down the steps, aggrieved, and slid around the side of the house, disappearing after pawing through some lilies of the valley.

Michael's wife, Kristen, emerged from their house—placid oval face, light eyes, enviably thick brown hair. I realized the obvious: she was pregnant. I went over to properly say hello. My instinct was that we—unlike Anna and I—could become friends. Michael stayed where he was with his cigarette but waved to us.

Twins, she said, and she was due any second. She was a nurse, and the technical aspects of her work went over my head, but she seemed to have a lot of expertise. She liked to read and called out to her husband that I taught writing. We talked about books, and she mentioned she'd seen me out running, and—gesturing down to her belly—suggested maybe in a few months we could go out together. I said that'd be great.

"Is that your cat?" she asked. The cat wasn't around, so this meant she'd seen me with it in the evenings. Not my cat, I told her, but it keeps coming by. "It eats chipmunks," she said.

We talked about how soothing the river was, how lucky we were to live near it. This is still my thought most days. It's something—when you feel lost or down—to walk out and face wild, crashing beauty. It exerts some pull on you as it rushes along, all gloss and froth.

The poet who lived down the street was going to Portugal for two weeks and asked whether I wouldn't mind coming by her house to feed her pet bunny. She was going to have a neighbor's child clean out the cage a few times a week, but she'd feel reassured if an adult could stop in too, and it'd be easy: just set out some lettuce or carrots and refill the bunny's water. I said of course.

Before she left, I stopped by so she could show me where everything was, and she mentioned that in her shed a feral cat often hid from the elements—she'd catch glimpses of it snuggled into some old cardboard boxes she'd stored in the back, and so she'd been leaving out tins of wet food. Would I mind putting that out too?

"I have a feral cat!" I said. "It likes being brushed, so I sit outside and brush it." I'd settled on my cat being savvier than other feral cats—more capable of pilfering food and attention before returning to its secret lair in the woods. This was why I never saw any of its brethren.

Her home, an old farm cottage, was tucked into the woods, trees looming over it as if a house in a fairytale. She had a skylight in her kitchen, and I could see pine boughs wavering above.

She was opening a bottle of wine. "I don't think that's a feral cat."

"It's always around," I said. "It runs along the river wall and eats chipmunks. It's desperate for attention."

She asked if I'd named it, and I admitted I hadn't. "I call it 'Cat.' I don't really like cats. But I feel bad for this one."

"I've named mine Winnifred," she said. "But I never see it except in tiny glimpses. Feral cats are normally very skittish. That's why I'm not sure yours is feral."

"Who is it, then?" I asked. "Or what is it?" I accepted a glass of wine, and we went to sit in her living room, which has a fireplace and lovely wood floors.

"Maybe a stray. Perhaps it ran out an open door and got lost. Or someone left it behind."

"I have pictures." I scrolled through my phone, showing her the cat in various states of repose and languor, blissed out from being brushed, sitting on the wooden slats of my side porch. The underside of its chin was white; its whiskers appeared transparent in the sunlight.

The poet laughed. "That's definitely an animal used to people." Her bunny, out of its cage, hopped into the living room, a black fluff ball with drooping ears. The breed was a cashmere lop, I'd just learned. The bunny's nose twitched and twitched. It stared marble eyes at us. "Pamplemousse," the poet crooned. "Here, bunny, bunny." The bunny did an about face and returned to the kitchen—hop, hop, hop—and the poet sighed.

We talked about her upcoming trip to Portugal. She was going to write a poem a day—a poem written that fast would be, pragmatically speaking, mostly junk, but she was hoping she could, through the process, learn her thoughts better as she traveled and explored new settings.

I was still mulling over the cat. Was it not wild? This changed things. "Do you think," I asked, "I should bring the cat to the Humane Society? That maybe someone would want to adopt it if it were a stray?"

"You could adopt it!" she said brightly. She poured us more wine. Her screens were in, and the air smelled of pine and crabapple blossoms. I shook my head, explained that I didn't like cats. "Well, it certainly seems to have chosen you. It's something to think about."

Then we went on to talk of all the writing we'd get done in the subsequent months when the days were long and our academic burdens were light.

On a July night thick with yellow light, the water rushing slipshod over rocks kept me company. I was sitting on my porch, noodling about with my novel, really watching the old grist mill across the river catch the sunset, its colors turning supersaturated: dirty white sidings, a rust roof, and behind it the trees were shadows with gold-burnished leaves. An older man who often mysteriously came and went from that dilapidated old building emerged from the mill's basement. At his side was his corgi, tiny ears, long torso, bright eyes. The corgi trotted to the man's red pickup truck, waiting until the man opened the door to leap in. The truck soon receded down the dirt road, disappearing into the trees.

I needed to finish working on a chapter, but I was thinking of the poet writing a poem a day while abroad, and how, if I did that, then maybe I could better learn my own thoughts about this place. I was missing something in what I witnessed—that something other the landscape was constantly suggesting.

I brought my laptop inside and went downstairs to see whether my cat was about. I scanned the river wall, the rock garden, the tomato plants Michael and Kristen had growing in raised beds. Occasionally, the cat would emerge from the vines, its light eyes watching me. Cricket call had just started. I listened for its meowing as it moved through the grass, announcing its loneliness.

Then I noticed something to the side of my porch, next to a bag of potting soil and the hairbrush. I knelt and felt some thickness in my throat. It was a small dead bird, its neck broken, twisted at an unnatural angle such that it looked to be attached and yet still dangling. It was taupe and brown and white—a striation almost like marble—with a tiny patch of white beneath its small beak. The eyes—round like dark seeds—were open and dull, black smoke within glass.

I went inside. I rummaged beneath my sink for a pair of gardening gloves and a plastic trash bag, steeled myself, returned downstairs. I had to close my eyes when I reached for the bird, which was stiff and soft at once. I put it in the bag, marched the bag to the trash, threw away this gift from the cat. Inwardly, I told the bird I was sorry.

Back inside, I spent time searching through photos of birds on the Vermont Audubon website until I discovered the bird was a vesper sparrow—a beautiful name bequeathed because a naturalist believed its song was heartiest in evenings. The other detail I thought captivating: often it could be found dustbathing in dirt roads, which were everywhere around here. I imagined this bird fluttering low to the ground in a kind of dance, winging up dust, until deciding to arc skyward into blue.

What to do with my own fluttering? My heart, a ragged pulse. Just a dead bird. Just the cat acting as it ought in the wild.

As I went to bed, I decided the bird would perch on the windowsill of the room the Blue Lady haunted. From now on they would be a pair. This, absurdly, finally settled me for sleep.

A few weeks later, I was walking along Grist Mill Road when the corgi came out at a quick trot to greet me. I stooped to pet it, scratching behind its ears, its fur surprisingly rough. The man came around the side of the mill. He had on work gloves and reading glasses. "Thank you," he said, "for being kind to my dog." He told me he'd seen me out running a few times, and I pointed behind me, across the river to my apartment, telling him I lived nearby. "Welcome," he said. I thanked him. I'd lived here a year, but this welcoming made its own sense. I'd finally become habitual in the landscape.

And it was right around then people started waving to me. I'd go for laborious runs through the sparse neighborhoods, a mix of older houses in some state of disrepair and others renovated into country-living pristineness. The mountain loomed in the east, and I'd raise my hand to the sheep farmer, whose farm I'd pass, the field dotted with pastoral woolen creatures; the old couple from Philadelphia who live across the street; the mothers out with their toddlers; the wizened thin woman with her pair of collie shepherds; the rangy runner often heading into the woods to run old logging trails. He told me he sometimes saw a bear back there, but it kept to itself.

Sometimes I'd run on roads out where no one lived, and the foliage —the thick tangle of green on either side—became junglelike in its density. I imagined the trees breathing, me breathing with them. There was constant rustle from within the woods—deer, squirrels, birds. Once, a fox trotted out from beneath a crumbling corner of an old barn. Its eyes were gold, its ears sharp, its fur a bristling orange. It crossed the road and into an orchard. As I passed, it stared from beneath a tree, keeping its sights on me.

Another day, I was kicking up dust, rendering the air diaphanous, and thinking of dust baths, of vesper sparrows, when I saw a bloodied bone on the side of the road. It was as if I'd conjured another animal's death: a joint—with torn fur—and the extended bone, wet looking. Blood dripped in a dark splattered path off into the trees. Dust glittered before me, and I inhaled sharply, trying to sprint.

I returned to my apartment, my cheeks flaming, my breath rough, to find Kristen—who'd had her twins two weeks earlier—on the river overlook. The babies were bundled and asleep on blankets laid out beside the Adirondack chairs. The neighbors from Philadelphia, an elderly couple, were also over. They had with them a bottle of white wine, which the husband was uncorking, and plastic cups. His wife was cooing over the babies. Everyone looked up at once and smiled at me. It was so earnest and sweet and unrelated to my thoughts of gore. I went over and accepted a glass of wine, which went to my head, and told them about the bloodied bone. A coyote or a bear, the couple from Philly said. It happens, it happens. Kristen, tending to her babies, had gray-violet pockets beneath her eyes. She said, "You saw a femur, it sounds like. I bet it's already gone. Animals clean up after themselves."

The next day, I forced myself to run the same loop—to check—and saw only very faint blood splatter. Had I not been looking, I wouldn't have noticed it at all.

Then the downstairs neighbor's epileptic German shepherd disappeared. Or, rather, Anna was no longer taking it out for its short, fraught walks. Meanwhile, she had joined the fire department. I saw her come home one day wearing black pants with yellow piping, a light-blue shirt with ironed-on insignias, a black cap like a policeman might wear. Kristen, in a moment of idle gossip, had told me this was Anna's second divorce, and I wondered how Anna could have so much happening in her life. My instinct was that she acted first, thought later. I couldn't decide if I admired this. Regardless, I hoped nothing bad had happened to her dog. I hoped her ex-husband had claimed ownership, but I couldn't ask.

One night, I was sitting on the stoop with the cat when Kristen came out in her sneakers and yoga pants, her hair in a ponytail. She told me the twins—in a rare moment—were both asleep, and Michael had suggested she get out and enjoy the summer night. She asked if I wanted to join her on a walk. I said I'd love to and stood. The cat batted a paw at the air, protesting my leaving it, but Kristen came over and scratched its ears, and it scrunched up its face in pleasure. Leaving actually got me out of a bind: as the summer had progressed, the cat had taken to rushing between me and the door when I'd try to go in. So I'd have to do this dance, keeping one foot extended to hold the cat at bay as I slid through the cracked door. When we set off, it stayed on my porch, attentive to our movement.

"Michael told me there's this sculpture in the woods," she said. We were moving at an easy pace down the sidewalk. A few kids were biking past the library, shouting to one another about where to go next.

"Sculpture?"

"Past the inn, there's a path in the woods that skirts the river. He said to go back and look."

This street: I knew of two published poets, one professor of political philosophy, and one dean. And I didn't know most people still. So I figured someone from the college, someone in the art department, was amusing herself, perhaps making something out of the abundant stone around here.

As we walked, we talked of how much her life had been upended these last few weeks, how it was exhilarating to feel a love she'd never felt before, but the weariness—a kind of bone-heavy fatigue, as she described it—was also new. She raised her left hand to show me her pinky and ring finger taped together. "A sprain," she said. "I've never sprained anything in my life. And all I was doing was setting Milo in his crib. I'm still not sure how I managed it." Milo and Pearl: the twins. All of a sudden the care for these babies subsumed everything else in her life. And it was not subtle, this love, it was fierce. I listened. I'd never felt this.

We went past the inn and crossed onto a small path in the woods. The sky was milky, thin clouds overhead, and we were in that high tangle of green just going sallow: end-of-summer leaves. They made me anxious, reminding me school was starting soon, that I'd barely accomplished any writing this summer—all I'd imagined for myself had been a bust. The trail was dirt and bounded by rougher forest ground— pinecones and exposed rocks and roots, fallen branches all around. The river, its rough rush, became more present.

"Oh," I breathed, stopping. I pointed. Almost as if it were transparent —a mesh wire figure of a woman: she appeared to be in a long dress, clutching her arms at her elbows, her head raised. She looked there and not. You could come from a certain angle and only see air. Or a bundle of wire. But it was more delicate than that—gothic, gray, sad.

Kristen went up to it and touched the figure's elbow. She shook her head. "Michael said to me, 'You have to see the chicken-wire ghost lady in the woods.' And I told him that was ridiculous, and he said, 'Go look.'" She touched the lady again. "Unreal." She laughed and then covered her mouth with her bandaged hand.

I couldn't touch it, didn't even want to look at it anymore. This place!

I asked Kristen if she thought this figure was the Blue Lady. She'd never heard the story. "I guess I don't think they're the same," she said, after I told her about this other ghost. "But I have no logical reason to say that." The light was going down, a quieting as I thought of it, and then something in Kristen's features shifted. It was as if her face had sagged, her skin loosened in the milky light. But I thought it was a trick of the evening in the woods, and the creepiness of this ghost woman barely there, adding to Kirsten's sleep deprivation. I suggested we get back, and she agreed. "I'm glad I wasn't alone coming upon that," she said. I felt similarly. We came back out after a stretch to the sidewalk near the inn. People were out for walks. We passed a light-blue Victorian home with a white picket fence, an older man out pruning some bushes. It all seemed so normal. And then that skewed too and became strange. The whole world was liminal. When we got home, the cat was nowhere to be seen.

Classes were about to start. The evenings were turning dusky, the sun setting earlier and earlier. I had the cat next to me, its fur too warm against my upper leg, its smell sour. Twice it had tried to climb across my lap, its claws needling my thighs, and I'd pick it up around its middle and set it aside. When I rose to go in, the cat rushed for the door, and this time it slipped through my ankles and darted up the stairs.

It stopped, looking down at me, then turned and wandered into my kitchen. I bolted up the steps and found it prowling my pantry, considering the shelving, the washer and dryer, the entry to the crumbling sunroom.

I could keep this cat, I thought, make it my pet. It wished to be loved more than twenty scant minutes a day. But I also thought of litter boxes, which seemed anathema to me, and this cat jumping on my counters, how my apartment would smell permanently of cat pee. And wasn't it right now bringing fleas and filth into my home, while I was without recourse to handle it? I didn't want a cat. I wanted a dog. I wanted a settled, successful life with a dog.

"Out!" I said. "This can't work."

I picked it up even as it tried to rush away, clutched it to my chest as it yowled and yowled, and marched it downstairs. I set it on the porch. It tried to dart toward the door to get back in. "I'm sorry," I said.

The cat stopped coming around. School began, and being busy was relief and anguish—here was work I felt capable of, as opposed to the constant failure that had been my writing summer. Christmas, I told myself. I'd write then. Plus, now I had to be very diligent about applying for jobs, focused on hoping something would come through.

Kristen hired a nanny and returned to work just as the school year started, so I saw her less, but we waved at the beginnings and ends of days. I wanted to ask her if she wanted to go running, but she had such a full life: working as a nurse and then returning home to so much family. Plus, I'd noticed, the lavender beneath her eyes had yet to fade.

I sat outside some nights, but the cat was nowhere. The cat had returned to its tribe in the woods. Or it had never had a tribe but had found some other sucker to rub its tummy.

Then it got cold. The leaves turned gold and fell, and after they fell we had frost—blades of grass encased in rough white. In November, it started to rain—nights the rain gusted I would sit inside listening to the wind pick up, imagining the Blue Lady also sitting by a window, looking out into the dark, perhaps conjuring her own apparitions out of the night air.

Once I heard a cat calling—less a caterwaul and more a sustained lament. I tried peering out my window, but my lights were on, and I could see only blackness. I turned off my lights and pressed my nose to the glass. The empty sidewalk was lined with bare trees glossy from rain. I went downstairs and stood on my porch, my arms wrapped about my sides. I watched for the bushes to shiver with movement, for some shadow to elongate as the cat soft-footed its way to me in the dark. I listened for its cry but heard only the wind shifting the branches, the rain splattering.

With the winter, my river came to a standstill, its rush and crash buried beneath ice. I spent my days in hypothesis. If there were feral quarry cats, then they had instincts about how to burrow under the snow to keep warm, to build themselves cat igloos, to find the fall's leaves and make from them nests. Or if they were smart as Winnifred was smart, then they found an old shed and took refuge in cardboard boxes, sustained by the tins of wet food left out by nice poets. Maybe the Humane Society was filled with volunteer angels who scoured the town rescuing animals who couldn't survive the winter.

There were days my lungs hurt to inhale the cold. I'd be out cleaning off my car, looking at the trees etched in ice, the snow powder-white, the sky a pale pink-blue. As if the summer had been a dream, some nonreality, and here was ineluctable truth.

I'd killed the cat. It had been out shivering in the woods and then had died. Some other animal had eaten it and scattered its picked-clean bones. They sank into the snow and became hollow. The cat was a ghost now, prowling about the woods with the Blue Lady when the Blue Lady deigned to be earthbound before billowing up on some gust of wind. The cat circled the wire sculpture, but that ghost wouldn't stoop to pet it, guarding its stillness, needing to stay a vanguard in the woods. The ghost vesper sparrow twittered and flapped its wings, shrieking for the cat to go away, go away before it resumed its perch on a windowsill in the inn, rapping its beak against the cold glass for good measure as my cat slunk off into the snow. Even as a ghost, it was alone too much of the time.

Downstairs, Anna's son started throwing tantrums. Seven in the morning was prime screaming time—as if he were a dragon issuing smoke from his nose. Rather than attempt to comfort him or quiet him or do anything at all, Anna would slam the door and stalk about in the cold, pacing in front of her apartment in a bright red parka, smoking cigarettes down to the nubs and flinging the butts into snowbanks. Once, when I was outside shoveling my driveway, she offered me a sharp look, probably thinking I was judging her. I was. The divorce had clearly unsettled her youngest child, but she had to go fight fires and date new men. Where before I'd found her active, I now found her irresponsible.

Of the twenty-five jobs I applied for, I was offered one—teaching in Indiana, a mixture of composition and creative-writing classes. It was a step down from the job I currently held, but my credentials looked static. I hadn't published anything new. The job would last three years with the chance for renewal, but already I knew that, come three years from now, I'd be angling for something else. The winter seemed endless, and yet I quailed at having to move again in six months. At Christmas I got no writing done.

One morning, I ran into the nanny and Kristen as they were getting the twins into the minivan for a doctor's appointment. The nanny was an older woman with no-nonsense short hair and glasses. She rubbed her gloved hands together and exhaled, pluming white breath, then smiled at me so we could agree on the cold. Kristen was snapping the buckle on Milo's car seat. "Put socks on one, and the other has wrestled her socks off," she said, as the nanny got Pearl settled. "Get one into a car seat, the other needs his diaper changed." Circles were still dark beneath her eyes. She asked me how my writing was going. I don't know what possessed me to be truthful, but I told her it had been terrible, that I wanted to throw my novel into the river.

She rummaged in her purse for her car keys, and when she looked up, I saw pity in her light-blue eyes—pity she'd been trying to spare me by first averting her gaze.

"I'm moving to Indiana," I said and started to ramble about how I'd miss Vermont.

Finally, in April, we again had light into our evenings. I bought a space heater—an impractical purchase—and went out onto my porch with it. I watched the ice in the river fracture—crack and float and gain speed—and hunted for the landscape's first traces of green. Squirrels ran along the concrete wall. Dog walkers began to appear, heading down the road to traverse paths in the woods. I thought about how in a few weeks I'd be teaching "Dog Heaven" again. My cat, which I had killed, was nowhere.

I leave in a month. I want to go, I don't want to go. The woods haven't told me their secrets yet. The ghosts are all going to have to keep themselves company, sit together and make up stories about one another. I'm going to be gone and can't continue to do it for them.

This week, downstairs, I heard yipping and high-pitched barking and thought Anna must be taking care of someone's pet. Then, yesterday, I saw Anna's mother, who pretends never to see me when she's puttering in her garden, gripping with both hands a leash. A tiny German shepherd puppy was bounding about in the grass, trying to nip at its tail. Anna's son was sitting on the lawn, banging a plastic shovel against a toy truck. And Anna was smoking some distance from them, under our plum tree. She smiled at me.

Today, out the window, I noticed the nanny had her car's hatchback open. She was sitting in the shade, fanning herself with her book. Kristen was also home. She'd been home more this last month, and I thought she'd finagled herself some time off. Then I saw light eyes peering from the hatchback.

I hurried downstairs. "Hi!" I called. The nanny waved. "Did you notice the cat in your car?"

The nanny set down her book and laughed, a belly chuckle. "No, I didn't notice. But I don't mind. I grew up on farms."

I didn't understand her logic, but that didn't matter. "This cat!" I said. It stared at me impassively and meowed, scrunching up its face and showing me its teeth. "I worried about it all winter. I should've taken it to the Humane Society. I wasn't sure if cats could survive the cold. I haven't seen it since last fall."

She joined me at her car. The cat dimmed its eyes, as if demure in the face of so much attention.

"I would pet it with a brush," I said. "It likes being around people."

"Kristen just told me she finds the cat soothing," the nanny said. "It's only been out again for a few days. Your downstairs neighbors took it in for the winter."

"Really?" The cat had been living downstairs all this time? Anna likely saved its life.

"Apparently some family down the street just let it out one day and never thought about it again. Your neighbor took it to the vet, got it all its shots. But they just got that puppy, and the cat and it aren't getting along. It really wanted out. We just started setting food out for it." She gestured to a small bowl of cat food near Kristen and Michael's front door.

"Is it eating? Last summer, I offered it tuna, and it didn't seem to want it."

The nanny had so many kind lines about her eyes. She was in cargo shorts. She grew up on a farm. "It's eating. All of us are taking care of it," she said.

"It never ate the tuna," I said. "Do you think it would be a good idea to find a family to adopt it?"

She craned her neck toward the river, a suggestion we walk toward the concrete wall. "Kristen said it climbed into her lap today and fell asleep." She pointed to a bird darting one limb to another, its wings a flutter over the water. "Kristen has breast cancer, and whatever comforts her right now is what I want her to have. They've just started telling people the last few days, so it's all right I'm telling you." Her squint said it wasn't, that telling me was a necessity to keep me from carting off the cat. No, no, no, I wanted to tell her. I'm all talk. I'm trapped in my head. It wasn't a feral quarry cat. It was a cat ill-treated by people on this street, and then treated much better by Anna. Meanwhile, I would've let it freeze to death as I thought about ghosts.

"Breast cancer," the nanny said. "She'll beat it for sure. And once things have settled more, I think they'll adopt it."

"Yes," I said. I felt like crying. "I'm sure she'll beat it. I'll leave the poor cat be."

Kristen was ill. Kristen was ill, and Anna was responsible, and the cat was alive, and it had never been a quarry cat. All these details I accumulated, considered, and meanwhile, I didn't know anything at all about what was really happening around me.

What was it that I told myself stories about a dead cat? About my neighbors? About this woods? About my future? I told myself so much, and I was wrong about the world. It was vivid, yes, but a dreamscape—a defense against actuality.

The cat meowed, plaintive, and I reached to scratch its ears. It closed its eyes and purred, asking I cast aside such thinking, and it offered me solace, if I could accept it—rough and low throated and not what I wanted, but what was there.

The Orams

THE ORAM BROTHERS LIVE up the mountain. Head east on the main road until it crosses the river and forks. Take the fork leading into the woods. Take the road less traveled. Don't pat yourself on the back for your poet jokes. That is a false poem, and that poet knew it. For a time, he lived on the mountain too, and when he was grieving the loss of his wife, he would eat cigarettes. Eat them. When he got jealous of another famous writer, he set fire in a trashcan and yelled "fire" so no one would hear the other famous writer read his work. Suffice to say, he knew all roads are not equally fair. The lesser traveled one—the one you take to get to the Orams—is in ruinous shape, filled with ruts and eaten at its edges by the woods.

When that rough dirt road branches again, a brown-and-white sign will say you're on a Green Mountain National Forest road. You are not. Or you are, but that is also false, and once you take this path—tire tracks, really—you'll see another sign saying Bertram Oram Road. This is correct. The Orams go back further than Bertram, but some assertion of self got Bertram the road. This was about one hundred years ago.

Bertram had been a logger, and Bertram Jr. had been too. Bertram Jr.'s two sons, Jasper and Wyatt, work for the inn and act as a night watchman at the college down the mountain, respectively. The boys live on Bertram Oram Road. They are neighbors, and both their homes overlook Oram Brook, which is shallow and meandering and bad for fishing. They claim this brook is named for them. When they say this, we wonder if their wits are still intact, since clearly we know otherwise. We believe this is one of their jokes.

Jasper and Wyatt go in for jokes, which mainly constitute the meanness they wish to inflict on you. Agnes Billings, who runs the inn—which was established one hundred years before Bertram got his road—says she once asked Jasper if he'd cover the front desk while she had lunch with Eustace, her sister down the street. And Jasper said, "Agnes and Eustace: those are names for cows if ever I've heard one." He was wearing a tool belt and had just examined some faulty wiring and wished, Agnes said, to have taken lunch for himself just then. She said, "You no longer wish to work here, Jasper?" He only had the job because she'd been fond of his father, Bertram Jr., who used to play the fiddle for her patrons. Bertram Jr. died of a heart attack when he was just shy of forty-five. His boys have been on their own since they were teenagers.

Jasper has flat gray eyes that only get flatter when you inspect them. He scratched his neck and said, "Agnes, I was joking." He gave a chortle —Agnes's word. Even his laugh was deliberately ugly. But she remembered Bertram Jr. playing quadrilles, even if none of her guests knew how to dance to them. We know how to dance to them, so many of us with French Canadian roots. At summer barn dances Marty Tremblay played mandolin, George Weathers played guitar, Bertram Jr. played fiddle. The barn was full of light and the sweet heady ferment of hard cider and beer. These nights: they helped Jasper keep his job.

No history, the boys claim, and yet history is their only preservation up here.

Likely the Oram brothers got their taste for insularity from their mother, Helena. Hollow-eyed and fretful, she came from a town on the other side of the mountain and then left her boys when they were still little enough to cling to her. We were never fond of her but don't think she left because of the town per se. We think in general she found life too burdensome. Which is an infectious attitude. Bertram Jr. was dead a decade later. And the boys are bachelors who care only for one another. Except even that care has proven fragile.

The poet once complained we took a long time to welcome him. What did he expect? He could write all the poems he wanted about rock walls and snowy woods: noticing well doesn't make you from a place. Yet we think of him fondly. We liked him better once we understood he wasn't just a dignified man of letters playing at rusticity, but a man who battled for what happiness he could grasp and who, on occasion, found the world too much with him. (We've read other poets.) Once he muttered to us he sometimes regarded himself as a joke. This notion of a joke isn't one the Oram brothers would understand.

The poet was a great fan of Agnes and Eustace's mother, Dorothea, who used to run the post office out of her house in a converted room off the kitchen. Back then the US Postal Service insisted post offices display most-wanted posters—pictures of terrible men and women who'd been active in lawlessness and destruction. The poet, who liked to sit at Dorothea's kitchen table, said she should put the posters on the back of the door leading to her back porch. Which is to say: where no one would ever have to see them. We thought this sensible and good. Now we wonder about looking away from ugliness, if there are ramifications for pretending in a kind of constant, essential decency. We will admit: this makes us happier. Also it might make us nitwits.

· · ·

The Galvin Cemetery, out past the elementary school and near where Oram Brook runs into the river, is a green field spotted with the decaying gray beauty of old headstones. This is where the first Oram, Rollins Oram, rests. He was born in 1787 and lived to be fifty-eight. What the cemeteries tell us: there are six generations of Orams. How it feels: the woods have always contained them. But nature's indifference is also its great patience. It will reclaim itself. At the very least, it will claim the Orams. That's what seems to be happening now.

When did the trouble start with those boys? Maybe when Helena disappeared. But we think earlier. And earlier still. For instance, their grandfather Bertram—who got his name on that road—was the last in a line of smugglers.

Down the mountain and due west is a large lake with waterways leading to Canada. And in Rollins's era, smuggling wood became a profitable activity for those with a certain amount of grit and a certain paucity of character. Rollins would, when the weather was fair, travel north with the logs on rafts. When the weather turned bitter and cold, he traveled the lake by sleigh. And down the generations it went until Bertram. By the outset of the twentieth century, smuggling had to have been all but untenable. We think waging a losing fight gave focus to Bertram's life, that it got him the road. Then Bertram Jr., that aberrant, decent Oram man, rejected the practice outright.

And now Jasper and Wyatt can't exercise their ill humors the way their forbearers did, transgressing and profiting all at once. Instead, they have their pranks, which they claim are jokes.

Once when he was a teenager Wyatt got caught stuffing ketchup packets in his pockets while in the McDonald's down the mountain. The manager, George LaCharite—cousin to Nancy LaCharite, who teaches second grade at the elementary school—said he couldn't figure the point. Go steal a bottle of ketchup from the grocery store, he'd suggested to Wyatt. Or buy a bottle? It costs about two bucks. Wyatt, standing by the counter with the plastic forks and napkins, flung to the floor the packets he'd been clutching. He walked out. "Don't come back!" George shouted after him, but felt as if he'd been forced to act in some bad play.

Wyatt eventually admitted Jasper had dared him to steal as many ketchup packets as he could. That absence of subterfuge, though: this doesn't sound like someone trying to successfully navigate a dare. (And can you really imagine such a mind trying to negotiate smuggling?)

Oram Brook intersects a small road that winds in a large loop and has at least three names depending where you are on it. As the road circles closer to the inn, its name is Country Cross Road because apparently our forbearers were, at points, without imagination or smugglers to spur them to greater specificity. And off Country Cross lives Beth Kirby. She works for the state's electricity company. Once she'd lived down the mountain and had gone into an office, but she finagled her way into a telecommuting position and moved back up here. She couldn't bear anywhere with sidewalks: it was all too noisy and loud. She lives in a gussied-up log cabin and goes in for wind chimes and window boxes used to house lavender. She grows shitake mushrooms on a log and then dries them for the winter months, claiming they are medicinal and will let her lead a long and terrific life. She has bright white hair, the envy of all those saddled with a rougher gray. She has a terrier—a tiny white thing named Gretel—who we secretly think of as matching her hair. Beth's house faces Country Cross, a narrow dirt road that, in the drier months, kicks up a lot of dust.

Beth's house is also one Jasper and Wyatt pass every day on their way to work. Jasper and Wyatt, who live in constant tree shade in run-down places with private-property signs tacked to trees, presumably to keep people from the junk in their front yards. As if anyone were considering stealing an empty chicken coop or two old snow tires or some mildewed vinyl siding stacked against a house, a garden gnome with a broken cap one or the other must've thought funny once.

Six months ago, as best we understand it, Jasper and Wyatt were gearing up for deer season—rifle, not bow and arrow, because they have no patience for such things. And they were squabbling because Jasper—two years older—wanted to go higher into the mountain range, while Wyatt wanted to go down the mountain and into some woods south of the college town. One of the other night watchman's uncles owned land with some old orchards on it, which meant herds were likely to be nearby. Jasper went on, though, about the ridgeline where—ten years earlier—he'd bagged a twelve-point buck. He wanted to return there. But he always wanted to return there, was Wyatt's point. Somehow, it did not occur to them they could hunt separately.

Jasper pointed to the deer head mounted on the wall near his wood-burning stove. It was set on a wooden plaque and was glossy eyed and tan, with white fur at its ears and throat. It had ample horns—the graceful twist up as if presenting the outline of a chalice. This was the best deer he'd ever shot. He'd named it Blue Barrow because he'd shot it near Blue Barrow Brook. It stirred in him a sense of a rugged and capable self.

Wyatt acquiesced and that weekend they went up to the ridgeline with a thermos of whiskey and a thermos of coffee, and they watched the sky go from pewter to a foggy white-pink. They shivered and tromped for hours and heard nothing but the rush and scurry of chipmunks. A bust by their standards.

Early Monday morning, Beth came out to her front lawn with Gretel. She dropped the dog's leash and covered her mouth with her hand. There, with the dew not yet off the grass and the birch trees in the back fields gray-white and late-fall ethereal, was, facing her, an animal head seeming to rise from the grass. Gretel ran to it, flattening her back and barking at its glazed eyes. She then looked to Beth and wagged her tail hopefully. Beth, coming closer, could now see the deer head was propped with two old bricks. Then she knew this was one of the Orams, because she knew their trash. A pile of crumbling bricks stood at the side of Wyatt's home.

Gretel lifted her tiny back leg, and her urine steamed in the cold November air as it ran down the wooden plaque. Blue Barrow's antlers were pearled with dew. "Good dog," Beth said. "Damn straight."

She returned inside to give Gretel her breakfast, asking the dog to wait just a bit before they went on their walk. She came back out wearing her gardening gloves and carrying a black trash bag. She got into her truck, still wearing the gloves, the trash bag covering her lap, the deer head on the trash bag. It was an uncomfortable drive around to Bertram Oram Road, one antler continuing to scratch at her neck. She idled between the two houses, laying the flat of her palm on her horn until the brothers stumbled out of their houses, still scummy with sleep. Beth opened her truck's door and held out Blue Barrow. "You foolish boys don't scare me!" And as Jasper ran at her shouting obscenities, she tossed the deer head in the plastic bag and slammed the truck door and drove to the town shed where people throw away their trash and recyclables. She left the truck running and flung the plastic bag in one of the big metal dumpsters. Then she drove home, taking the long way around. She was fretful that during this interlude they'd done something to her dog, but Gretel was safe, tail a frenzy and on two legs to watch through the window as Beth pulled in. They walked to the elementary school and back. Gretel has a bright-blue leash Beth loves because it reminds her of September sky. And this soothed her, as did the walk and the earthen smell of decaying maple leaves, and she let her heart calm into more decent rhythms. "They will not mess with us again," she told Gretel. "Those goddamn Orams." She waved to the school bus as it passed.

Jasper, after he returned from the shed stinking of trash and holding up urine-scented Blue Barrow as if a boxer victorious, started shouting he would punt that old woman's dog into the treeline, and Wyatt, who had waited on his lawn, laughed.

Jasper lowered Blue Barrow, each fist gripping the base of the antlers. "You did this," he said.

"Your face," Wyatt said. Jasper had scarlet streaks up his cheeks as if he were a blushing drunkard. "I'm sorry, Jasper. I put it in her front yard to scare her. A prank. I didn't think she'd take it to the shed." Wyatt put his hands in his pockets and glanced up at the pine tree they were standing under. Both brothers knew he was lying. He'd just wanted to punish his brother for not letting him choose where to hunt. That Beth had arrived here radiant with indignance—that she'd thrown Blue Barrow in the trash? That was the best outcome Wyatt could've hoped for. That and the dog pee.

"A prank," Jasper said.

"A prank on old lady Kirby with her yappy dog," Wyatt said.

Jasper nodded and brought his stinking prize inside.

Wyatt and Jasper have a history of doing rotten things to one another— firecrackers set off in the kitchen, bear scat left on the front steps, trading out good light bulbs for dead ones. Jasper once put a plate of worms in Wyatt's refrigerator. Wyatt once let the air out of Jasper's back tires. They each, once a year, decide it's delightful to capture a woodchuck and put it in the other brother's garage. Or they take rocks from the brook and fill up the other's bathtub. But Wyatt—out of boredom, out of malice, out of a thwarted need to do something bigger boned in his nefariousness—raised the stakes too high, too fast.

Just over a month later, on Christmas Eve, Jasper came into Wyatt's home after his younger brother had gone to bed. Wyatt went in for Christmas trees, always decorating them with the old ornaments he and his brother had made in elementary school: paper snowflakes and pinecones dusted in glitter, red-and-white pipe-cleaner candy canes. Little bells cut from cardboard and tied with ribbon to adorn the tree. Wyatt had his and Jasper's decorations both since Jasper always said he could go two feet out of his home and stare at pines anytime he damn wanted.

Crowning Wyatt's tree was a construction-paper star six-year-old Wyatt had decorated with a large smiley face in red crayon. Jasper, in the dark, cluttered house, dragged the tree until it was under the smoke detector. He then delicately scraped a match against a matchbook's striking surface, lighting a bit of orange flame he set to the star. Before slipping back next door, he set fire to several top branches as well.

When Wyatt—awakened by the wailing fire alarm—stumbled into his living room, he suspected he was in a terrible waking dream. His tree was billowing brown smoke and its pine needles were turning to ash and flaking to the floor. The air smelled of burning pipe cleaners, acrid and poisonous, along with the sweetness of pine sap. Wyatt, running to get a bucket of water to douse the tree, which in portions glowed dark orange, thought how he'd done nothing to deserve this, then remembered he had, then decided they were not at all equal because Jasper could always bag another deer if he were such a hot-shot hunter, but Wyatt could never replace the glittered and crayoned decorations of his youth—their youth. He threw the water, then covered his ears because of the fire alarm's cries. The treetop turned to wet char—its own bad smell—and he dragged it to his snowy backyard, a few steps from the brook, which was crusted over in delicate ice. The tree in the snow hissed and gave off ugly fumes, which wafted up in the starlight. Wyatt noticed Jasper's bedroom light, a pane of sulphered yellow in the dark.

Christmas day, he hauled the tree to the shed. He'd managed to save a few ornaments—those not charred or melted or ruined by snow—and had put them at the top of his closet. Rather than return home, he went to the inn's taproom, which was open for those who liked some company holiday day—who enjoyed a roaring fire while having a few slow pints. Wyatt sat at the tavern all afternoon, drunkenly talking to anyone who would listen about that jackass, Jasper.

Along the tavern wall farthest from the fireplace is an old church pew with red velvet cushions. When the sun fell, Wyatt went and passed out on it, the fire's crackling not drowning out his snores. Agnes, deft, got his truck keys from his pocket and handed them off to her husband, Bruce. The two managed to get him up, and Bruce drove Wyatt home while Agnes followed. Leaving the bar unmanned was not a problem. Everyone was sleepy and calm from rich Christmas meals and local beer and the occasional fortifying shot of whiskey. Even if it hadn't been a holiday, Bruce and Agnes could've trusted the patrons. We go back. And we are decent. Or we believe we are, which—in most circumstances—is enough. And, my God, Agnes said. No one wanted to hear one whit more about the smell of melted glitter and Elmer's glue, or watch Wyatt, his eyes red with old smoke and fresh drunkenness, look as if he were about to cry huddled over his pints.

This was Wyatt's version of eating cigarettes. Maybe if he'd written some poems we would've lauded him.

The apparent détente ended during the sugaring season. The boys have a small sugar shack on family land, which goes back at least to Bertram's time. A tiny operation, but also a ritual of work both take pleasure in. When winter days warm but the nights stay cool: that's when the sap starts to run. One Saturday afternoon Jasper had gone to get the equipment to tap the trees—the buckets and spouts—when he took the padlock off the door and found Jasper had taken an axe to the evaporator. A wood stove with old metal vats attached was now dented and gnarled into disuse. Wyatt with his lack of foresight, Jasper thought. The evaporator was an antique but had still worked for their purposes. A new one would set them back well over $1,000, which neither had. His kid brother couldn't even come up with something clever enough not to hurt them both.

As kids, they'd come out here with their father and had watched him take stock of the sap boiling down, watched him feed the stove with logs. The evaporator has a long stovepipe that lets off sweet-scented steam, and the scent is as delicate and as springlike as either could imagine. They'd stand out in the snow with their dad—and even their mom a few times too—stamping their feet to ward off the cold, the snow crunchy and crystalline, the light streaming through the bare branches, and they would have bowls of snow upon which their father would pour still warm syrup. The syrup would cool into sugared glass they'd eat with pickles. When they were really young, they'd worn mittens, which had made grasping the spoons with which they ate cumbersome. The thinnest strands of syrup spun into amber filaments.

Wyatt had ruined the sweet quiet and fragrant air of the woods in March.

Then one night in April, as Wyatt was driving home—the light getting long again in the evenings—he had to stop short before he could turn into his house. There in the dirt road, the pines throwing longs arms of shade across it, was all his fishing equipment. Or what had been his fishing equipment. The poles were snapped, the lures and bobbers all smashed, it appeared, with a hammer. His net had been ripped. The tackle box looked as if his brother had run over it with his truck, collapsing its middle. His waders were scorched with lighter burns—Jasper with his pyro instincts again. Wyatt hauled the mess into the back of his truck, then parked in his driveway. He sat with his forearms folded over the wheel, his forehead resting at his knuckles.

Inspiration came as the feral cat Jasper took semi-care of slunk around the side of Wyatt's house. Never named, a brown-and-gray cat with yellow eyes: especially during the winter months, it stayed close in its prowling. Jasper always left his shed open and had filled an old plastic laundry basket with straw. The cat slept there and ate the dry food Jasper put out for it in a shallow bowl.

Wyatt opened the truck door slowly. The cat gave him a sharp glance and then sat, using one front paw to scratch its ears. Wyatt went inside and then returned outdoors with a plate of tuna, which he set on his front steps next to an old metal chair. The cat darted for the tuna and hunkered down to eat it. Wyatt watched its sharp teeth as it took small bites. He let the cat clean the plate before reaching out to grab it by the scruff of its neck, and he brought it yowling to his truck. As he slammed the truck door, Jasper came tearing out into his yard, but Wyatt was already off, taking the sharp twists as quickly as he could down the mountain. The cat didn't stop hissing, its tail raised, its back against the passenger's seat door, until Wyatt stopped at the mountain's base, six miles down. Some quiet houses, some tidy mowed lawns, some sidewalks. He sprung from the truck, and the cat leapt after him, crying, still hissing, yellow eyes like lanterns. Wyatt jumped, literally, over the cat to get back into the truck.

As he returned home, he thought how some soft neighborhood

type would put food out, maybe build the cat a nest of hay, even as he also thought he'd just doomed the animal. But if Jasper was going to keep destroying what Wyatt deemed valuable, Wyatt would do the same right back. Never mind that Wyatt had started it. He'd argue he didn't start it. If Jasper hadn't spent decades bullying him about where to hunt—and bullying him about other things too—he wouldn't have done what he'd done to Blue Barrow.

This circular logic, this dragon eating its tail, this uroboros of ugliness. It doesn't make more sense as we study it. We did our best tracing the brothers back to Rollins Oram and only feel foolish for our efforts. We cast back too far and also not far enough. We neglected a thousand details both large and small. We never told you about the time Jasper, as a child, convinced a very young Wyatt to swallow a spotted salamander he'd found in a vernal pool.

Bruce told Agnes he'd discovered Jasper by the inn's back shed hurling old wood-varnish tins at trees. Seeing Bruce, Jasper had crouched, back to a maple, hands gripping his knees, mumbling into his chest how Wyatt had deliberately set out to hurt his cat.

Studying is no good. Or, studying is of no help. But what should we have done, gone hunting for that cat down the mountain?

We went hunting for that cat down the mountain. Parked at the tiny community library and walked up and down the sidewalks, not so surreptitiously looking into backyards, glancing at the river, and considering all the woods, which—though less assertive in their presence—are still everywhere. We listened to birdcall and thought maybe the cat would learn to hack it in these strange surroundings. We smiled at a few people out for walks, listening to their iPhones, walking their Labradors, pushing their strollers. They smiled back but were unsure: we were not familiar. We returned home catless.

Perhaps it's important to say Wyatt and Jasper have beautiful singing voices. As kids in church, they were both sweet boy sopranos. At

Christmas, Jasper sang "All We Like Sheep Have Gone Astray." And Wyatt, one year later, his bangs too low and getting in his eyes, sang "Unto Us a Son Is Born." (Hilda Tremblay, our church choir director, has a soft spot for Handel.) They each settled into tenors. Not that they continued going to church. We don't think anyone has seen them in church since Bertram Jr. died. But around town, we hear them. Agnes says Jasper is always humming when he's focused on a task: that's how she knows he's focused. And when Wyatt goes into the general store for smokes, for milk and bread and peanut butter, he always sings along to whatever's on the radio. Has a mind for it is what Clive Cushman, the store's proprietor, says. Clive is in the church choir and wishes he could entice one—or both—of the brothers back into the fold. A good tenor is rare indeed and even more rare up here in our tiny old town.

We are fretful we've said nothing good of them. They have some good in them. This is true. At least, it's not false. They've gone long stretches of their lives without doing anything overtly bad. They contain multitudes. (Poets! There are so many of them.)

Then there are days when we remember they claim the brook is named for them. And there are days like the day before our community house.

Our downtown, if you could call it that, has a country store, the inn, the town clerk's office, the new church (new in 1864), and the old church, which we now use as a community house. The building is narrow and white with a gabled roof. It is, according to our historical society, a fine example of Greek Revival. Sometimes we have local musicians put on small shows. Hilda Tremblay plays mandolin just as her father did. And sometimes we have French Canadian groups travel here and perform for us, which lets us feel nostalgic for times we never knew.

The historical society also hosts talks in the community house. The poet is a popular topic, but these official stories, as we think of them, only make the poet sound genteel, which is false. For instance, once a young writer came up here. He worked for a fancy magazine but had the flu, and so—as the poet was giving a reading—the writer got up to leave, as he was feeling woozy. Our poet threw the book he'd been reading from at the writer's head. Then he called the fancy magazine and got the writer fired. The young writer himself became famous years later, and he gave an interview in which he said our poet was the meanest man who ever drew a breath—an old fake.

Should the historical society discuss this? We don't know. The poet loved horses. He loved dinner parties. He chopped his own wood. He gossiped at Dorothea's kitchen table and advised us about most-wanted posters. We draw from the best of his poems solace. And we've heard that other famous writer wasn't very nice either.

As you enter the community house, you'll find bookshelves built into the austere white walls. They are sparsely filled with dark-red and dark-green volumes, delicate gold lettering adorning their spines. Local works, old almanacs, some volumes of maps. Poetry collections. A framed photo of the poet in a tweed suit jacket and a thin black tie, his face craggy, his hair a thick mess. We think of the space as a temple and the bookshelves as an altar to our old best selves.

A Saturday morning in May when beauty was thick upon us after months of harder weather, and the crabapple trees were explosions of mauve and rose petals, Homer Cushman was going into the community house. He manages the space, and a concert had been planned for that evening. He was getting the money box and some music stands from his back seat when he saw, in spray paint across the building's side, WYATT ORAM IS AN ASSWIPE. This in a jagged lizard green, garish against the pine-dark shutters. Paint thinner, he thought. Maybe the country store across the street would have paint thinner so he could clean this ugliness away. He felt a great weight between his shoulder blades. Those Orams. They could at least have the decency to keep their misdeeds to the woods.

Then he noticed Jasper's red truck, not quite hidden behind the community house. With a pair of binoculars, Jasper was watching through his windshield the country store, where, Homer realized with some horror, Wyatt's dark-gray truck was parked.

Poor Homer. His shoulders are stooped and his hair gray wisps. He studies the migration patterns of birds. His grandfather ran the farm on which our poet kept his writing cabin. When reporters or other writers or even the chattier local types wanted to talk to our poet, they'd stop first at Homer's grandfather's farm. His grandfather would then call our poet and ask if he were in the mood for visitors. Only if the poet were feeling sociable would Homer's grandfather let the visitors pass. The poet was so famous toward the end of his life, and we wanted to protect him from the crass and intrusive world. Homer had admired his grandfather for not letting everyone cross the poet's threshold. His grandfather had displayed judgment.

Homer approached Jasper's truck, tapping on its window. Jasper glanced sideways and brusquely shook his head before raising the binoculars once more. Homer had judgment too, it just wasn't coming to him then in sensible form. He started to walk away, still trying to think what to do, and behind him he heard the truck's window go down. "Get the fuck out of here," Jasper said.

Across the street, Wyatt emerged from the store with a paper bag on his hip. Homer became a bird at roost. Maybe if he just stayed still, Wyatt wouldn't notice anything and would drive home, and then Homer could buy that paint thinner.

"Hey," Jasper called, his elbow hanging out the truck's open window.

Wyatt was putting his groceries in the truck. He glanced about. Homer could see them both. They couldn't see each other.

"Hey. Hey, Wyatt. Come here."

Nancy LaCharite pulled into the country store and said good morning to Wyatt, who ignored her. He put his keys in his pocket and crossed the street.

"Hello, Wyatt!" Homer waved in broad arcs. "Good morning!"

Wyatt squinted at him, not convinced.

"Hey," Jasper said, his truck covered in tree shade. "Wyatt, come see."

The crabapple branches were a mauve rustle near the whitewashed building. Wyatt came into the dirt parking lot and studied the lizard-green scrawl, hands on his hips. Nancy LaCharite emerged from the store holding a box of pancake mix. Clive stood in the doorway chatting with her. Both looked toward Wyatt and their conversation dimmed. Jasper got out of his truck and came next to his brother, also placing his hands on his hips. He scratched his neck—a tell, Agnes has said, of when he's about to do something bad or has already done it.

Wyatt licked his lips. He went up to the building and rubbed the flat of his hand against the lettering—to see if it would come off, maybe. Then he turned and charged his brother, headbutting him as if he were a bull.

Jasper stumbled but didn't fall, and he reached into his back pocket for a knife and slashed at Wyatt's cheek. Wyatt leapt back. His eyes were wild. Like an animal's, Homer told us later. An animal that's been poorly shot and is going to die slow but doesn't know it yet so still thrashes. Jasper, holding the knife low at his hip, came at Wyatt again, and Wyatt bolted across the street, almost getting tangled in some bikers out for a hilly ride. They in their fancy attire shouted, "Watch the road!" and were gone in a flash of neon and spinning wheels.

Nancy dropped her box of pancake mix and started to cry. Clive had pulled a phone from his pocket and was tersely muttering into it. But—please remember—we have no sheriff up here, and we have no hospital. Wyatt climbed into the back of his truck and pulled out a shotgun, which by no right or measure should he have had with him. He walked back across the street, his right elbow out, the gun leveled at his bleeding cheek. Jasper grinned. His eyes were flat and the color of rain. "Asswipe," he said. "Asswipe, asswipe, asswipe."

Wyatt shot into the trees. We are all of us accustomed to gunshot but not in May and not near the community house. Agnes came out of the inn, standing before its blue door, arms clutched at her elbows. She shouted, "Homer, get back!" But Homer was a roosting bird. He could imagine a Heaven that would welcome him but he couldn't move.

Wyatt lowered the gun. He was crying. "You are very bad!" he shouted at his brother. None of us expected something so plain. Then he raised the gun, but it was Jasper's turn to charge, toppling Wyatt. The gun went off and Jasper thrust Wyatt's side with his knife. Homer heard Wyatt's shirt tear, a messy rip. The gun clattered as it hit the dirt. The air smelled of cordite.

Eustace, who lives down the street, came out. She had on her apron and reading glasses, and she wailed but ran straight for them. She cried, "Your father would be so ashamed!" She was so fast and strong as she kicked the gun out of their reach. The boys were a twist of limbs, of heavy breath and curses. Both were moaning. Wyatt had blood seeping from his shirt, Jasper from his pants. Then Clive was also across the street and slapped one brother—or both—and got the knife, too. He hugged Eustace and told her she was brave. Agnes arrived with cries that her sister was a fool, and Nancy, shivering, stood aside with Homer. Bruce joined them and with Clive dragged one brother from the other, then cordoned them off. Neither brother could stand, but both were moaning and swearing they would kill the other—*kill* the other—as soon as they could, so this still seemed more than precaution.

Jasper's thigh had been shot, and the blood seeping through his jeans looked like tar. Wyatt had had the knife go under his ribcage. They were both pale and gray and sweating. Nancy called her husband and said don't bring the kids but please come right away. Clive phoned his wife and asked her to man the store, and he'd explain it all later. Homer found he could move again and asked Clive if he had paint thinner and Clive said maybe, go check, take whatever you want.

Agnes had a ladder, and Bruce knew where they kept the plastic cleaning buckets. They went to get cleaning materials. Vinegar, maybe, Eustace said. She was standing watch over Wyatt at that point. She kicked—hard—the flat of his boot. He called her a cunt. She pretended she didn't hear.

Finally, the distant wail of the ambulance and the police as they traversed the steep roads. Everyone there swore it took an hour, and yet it took twenty minutes by the police log records. And that was lucky too, the sheriff explained. A calm morning, and they had nowhere else to be. He came upon a dozen people—and it grew to two dozen as the brothers were put on stretchers in the ambulance—attempting to clean the side of the community house. They had blue gloves and buckets of suds and baking soda and vinegar and paint thinner. Anyone who had driven by—or had heard of the violence via phone—arrived and joined in. This wasn't cheerful work, but very quiet. The sky was blue and without clouds and crabapple blossoms were perfuming the air. But the scent turned their stomachs; it seemed a sweet poison. They felt easier breathing in paint thinner and vinegar and chemical cleaners and soap. They worked with brushes and sponges and hoped they were making things better.

The wording remains, if blurred and paled. We will be repainting the community house this coming weekend.

Both boys spent some time down the mountain at the hospital but came back up last night with the prognosis they'll each recover. They had to take cabs (pricey and unusual) to their homes. No one would've volunteered to pick them up, nor did they ask. Beth Kirby says she saw their lights on. She says those goddamned Orams.

They've made it impossible we look away. So now we're all looking, waiting, worrying, trying to think what to do. We don't know what will happen next. We know what will happen next. We wish it were over already. We wish they were posters we could put on the back door to the back porch, but we also think how fundamentally inadequate that makes us. We wish we were better.

We wish the poet were still with us to talk to us. We would like some counsel even if his wisdom didn't always measure up. Our poet said a poem is a momentary stay against the confusions of the world, but even if we find brief emotional or intellectual respite, those confusions: there they are, waiting for us.

The Orams will rise from their beds and then what, then what?

The Chair

THE CHAIR IS LIGHT BLUE but shades toward gray in the sun. China blue but more somber, more delicate. It's an Adirondack chair, which are common in New England, but when she first saw it, she found it unique, unusual, a splendid wedding gift.

They married right after she graduated. She was twenty-two and Morty was twenty-nine. The gifts their friends and families bestowed upon them were staid and correct: towels, saucepans, a basic china set. But after the ceremony, Richard—bearded, his hair shaggy as an undergrad's—told them if they wanted their present, they'd have to come over to his house. They'd not planned a honeymoon, so they went the next day. At the front door, Richard asked them to meet him at the garage. He lifted its door from the inside and there on the concrete: sun illuminated its wooden back, its wide arms. It looked like a minimalist throne. She hadn't suspected Morty's peer was so gifted in carpentry. She reached on tiptoe to kiss his cheek. Morty shook Richard's hand and said he was lucky to count Richard as a friend.

Morty's accepting the position in Vermont had given Richard the idea. He'd been once as a kid and remembered loving these simple, stark chairs: no cushioning and yet comfortable, perfect for reading a book on a nice day. The paint color, too, was part of the gift. Richard knew Morty's full name—Mortimer—translated roughly from the French to mean dead sea. He didn't know what a dead sea looked like but had imagined it pale. Then Richard flushed, and Cappie thought he worried he'd too baldly admitted his affection for Morty, a thing men always struggle with. "I'd meant for there to be two chairs. But the semester flew by." He glanced toward the house—she imagined toward his study, to the blue-book exams stacked on his desk.

"This is the most thoughtful gift we've received," she said. "We love it."

Richard invited them in. He and his wife, Tabitha, had a small cottage in Cayuga Heights. Cappie loved this tree-lined neighborhood, the quiet houses tucked back amid oaks and elms. Morty lived north of campus in a brick apartment complex populated mostly by graduate students. Her first two years, she'd lived in Mary Donlon Hall; her junior and senior years, with a few girlfriends, she'd rented a seedy apartment on East Seneca near Collegetown. Tabitha suggested lemonade on the back patio and a game of bridge. The backyard was thick with sunlight, which, as Cappie wore a sundress, warmed her collarbone and shoulders. Tabitha had put mint leaves in the pitcher of lemonade; they floated on the surface. She poured them all glasses as Richard found a pack of playing cards. Morty and Richard discussed how their students had done this semester. Tabitha told Cappie the wedding had been beautiful. Cappie thanked her, although she was privately relieved the day was over. They'd been married on campus, in Sage Chapel, gothic and rich with its apse window and vaulted ceilings, its gleaming brass lamps and mosaic designs. At the last moment, her mother had volunteered the nondenominational church displeased her. The crypts holding the college's founders were distasteful. The space was remote, overly ornate. All this, Cappie had felt, was implicit criticism of Morty, with his imperiousness and academic prowess. Buried even further down was jealousy: her daughter—easily, without drama or strife—had fallen in love and would spend her life with a successful man. So many, too, had borne witness: it had made the wedding seem a performance rather than a ceremonial joining. It had lacked intimacy.

That morning her parents had driven back to Ohio. Her more distant family had similarly dispersed. Morty's parents had returned to Albany. This afternoon was the first time she felt properly married. They could do as they chose, together.

Hemlocks threw shade across the grass. She sipped lemonade, tart and icy. The day was so warm and tranquil.

"What a good friend he is to you," she said to Morty later that evening.

"We came in together," he said. They'd both been hired when they were just twenty-seven, straight from getting their PhDs. "It bonds a fellow."

Now that she's ordered the hospital bed, she hopes to let the moniker go. She deliberately spent a mint to ensure what arrives will not be ugly or sad and can pass reasonably as furniture. She's tried calling it a daybed—though that's not what it is—but so far Morty hasn't deferred to this mild form of erasure. Increasingly, maneuvering the stairs has been difficult for him. Then, last week, he fell. Her heart went so fast to see him in tears and wheezing, because to cry was to increase the labor of drawing a breath.

A broken ankle that will mend. And chronic bronchitis, the doctor said, badly inflamed bronchial tubes. The doctor did not say dementia, but she's started to become anxious. He doesn't remember where things are, which means he spends more time in his agonized lumbers throughout the house. He's also begun to lose track of time, surprised when she tells him dinner is ready or she's about to leave for her job at the library. There's also his surprising decision to want the bed in the sunroom. When she questioned his choice, he quickly delineated the ways this was, in fact, pragmatic. The sunroom is right off the kitchen and closer to the downstairs bathroom than the study at the hall's end.

Of course, the study is barely farther away from the bathroom. And she brings him all his meals, so his time in the kitchen is minimal. The study is carpeted. It's warm. Instead, he's choosing a room half made of glass, with slick tiled floors. And particularly now in January, when the landscape is all ice and snow, he seems deliberately to have chosen an inhospitable space.

They're considering the sunroom now. She has some wicker chairs in there, a low sofa with natural fibers, a glass-top table. The Adirondack chair sits in a corner. Weather in Vermont is so fickle, even in its nicest months, and she decided decades ago she'd prefer to keep the chair inside, where the rain and humidity can't get at it. The room is long, if narrow, and she could move the furniture to the far end so Morty's bed isn't crowded. Although that might look a jumble. She asks what he wants.

"Let's move most of the furniture," Morty says. "But I think just get rid of the chair."

"The chair Richard made us? I'll put it in the garage for the time being."

"That will clutter up the garage." Morty's foot is in a cast. He leans on crutches. She bought him several pairs of cheap loose-fitting pants and cut the right pantleg from the knee down so he can still be in trousers. Not getting dressed, he said, made him feel like an invalid.

"Then I'll put it in one of the upstairs bedrooms. It's no trouble."

"You can't carry it up the stairs."

"Of course I can." She worries they're treading into unsafe conversational territory. He's weakened in ways she is not.

"Get rid of it," he says.

· · ·

It's a Tuesday morning, and the hospital-daybed has just arrived. She's already helped Morty down the stairs, a terrible ordeal because he's practically a foot taller—six two to her five three—and she can't, with her tiny frame, support him well. This morning he was especially short tempered, exhorting her to stay still, stay still, as he squashed her against the railing. She'll be glad not to do this again.

She asks the movers whether they can arrange most of the furniture at the room's eastern end. She goes to lift the Adirondack chair, which is cumbersome if not heavy. She has to stretch her arms wide and bend her knees and round her back. A mover asks if she'd like help: two people carrying it would be easier. Morty, supervising from the door-frame, frowns. She says yes, could he help her get it to the garage? They walk together, her forward, him backward, through the kitchen and mudroom. Trying to go through the mudroom door to the garage, they discover the chair is wider than the doorframe, so they have to angle it. She squats; by virtue of her height, she holds the lower end. Bringing home the chair from Richard and Tabitha's had been so simple. Morty, that spring, in a rare splurge, had bought a Chevy convertible. He'd decided driving it to Vermont would make the move feel more like an adventure. Richard carried the chair to the car and lowered it into the wide back seat, admonishing Morty not to let it jostle. Evening was upon them, lavender air and crickets, and Morty drove slowly out of the neighborhood and north across campus. He joked they should've had her perch on the chair. She could've given all of Ithaca a queenly wave while wearing a sash that read "Just Married" on the front and "Magna Cum Laude in Government" on the back.

She and the mover set the chair next to the recycling and garbage bins. She'll figure out a more orderly arrangement later. She thanks the man, a touch humiliated to find she's sweating. Back in the sunroom, Morty is leaning against the side of the bed and trying to hoist himself onto the mattress. The other mover reminds Morty to use the remote control to raise the bed into a more upright position. Then he'll be better able to get himself onto it. If he wishes to be supine, he can again use the remote. Morty thanks them both and begins pushing buttons. She sees the men out, tipping them well. Supine, she thinks. An elegant word for an inelegant posture.

When she returns, Morty has the bed's back elevated such that it resembles an ungainly chaise longue. He sits in it with a crutch across his lap. "This will do," he says.

She's glad and tells him she'll bring down a side table, his alarm clock, some pillows. She'll make him a turkey sandwich before she goes. He asks if she'll also bring him the most recent *American Economic Review* and his laptop. While testing out this monstrosity, giving being bedridden a go, he'll read.

"Six more weeks," she says.

He's looking out the windows to the tamaracks crusted in snow, acting as if he doesn't hear her. She knows his fear because it's hers as well: this marks the beginning of some diminished future.

The gym at this hour is generally quiet since most students are in class. Although, as she walks into the locker room, one clutches her phone, discussing Arabic. "No, mom, you'd *love* it. It has a root system, so it has all this logic. Like, if you wanted to say 'cousin' you might say 'son of an uncle.'" These young women talk constantly with their parents—confessional, mundane, cheerful conversations. The cafeteria finally got oat milk. *Paradise Lost* is so boring, even the part about Satan. Cappie likes their assertiveness: sure their thoughts matter, confident in their parents' love for them. Among themselves, they frequently talk about what they're bothered by: an instructor who doesn't provide a clear rubric and then grades too hard; having to get a Brazilian wax for a boyfriend who doesn't even carefully shave. From the world, they demand fairness, which strikes Cappie as young.

She sits on a bench, pulling a T-shirt over her head. Nearby, two long-limbed girls, both wearing a high ponytail and form-fitting yoga pants, are deciding which cafeteria they'll have lunch in after they work out.

The fitness center—rows of bikes, ellipticals, treadmills—is a clean white space with large windows. She gets on an elliptical. To the east, the Green Mountains are dark blue in this frigid weather. A man whom she suspects is a coach, given his rangy bearing and focus, sweats copiously on a StairMaster. She puts in her earbuds to listen to *This American Life*. She started attending the gym a few years ago: all the articles about physical fitness improving cognitive function convinced her. It's open to staff and faculty, including emeritus, and their spouses, although Morty has never gone, claiming he'd find working out among the students distasteful. Maybe after his ankle heals, she could get him to walk on the indoor track. He's been retired three years; he'd be reasonably anonymous by now.

She has to go for thirty minutes and make sure her heart rate stays at 120 bpm. She sweats lightly, conscious of her loose skin, her wrinkles, the way her movements are not vigorous compared to those surrounding her. The young women from the locker room run on the treadmills. Each is serious: shoulders back, elbows close to their sides, ponytails swaying as their feet strike the treadmill's belt. She loves the undergraduates best for how they work to be strong. She wishes she'd had a space like this when she was in college.

After her workout, she does some stretching on a blue mat. She drinks some water and feels calmer after a difficult morning. This business about the chair was likely his misplaced frustrations about his ankle, the bronchitis, needing the hospital bed. But better to let him come to this conclusion; if she says it, he'll interpret her remarks as condescension. The girls—flushed, sweating—are stretching too, impossibly limber. When Cappie was just a little older than they are, she was ready to be married. In the locker room, the girls never talk of marriage. She doesn't know if it's a deferral of adulthood or a stronger assertion of self. The world changes. It's not worse or better, she thinks—just different.

In the locker room, as she's taking off her sneakers, she hears the girls return to the row of lockers behind her.

"Are you mad at me?" one asks.

"No." The other opens a locker, then slams it. "Are *you* mad at *me*? Why are you asking me this?"

"You've been very quiet today. I thought maybe you were mad."

"What would I be mad about?"

"I don't know. That's why I'm asking."

"I'm not mad."

"LOL, now you're going to be mad, since I asked."

"I just don't know why you're asking."

"Because you seemed mad, and I was worried."

"Well, I'm not. Ugh, but maybe now we're both mad at each other." One laughs and the other joins in, both uneasy.

Cappie feels heartsick: the vulnerability of the conversation; the way it went nowhere; how one probably is angry at the other and yet there will be no honesty between them.

She gets up to go, and as she passes them, they both look over. The silence turns expansive, weighty. Cappie leave the gym angry. She knows, by virtue of being an old woman, she's often invisible to others. But to be so purely nonexistent those girls wouldn't consider she'd not want to hear their strange, sad argument?

She drives to the library. Gray marbles the sky. Snow is predicted this evening. Life's turbulence is never behind her. It's never behind anyone. And the problems themselves stay constant. Loving someone else, needing them, too often becomes a crisis of the heart.

When she found out her senior year she'd gotten in early admittance to Cornell's law school, she called Morty at his office. This was exceptional news, he said. He was proud of her; they'd celebrate that evening by going to the John Thomas Steakhouse. This was where he'd taken her when he'd proposed—a thrilling indulgence, lobster bisque and porterhouse steaks. Her roommates said she could not defer celebration so long; they were going out right this minute. So the quartet walked to The Palms—replete with a tacky sign of a palm tree out front and high wooden booths inside that patrons, for years, had carved their initials into. They ordered pitchers of beer and drank through the afternoon, every so often lifting their glasses to Cappie and toasting her success. She called Morty again from the bar's phonebooth, asking if he could pick her up there as opposed to her apartment.

"You are bombed," he said.

"I am," she agreed. "Yes, yes."

By the time he came in, it was evening—dark and blustery out—the cold wafting in as more patrons started arriving. The Rolling Stones were on the jukebox. Morty found her and her roommates. He was bundled up in long wool coat, a scarf. He was carrying a large pizza—mushrooms, sausage—and he glanced over his shoulder, but the bartender had chosen not to notice. He sat down next to her, taking off his gloves, slipping his cold hand into hers. Her girlfriends cheered for the pizza, and they all ate the warm greasy slices, ravenous and happy and drunk. Morty went to buy the next round. One of her roommates leaned in and stage-whispered, "He is *good*, Cappie."

After she graduated, they planned to buy a house—she wanted one in Richard and Tabitha's neighborhood. She'd go to graduate school while he continued teaching, and eventually she'd set up a small practice in town. Then his former graduate advisor from the University of Michigan called: a good liberal arts college in Vermont was looking for someone to bolster their program in labor economics. He'd be given a real say in how to shape the major, what classes to offer, who else to hire. She remembers him taking the call. She'd been in the living room, sitting on his threadbare couch, studying. From the kitchen, he'd sounded surprised, then excited, then formality crept into his voice she knew had to do with his anxiety or need to stay in control. She went into the kitchen. It was at night. She was wearing slippers. He sat with his elbows on the table, his hands to his cheeks. He looked up and tried to smile. He explained the offer, how good it was.

She took milk from the refrigerator, poured herself a glass, asked whether he wanted some. He shook his head. "I can go to law school in Vermont," she said.

"There are none that I know of."

"We'll work it out." Her belly was lead, and the milk had been a bad decision.

"How?" He was like that, not letting niceties stand. Problems had solutions or they didn't. But he pursued the line of thinking.

She didn't know, she said. But he was unlikely to have such an offer come along again. She'd proven herself capable of getting into a good law school. When the time came, she'd do it again.

He pushed back the chair and came around the table. He dropped to his knees and hugged her waist, his head pressed to her stomach. In that spartan kitchen, she stroked his hair.

Six years after they moved to Vermont, a law school opened, but she'd have needed to drive over a mountain to get there. And by then, she had three-year-old Melody. And Morty was suspicious of such a new school. What if it weren't rigorous enough? A well-intended snobbery. So she continued to put the thought aside while she raised their daughter. When Melody was sixteen, whip smart and self-sufficient, she began considering it again. She brought it up to Morty, who brought it up to his colleagues. It turned out Vermont was one of four states where one could do an apprenticeship—clerk under a lawyer—in lieu of going to law school. The statistics about people passing the bar this way were dismal, but she wanted to pursue it. She was in her late thirties. The time for sitting in classrooms had passed.

At night, she took over the study. And during the day, she clerked with a very decent older lawyer who had an office next to an old mill overlooking a river and falls. At her desk, she'd watch the placid water giving over to foamy spray. She took notes when clients came in. She drank strong coffee from a pot the lawyer constantly had running. She learned the fundamentals of trust and estate planning, probate proceedings, real estate law. When she passed the bar exam, she called Melody. Her daughter was twenty-one—a junior at Yale, almost the same age Cappie had been when she'd thought she was about to begin law school. Her daughter was delighted, said she was going out that night with friends, and they would all toast her.

She began practicing law when she was forty-six and retired when she was seventy-two. She had the small practice she wanted in the beautiful town she had come to love. And Morty adored teaching at the college. He was there fifty years before retiring. They have their beautiful, smart daughter, who is, astoundingly, on the later side of middle age, a mother herself to a child she had when she was forty. Melody and her husband, Tim, met in grad school. They got hired together to teach environmental policy at Colby. Their daughter, Presley, is in fifth grade and very quick with numbers. She has the same wheat blonde hair Cappie had for so many years. She loves all things Harry Potter. Cappie wouldn't have had Melody so young if she'd gone straight into law school. Who knows what might've happened? Only that the goodness of her life wouldn't have taken this shape.

She's at her desk at the library, perusing book reviews—which is part of her job as a volunteer librarian. She also has her email open, and the daily email from the Town Hall Forum just arrived. It's a compilation of postings from fellow town members: someone is selling bedroom furniture or wishes to know where to purchase firewood. A person saw a bear in her backyard and recommends people defer putting out their bird feeders. As she's perusing the items, she sees one titled "Adirondack Chair" with the subtitle: "Free Item."

We are looking to give away a handmade wooden Adirondack chair. Light blue. Dimensions upon request. Good for a sunroom or covered porch. Please contact Catherine Rush: cappierush@ gmail.com.

Already two new emails have come in, both titled "Re: Adirondack Chair." One reads, "Can u send pics?" The other says, "If the chair is available, I'd be interested in taking it off your hands." A third arrives from the owner of a used furniture shop. He could be by in half an hour.

She closes her laptop. At the front desk, the other librarian, a woman in her fifties with taffy-colored hair, glances behind her. "Everything okay, Cappie?"

Cappie says it is. She'd call him but has no privacy for a heated conversation. Once home, she'll tell him not consulting her was poor form. It was rude. She'll say, furthermore, she's not giving away the chair.

She calls hello but hears only the refrigerator's hum, the subtle creaking of the house. She sets down the mail on the counter and flips on a light. The entire house is dark. She'd assumed Morty would've moved from the bed, after testing it out, to the living room couch. There he'd have more light, more heat, more to do—the TV if he wanted to watch sports, the radio if he wanted to listen to VPR. She opens the door to the sunroom. In the dim, the snow falls gray and soft, covering the trees. Morty is asleep, his cheek turned toward the windows, the snow. His right arm is sprawled across his chest. A streetlamp casts a small sheen across his bald head. His breathing is wet, uneven.

One crutch is propped by the side table. The other lies flat across the tiles; it must've slid and clattered out of easy reach. With just the one crutch, he wouldn't have had the necessary balance to get out of bed. He's been confined here for God knows how long.

Chill comes upon her. They have a space heater upstairs. She'll bring it down.

He stirs. She goes and places the crutch beside the other. "An umbrella stand," he tells her.

"Yes?" Her heart rushes, murmurs.

"An umbrella stand for the crutches. So I have a place to store them. I ordered one from Amazon while you were at the library."

"I'd like to stay home for the next few weeks," she says. "I'd feel better if I weren't out during the afternoons."

"Nonsense." He's pressing buttons, tilting the bed to an angle that lets him reach the crutches. He stands, his arms only trembling a little, and she gives him room. He heads for the bathroom. She takes out the makings for a salad but is too distressed to chop the red pepper, to get the spinach into the bowl. He's been sitting in the dark cold for hours, unable to move.

He returns to the kitchen. "I posted about the chair to the Town Hall Forum."

"I saw." She reaches into a drawer for a cutting board. "You should've told me first."

"It's a relic," he says darkly. He sits at the kitchen table, carefully leaning the crutches against the chair.

She sets down the cutting knife. "Don't do such a thing again."

He nods. He's toying with a place mat, rearranging its fringe.

"I've had fifteen emails about it," she says. "In the morning, I'll sort through them, decide whom to give the chair."

Last night, the sheets felt confining; the radiator's hisses and burbles kept her awake. She crept downstairs to make sure Morty's crutches hadn't fallen. In his sleep, he clutched his blanket, coughing. The space heater whirred, but the room remained frigid. At three in the morning, she searched online for space heaters, ordering three, not caring if he protested. When she returned to bed, she dreamt of Tabitha.

Approaching her twenty-fifth reunion, Cappie started receiving emails from her old roommates, who thought they should reconvene at their old haunts, drink beer in the reunion tents on the arts quad. Cappie looked into making arrangements. Cornell would set them up in dorms on North Campus, but Morty wanted no part of that. He suggested they ask Richard and Tabitha if they could stay with them instead.

The couple had moved to a magnificent Tudor off Triphammer. Getting out of the car, Cappie irrationally wished they still lived in their little cottage. They came outside to greet Cappie and Morty, hugging them. They'd both gone mostly gray. Richard's hair was short, his beard neatly trimmed. Tabitha still had strands of the reddish-brown Cappie remembered, now mixed into a wiry silver. Morty and Richard retreated to Richard's study, wood-paneled walls and built-in bookshelves. In the kitchen, Cappie and Tabitha drank a Finger Lakes riesling, chatting about what their Christmas cards had revealed over the years. Tabitha had three children—all at good colleges or graduate schools. She was writing poetry and had published some poems. She congratulated Cappie on becoming a lawyer. Cappie regretted having to rush off to dinner with her old roommates. That weekend, as she flitted in and out of Richard and Tabitha's house, the conversations always felt warm and natural—surprising given they hadn't seen each other in so long.

In the dream, Tabitha and Cappie were young. They stood at the kitchen counter drinking sweet white wine. Tabitha said, "Your checkbook is in Alabama on Tuesday." She said, "How perspicacious the dullard lamp." She said, "What is the wherefore of who." She smiled and her teeth glistened. Her eyes were alight with confrontation. Cappie gulped wine, which burned her throat. She said, "Are the ducks ready?" She yelled, "Yes, when!" She shouted, "Archdukes and headbands tread not for galas!" Tabitha's laughter was snide. She yelled back. And this volleying of nonsense sped up, became angrier and angrier. When she woke, her heart was juddering. The dark room was too big without Morty by her side.

At the kitchen table, Cappie rubs her temples. She must sift through these emails. Eleven more have come. She rises to check on Morty, who's on the couch staring out at the fresh half foot of snow that fell during the night. *BBC World News* plays in the background. He looks over and asks if everything is all right. She realizes she has no concrete reason to have come in, so pretends she's thinking about making more coffee and asks whether he'd like some. He tells her he's fine.

To hell with sifting, she decides, and picks the first polite email she opens. She writes the woman, Gwen, asking if she could come by today. Gwen immediately answers: she's teaching a class late morning but could be by at two. Cappie writes a form response to the rest, saying the chair has been spoken for. Next, she emails the library: she's taking time off to attend to Morty as he recovers from his broken ankle. She apologizes for leaving them in a bind. At breakfast, she told Morty she was doing this. He didn't fight her. She suspects he's relieved.

She goes to explain someone will be by this afternoon for the chair.

He nods without looking up from the newspaper. The BBC announcer talks of an Arizona man pulled over for putting a fake skeleton—a leftover Halloween decoration—in his passenger's seat so he could use the carpool lane.

Cappie invites the woman in. She's in a puffer jacket, jeans, boots. Cusping middle age but with looks that skew young: doe-eyed, a soft, round face. A few smile lines appear as she introduces herself and thanks Cappie.

"What do you teach?" Cappie puts on her coat so she can help Gwen get the chair into her car.

"Writing. A mixture of comp and rhetoric. Creative writing when I'm lucky."

"And you're a writer?"

Gwen nods. Her smile has some flicker of wariness. She doesn't want whatever question she anticipates Cappie asking next, and so Cappie decides to have the good sense not to pursue the conversation. She's trying to discern how much older Gwen is than the undergraduates she teaches, whether she feels distant from them or identifies with their mindset. She's not sure why this preoccupies her.

"And what do you plan to do with the chair?" Cappie says.

"I have a crumbling sunroom—nothing as nice as yours." She gestures toward it, perhaps not noticing the bed, the furniture's peculiar arrangement. "But my apartment overlooks the river. In warmer months, it'd be nice to have an Adirondack chair to read in."

From the hall, Morty comes into the kitchen. He stands in the doorframe, trying not to lean too heavily on the crutches. "Hello," he says. "I'm Morty."

"Gwen," she says. "It's nice to meet you. You have a beautiful home." Her gaze displays too much equanimity, as if she's working not to betray she's unnerved by his liver-spotted skin, his raspy breath and crutches. Cappie briefly sees him as she does: an eighty-three-year-old man, frail and ill, with crust at his eyes, his lips.

"My wife tells me you teach." Gwen nods. "At the college?" Gwen nods again. "Tenure track?"

Blotches of pink rise at her cheeks. She shakes her head. "It's a visiting appointment."

"Tenure will come." Morty readjusts his crutches, coughing violently into his shoulder.

"Morty taught fifty years in the economics department," Cappie says. She starts to list the books he's published, the grants he's been awarded, but Morty lightly shakes his head.

"It's no longer the same," he tells the young woman. "What I got, the way I started: no one could have that now. That world no longer exists."

"Exactly right." The color remains bright at her cheeks. "The market is flooded with people like me."

"You'll get what you want," Morty says. "Keep pursuing it." He hobbles away from the doorframe back to the living room.

Well, good. They shared some current of understanding. Gwen will recognize she was mistaken about Morty, didn't initially understand all he possesses.

Cappie and Gwen go into the garage. Cappie raises the garage door, and they carry the chair to Gwen's car. Cappie talks of Richard, how he had surprised them all those years ago. She tells her how they'd driven it home in the back of Morty's '66 Chevy, imagining her perched on it like some silly parade queen. She discusses how its craftmanship is so remarkable that over fifty years later it's still sturdy and comfortable—perfect for summer days. As she rambles, they try to fit the chair into the car, but its arms are so wide, its back so tall, that no matter how they tip it, no matter how much Gwen pulls the front seats forward, they can't get it in.

The sky is heavy and white, and flakes begin to fall, dusting their shoulders. Cappie's arms tremble with the exertion of trying to make something fit that won't. They set the chair down in the driveway. Snow gathers on it, the crystalline flakes softening and blurring as they hit the light-blue wood.

Gwen, peering into the back seat, pulls her head out. "I don't think it fits."

"I need you to take the chair!" Cappie cries.

Gwen, her hair becoming matted with snow, blinks her dark eyes at Cappie. She toys with her jacket's zipper. "Let's try the trunk," she says.

They lower the chair in. It doesn't nearly fit to close the trunk, but Gwen suggests bungee cords, rope. She'll drive to the hardware store and return in five minutes tops. They carry the chair back to the garage so it doesn't continue to get snowed on.

"Be right back," Gwen says. She drives off.

Cappie was wrong to raise her voice, wrong to impose any sort of emotion on the transaction at all. This poor woman stumbled into their lives.

In the garage's dim, her frozen breath escapes in plumes. Just beyond, this gray daytime, bewitched and strange. She should go back inside or Morty will worry. Instead she wipes away the accumulated snow from the chair's seat. She sits, her elbows resting on its arms, her head tilted back against its cold wood. She will stay here awhile, even if Gwen doesn't return. The snow falls so thickly, it blurs the neighborhood, altering it, making it almost indistinguishable from the sky.

The Bear Is Back

RILEY IS ATTEMPTING cartwheels on the front lawn, imploring me to watch. I tell her to hold on a sec, let me finish unbuckling Hubbard from his car seat. Hubbard, asleep, still clutches his Darth Vader plushy. If I can get him inside without waking him, he could have a full nap. Otherwise, this afternoon, we're in for a tantrum.

"Daddy," Riley calls. "Look!" Her cartwheel is floppy limbed—a sad-starfish tumble—but she rights herself, hands high and exultant.

"Well done." I cradle Hubbard against my shoulder and grab the day bag. "Riley, could you come help Daddy? I need the car door closed."

She does another cartwheel. My shoulder starts to go numb. One more cartwheel. "Riley, now please."

She jackrabbits over and slams the car door. Hubbard shifts, opening his eyes and dropping his toy. "Darf," he says softly. He kicks me as he tries to reach the far-below driveway. I drop the day bag and bend my knees, but I'm about to topple over. I straighten, murmuring I'll return for the plushy once I have him and Riley inside. Wrong. Answer. His tears begin to dampen my neck. Riley picks up the day bag and walks beside me. She puts her free hand to her ear in protest of her brother's wails.

Someone is calling. A neighbor stooped in our driveway—fine gray hair, an expensive-looking fleece. As she approaches, I think we should retire the term "elderly," at least for those older without a whiff of frailty. She hands the toy to Hubs, who immediately quiets. "Darf," he says. His beloved.

"Do you want to see me do a cartwheel?" Riley asks. The woman nods, and Riley runs to the lawn for more of her starfish routine, managing to catapult a sneaker with one particularly emphatic turn.

"Thank you so much." I set Hubbard on the front step. "Hubbard, can you say thank you?" Hubbard watches our neighbor as if she might be an apparition he must study until she winks out. "Say thank you, Hubbard?"

"Congratulations," he tells her.

She laughs. "It takes a village. Especially right now."

"Daddy, I can't tie my shoe!" Riley calls.

"You can," I say. "Try again."

I pick up Hubbard and settle him on my hip, and he bats his soft toy against my arm as my neighbor and I discuss a local dairy dumping its milk because its contracts with local schools and the college are on pause, and the cows are producing more than the dairy can sell in stores. People continue to post about it on our local listserv, some wringing their hands over the waste, some imploring the dairy to give away the milk, and some countering that if the dairy could've found a better solution, it would've, so stop hectoring the farmers. She tells me yesterday she saw a mama bear and her two cubs while out walking, that generally one doesn't see them until the summer, but she believes with everyone inside nature is reasserting itself. I'm impressed. We've lived here four years and have never seen any bears. She says she believes my wife and I work for the college, is that right? And I say yes, in the English department, and she tells me her husband taught in the economics department fifty years before retiring last year, and he's been so curious about what it's been like for professors this spring. I say Clarissa has been having a time of it—an under-understatement—and finds everyone is depressed, no one engaged. I reluctantly allow that I don't know firsthand: I run the writing center and only teach one comp class in the fall, nothing in the spring, and practically no one has signed up for any tutoring.

"This is all just a wash until they find a vaccine," she says. "Higher ed isn't nimble enough to cope with such large challenges."

"Yes," I say. Yes. I like this woman. "Charles."

"Cappie." Her smile is just this side of sly. "Maybe in a few months, we'll have you over for a glass of wine."

I say we'd be delighted. As we've been talking, Hubbard has peed, and I'm fairly sure we both smell like urine, but I really do feel brightened at the prospect.

Riley opens the door, bellowing, "We're hommmme!"

Clarissa is on the couch, her hand draped across her eyes. She's sprawled as if nursing a hangover. I tell her about meeting Cappie, about her and her husband eventually having us over. I set Hubbard on a changing blanket on our living room rug. "Hold still, bud."

Clarissa removes her hand from her eyes. "That's nice. Cappie and Mortimer. I'm not sure her husband is well."

"He taught in the economics department fifty years. The oldest of the old guard. How was class?"

She shakes her head and sits up. "Riley? Did you get your smoothie?"

"I forgot."

"Well, could you do it now?"

Riley watches me change Hubbard's diaper, squatting as if a coach ready to offer encouragement.

"Riley."

Riley turns, her lips full. She goes to the kitchen and comes back with her smoothie. She's been resisting eating the last few months, so in the mornings we make a batch of smoothies with whole milk, banana, frozen fruit, and insist she drink several prepoured sippie cups of it a day. It's that, basically, and bread she's willing to eat. She returns holding a sippie cup. "I would like a straw."

"Riley, we need you to behave like a big girl," I say.

"Get yourself the straw if you want it," Clarissa says.

Riley stills. Her eyes turn a hot blue, swimmy with tears. Her lower lip crumples.

"Oh, God." Clarissa rises. "All right. I'm sorry, Riley, I didn't mean to lose my temper." She hugs Riley, who flings her arms about her mother's waist and sobs. Clarissa pets her hair.

When I return from throwing away Hubbard's diaper and washing my hands, Riley is at the dining room table with her smoothie set to the side while she colors in her unicorn coloring book. Hubbard is on the floor, banging his plushy Darth Vader and Boba Fett together and saying, "Ya, ya, ya!" Clarissa sits staring into space.

It's 3:43 in the afternoon. These endless days.

"One of my students had a meltdown today," Clarissa says. I join her on the couch. "We're discussing 'Cathedral.' Some kids were talking about how social isolation makes you read this story differently—they think the narrator is even more of a prick because he's such a jerk about his wife wanting any other companionship." She looks at me warily. "Not that you're not my end-all be-all, my love."

"I might be in love with Cappie," I say.

"Then one student starts *crying*. She is just so *over* this. This was how she was finishing her senior year? With her little brother banging on her door to play Dungeons & Dragons and her mom frantic about the family cat, who isn't eating, but her mom is afraid to take the cat to the vet? I told her to log off, to get some rest. The remainder of class was a complete failure. We didn't even get to the end, to how Carver earns the epiphany—the subtle shift in how the character perceives his world, that quiet transcendence. There was so much we didn't unpack. No epiphanies for us. I'm failing them."

I say, "You're doing what you can."

I refrain from saying what I want to say, which is: let's switch. You spend every day with our children. I'll teach literature. I'll even handle it with equanimity if no one has any epiphanies about the construction of epiphanies.

"I'm doing what I can," she repeats. She's testing this idea, trying to decide if it provides solace. Day to day, the answer varies. She rises and goes to the kitchen.

The kids are momentarily peaceful. I scroll through my emails, skimming the community listserv. Generally, I pay little attention to these posts but have recently found them engaging. I must not be alone, since the listserv is now being posted twice, sometimes three times daily. Someone is offering a free bin of used tennis balls; someone is selling a mountain bike. Another describes how a peahen (a female peacock, the post explains) has wandered into a couple's yard. They can't figure out where she's come from. Would anyone like to adopt her? If so, please schedule a time to come by. Sometimes, Clarissa and I are still startled by how small a small town in Vermont can be.

Clarissa sets down a bottle of wine and two glasses, pouring us some, saying Cappie had a good idea.

Drinking in the afternoon: I almost tease her about still having Carver on her mind, but I don't want to revisit what has upset her. Just, I notice, as she's not nudged Riley about the untouched smoothie at her elbow. We need a break from ourselves. Because we can't have that, we must settle for overlooking things. I tell Clarissa about the peahen, suggest we swing by.

"I want a peacock," Riley says serenely, not looking up from her coloring book.

Clarissa drinks some wine. "We don't have enough land for a peacock."

"Could we move somewhere with more land?"

"Nope."

Hubbard sets down Boba Fett. "Peach hawk." I laugh, and he laughs too. "Ya, ya, ya," he says to his toys.

"Here's one in our neighborhood." I read: "'The Bear is Back.' 'As we call him, Butternut has returned. He was in my yard around seven this morning, and a neighbor said she saw him trying to open her compost bin at five am.'"

"The bear is named Butternut?" Clarissa says. We live at 17 Butternut Ridge. "That seems less than creative."

"How do they know it's the same bear? Cappie saw one with cubs yesterday. We apparently live in a beritable bear-topia."

Riley pauses in her coloring to study her mother laugh. She smiles, a beam of light. "I have a better name."

"We're all ears," I say.

"Hooligan Hello!" Riley snaps her fingers—I didn't know she could—as if inspired.

"Do you remember where you learned the word 'hooligan'?" Clarissa asks. Riley shakes her head. "Well, I'm for it."

"Hubs, do you want to name the bear?" I ask. He studies me seriously. "If you saw a big black bear, what would you name him?"

He glances down, shy. "Darf," he whispers. He's sure he's gotten this wrong.

I expect Riley to pounce and make fun of him. "They are both black," she says.

"Miss Viola!" Hubbard shouts, sudden and gleeful. He smacks his plushies together, then gets a plastic brontosaurus from his toy bin.

Miss Viola is the mean teacher in a picture book Hubbard is currently obsessed with. She wears a black dress, and I wonder if he's processing this via color. We all praise his naming abilities.

We devise a list of names for this bear who is surely multiple bears. Hooligan Hello, Miss Viola, Richelieu (the name of a nearby river), Robert (the blind man's name in "Cathedral"), Robespierre (because the alliteration struck me as funny). Derriere Derry Bear. Frangipane

Peary Bear. Exeunt Pursued by a Bear Bear. Hubbabaloo Hubby Bear. All Riled-Up Riley Bear. Gus. Lila. Mille Feuille. Clarissa jots them down, and we agree we're the height of wit and hilarity. Hubbard lies on the floor before the fireplace and falls asleep. That nap he needed. Clarissa carries him upstairs. Riley asks if she can watch PBS Kids, and I switch it on for her. For the first time, I post to the listserv, offering a bit of levity: our family's list of alternate names for Butternut.

"Boo-boo?" Hubbard asks. "Hot? Boo-boo hot?"

"That's right, bud," I tell him for the tenth time this morning. "Daddy hurt his arm, but he's okay." As I was taking the kettle off the burner to make coffee, I jolted because Riley wailed—a fight, it turned out, about not wanting to say hello to her preschool class on Zoom—and my forearm brushed the blue-orange gas. Since Hubbard had seen me yelping, I showed him the wound—an angry welt just south of my elbow—to explain what had happened. Cause and effect. Stupid and stupider of me. Hubbard can be obsessive about what upsets him, discussing it over and over. Had Riley been this way too and we hadn't noticed because Hubbard had been an infant and we were sleepless automatons? Is this the human condition writ tiny? Or is this evidence of the particular ruminative person he'll become? Or is it—right this instant, when he is soft and malleable—he breathes in our pandemic dread and it reshapes him?

"Boo-boo?" Hubbard asks again, shaking his head when I offer him more sliced apple.

Clarissa comes downstairs, explaining Riley is in time out. "Your bear posting is up. They categorized it as 'for discussion.'" She sits and I pour her coffee.

"It seemed funny in the moment."

"It seems funny now. There amid the people searching for cheap microwaves and imploring one another to wear masks. I find it charming."

I grab my phone to see, which is silly, since I wrote it. "Another email from the administration," I say. "I bet they really value us during these trying times."

She glances at her phone. "I didn't get the email."

The blather is thick, the passive voice abundant. The gist: They value me so much. We'll all get through this together. They're putting the writing center "on pause" for the upcoming academic year. I will be on furlough during this time. I am to inform the returning tutors and administrative staff.

The vice president for academic affairs, who makes $300,000 a year —more than double the operating budget for the writing center—signs the email.

"What the fuck is the endowment for?" I ask. "They have over a billion dollars! And they can't afford to provide basic academic services?"

"Boo-boo?" Hubbard bangs the table with his yogurt spoon. I reassure him I'm fine.

"Call Marion. Actually, let me call her." She takes my phone and retreats to her study.

Hubbard requests to watch *Sesame Street*. I sit beside him, thinking of the first English department gathering Clarissa and I attended here. A mile from campus, an old ramshackle Victorian house with a wraparound porch, wicker chairs. A stone patio where everyone mingled, the western light fading through tall spruce at the edge of the extensive lawn. After years in Virginia, we thought the night chilly, but most were dressed as if it were still full-throated summer. Marion, the chair, had greeted us with glasses of sauvignon blanc and steered us to shade beneath a maple tree. Clarissa had just gotten *the job*— the tenure-track position at the pretty little liberal arts college—we'd begun to despair, after several years on the market, neither of us would ever get. Adjuncting is a hard-scrabble life, and we'd agreed: if one of us ever bested the odds and got a plummy gig, the other would follow and we'd make the best of it. Perhaps in a more populous state, I could've looked into work at a nearby college. Except the nearest college was well over an hour away and not hiring. Instead, luck came into play. A kind of luck. The director of the writing center—who'd had the gig thirty years—had had a health scare and decided to step down. It was too late in the academic year for the department to put out a national call, so they'd been quietly trying to decide what to do. And there I'd been at Clarissa's side during the on-campus interview, listening to her give her talk. My specialty is the twenty-first-century novel: post-postmodernism or metamodernism, as the hip kids say. I wasn't interested in rhetoric and comp or pedagogy. But I had the PhD, and they wanted to sweeten the deal for Clarissa, whom they loved. It promised reasonable hours. It was teaching of a sort. It just had nothing to do with my ambitions.

Clarissa was being chatted up by a professor who'd done his graduate work at Columbia in the early seventies—bald, jowly, an easy smile. Half the people there had similar stories: this was, for a party taking place within spitting distance of dairy farms and mountains, a very New York crowd. It was also a very aged one, a sea of lined faces and thinning hair. A man who taught creative writing told me a marvelous story about being in Paris and drinking rum out of tin cups with Philip Roth. He called him Phil. I laughed heartily. I was trying to gauge his age, whether he and Phil were peers. I was trying to gauge the ages of most because I was trying to calculate when another might step down. Then I'd be there—juggling chainsaws and breathing fire and whatever else they wanted.

Riley walks in and sits beside Hubbard. "Are you done with your time out?" She nods vigorously. "Did Mommy say you were done with your time out?" Riley explains Mommy is on the phone but Mommy had said her time out would be half an hour and Riley had decided if she read four of her books twice, then that would be half an hour, and she hadn't known Carey was going to be on the Zoom preschool gathering, because then she wouldn't have been so upset because Carey has been to a horse farm and pet a horse named Zeke and also she really likes Barbies.

"Ow!" She rubs her ribcage. "Hubbard! He elbowed me!"

Hubbard stares ahead with a determined little scowl. I ask him not to hurt his sister.

Clarissa comes in. She holds my phone out to me and shakes her head. I have to fight not to cry before my children. She gestures I follow her into the kitchen. I consider admonishing the kids to behave but know that will just spur them into greater cacophony in less time.

"Her hands are tied," Clarissa says. "Which I know sounds like bullshit, but she sounded really upset. She just got the email this morning too. She suspects this is happening across the college. Whatever they can get away with cutting, putting on hold, they're doing it. Even if the school opens in the fall, half the parents are going to insist their kids defer. They're going to be out so much tuition money."

"The endowment."

"I don't think it's rational. They're panicked. Maybe you could adjunct online at another school? We could share Zoom doom."

"I've spent the last four years barely teaching. And what college would choose someone they can't count on for more than a year?"

"I know this isn't real solace, but I bet a lot of people in this town woke up to bad news. Marion told me the art museum is going to be closed. So the art historians, the curators, the museum director. And I bet sports are going to get canceled. All the coaches. Musical activities. The chorus director, the band conductor."

I'm trying to listen, but it's just a buzzing in my ears.

"Hubbard!" Riley shrieks. "Stop!"

We find them on opposite ends of the couch. Hubbard has returned to scowling. Riley slaps the arm of the couch. "He keeps elbowing me!"

"Hubbard," I say, "I asked you once already to stop. Please apologize."

He goes to his toy bin, taking out his brontosaurus and wagging it at us as if in chastisement. "Ya, ya, ya! Ya!"

We don't have time for this. We need to be out before ten—Clarissa's first class. Clarissa gets the day bag ready while I carry a flailing Hubbard upstairs and sit with him. His stare is dark, angry. He holds my gaze longer than I would've imagined, then resolutely stares out the window to the tangle of tree limbs. I'll take the silence. Clarissa calls up the bag is ready. Hubbard allows me to get his shoes on without squirming, and we walk downstairs holding hands.

Adventure time. I drive through our winding neighborhood, rich with trees, its houses set far back, so Riley and Hubbard can look about. I've discovered they like this. They call out their observations. The lady with the big sunglasses is on her bike again. There is a sign with a turtle on it! (People don't want baby turtles to get hurt after they hatch, I explain.) Riley articulates more than Hubbard, but every time I check the rearview mirror, he's clutching Darth Vader and staring out, focused. Today they're both pretty quiet. The neighborhood is quiet. I do another slow loop. Part of the difficulty of these days is figuring out how to kill enough time, since Clarissa also needs quiet to prep. And it occurs to me belatedly: we can't both teach next fall. Even if I could secure the work, the kids, at this rate, won't be returning to preschool. And to have them home is to constantly chase after them. If we ended up teaching at the same time? The house would be burned down before fall break. We could hire a nanny, but that would cost more than I'd earn. Adjuncting means working for peanuts.

Riley points to a woman kneeling in her front yard. Planting tulips, I suggest. Riley announces Mommy also should plant some flowers. I say maybe we, as a trio, could plant some flowers this week. I ask Hubbard if he'd like to dig in the dirt, but he ignores me. Riley says she wants no flowers unless Mommy also helps with the planting.

Nothing in our lives feels sustainable. And it's all going to go on and on.

"Do you think we'll see Butternut?" Riley asks.

"I hope not." I say bears generally live in the woods, where it is better and safer for them. Riley suggests we walk in the woods, and I say we're going to the path along the golf course. There, we'll definitely see squirrels and birds. "And remember the owl? With the glossy eyes and the twisty neck, how it watched us?"

"Whoooooo," Hubbard croons. "Whoo, whoo!"

The campus has adjacent to its fitness facility a golf course, and encircling the golf course is a walking path bordered with trees and brush. We strike out on their favorite portion, crossing a wooden footbridge over a marshy patch, tufts of tall grass sprouting all askew. We go into a cluster of pines, where chickadees flit through the branches, blackcapped heads, cream-colored breasts. We practice singing their call, which sounds to me like a kind of sighing. Hubbard asks if this is an owl, and Riley says, "No, Hubbie, a chickadee-dee-dee!"

An older man wearing a mask glares as he passes by, but there's well more than six feet between us all. I think of explaining the *New York Times*, just this morning, published research suggesting the chances for transmission are greatly reduced outdoors. And also telling him he's an asshole. But I'm in a jerky mood.

After our walk we have a picnic on the athletic fields, Hubbard eating salami and dried apricots and crackers, Riley listlessly drinking her smoothie. Then they run shrieking about. A few other parents have similar setups, but we're all far from one another. So far, Riley and Hubbard have been good about not trying to play with other children, but Riley watches them with such unabashed interest. She's a deer catching another animal's scent in the wind.

This is generally the point in the day at which I'm most at odds with myself. I'm so grateful for this abundance of outdoor space. I'm also nearest weeping.

Hubbard runs up, asking for more apricots. I hand him one, and he wrinkles his nose as if perplexed. "This isn't what you wanted?"

"Hot?" he says.

"Daddy is okay."

"Okay, Daddy." He eats the apricot and takes another, putting it in his pocket. I don't correct this. He runs back to his sister.

I look at my phone: thankfully, no more emails from the administration. The listserv posting has arrived. At least half the postings are about bears. And several are about me—how terrible I am. A woman writes to remind us black bears just emerged from hibernation in April, so they're likely still hungry. Last Thursday afternoon at 12:04, a man saw a two-hundred-fifty-pound bear casually crossing Sycamore Road, and why is it every time he wishes he had his camera, he's left it at home? A woman saw a bear trying to get at her hummingbird syrup, so please, everyone, bring in all your birdfeeders at night. More advice, all the advice: keep your compost bins locked, pour Pine Sol around your compost bins, be careful driving in the evenings when both bear and sky are black. Bears are afraid of ringing bells, bears are shy, bears like compliments. In the I-am-a-jerkface category: one person does not appreciate my trivializing these beautiful wild creatures. They are beasts, not pets. She believes in being deferential to Nature, which she has stupidly capitalized. Another believes I was inappropriate. More appropriate: naming the bear Awehsoh, which is Abenaki for "bear" and would hearken to those who lived in this region before us.

The kids are running in circles, flinging out their arms, pretending they're so dizzy they collapse.

One from the woman who wrote the original Butternut posting. Was the point in contributing this "creative" list to highlight that Butternut, as name, was not inventive? Surely I had better things to do than mock the neighborhood's small traditions? A bit of fun for years to be the first to sight Butternut in Butternut Ridge. A particularly disdainful one: "Too clever by half, this list of 'names.' Flatlander nonsense. Respect where you live. This isn't Disneyland."

Riley squeals with laughter. Hubbard joins in, giggling. They're lying in the grass, arms out as if to make snow angels.

I am all thumbs, tippity-type: "THIS is the topic people have decided to focus their moral righteousness and fury upon? Over some hypothetical names for a bear? How dispiriting. How rude of you who wrote. How empty your lives. I have news for you: there's a pandemic. Try getting upset over THAT and stop taking out your frustrations on me."

"Hubbard!" Riley cries.

The kids are sitting up, side by side, and Riley is rubbing her ribcage.

Hubbard with his soft cheeks and big eyes and mean mouth. It doesn't add up.

"Hubbard, if you do that one more time, I am going to put peanut butter on your elbow, and then you are NOT going to be able to lick it off!" Riley stands, dusting grass off her knees. She starts marching toward me. I hit send and put away my phone.

Hubbard has lifted his elbow and is testing various angles, trying to bring it close to his mouth. I find myself doing the same. Riley has hit on some elemental truth: you cannot lick your own elbow.

Hubbard tips back his head to the sky. His wailing is terrible, his wailing is pure. It is a banshee cry interspersed with jagged, rasping breaths. It is a siren. I run for him, picking him up, patting his back, but he doesn't quiet. He doesn't even diminish. The other parents stare, horrified. Riley watches us return with apprehension. She clamps her hands to her ears. I set Hubbard down. Ring the alarum bell. Murder and treason! He's pale, but with blotches of scarlet on his cheeks. He howls, he laments, he's this wide black mouth.

"Riley," I say. "I need your help right now. We need to get everything in this bag and then I need you to go open the car door on Hubbard's side."

We assemble all our gatherings—the toys, the containers of food, the picnic blanket—and then Riley runs all flailing limbs to the car, opening the door. I jog too, Hubbard on my hip. He buries his head at the crook of my neck but doesn't let up. I get him in his car seat. I get Riley buckled in. I roll down all the windows, hoping the drive might soothe him. But as I keep glancing back, he never once rises up from within himself to reengage with the world. Such despair, such private sorrow, little Hubbard.

Riley is sitting with her eyes too large, her lips in a grimace. She's continued to keep her hands over her ears. I consider driving around town to give him a chance to calm, but I don't want her to have to put up with this any longer, either. I drive home.

We're trudging up the driveway—I've left the car doors open and don't care—knowing we're early. I'm grinding my teeth. Hubbard sounds as if someone is stabbing him. For a full half an hour this has not let up.

Clarissa flings open the front door. "Is he hurt?" I shake my head. "Did you lose Darth?"

"He's upset." I have to shout this to be heard.

"This is not what I meant to happen!" Riley wails. She pushes past her mother and runs upstairs.

"For fuck's sake!" Clarissa says. "I just canceled class because I thought my baby was dying!"

"I don't care," I say and ignore whatever look she tries to give me. I bring him to the living room and set him on the couch. His eyes and nose and mouth are crusted with tears and snot and saliva. I pet his hair over and over and over. He burrows into my side, his yelling directed at my abdomen.

And then he's done. He's asleep. He's snoring.

Clarissa has walked out only to return with Children's Benadryl, holding the spoon and bottle out as a kind of offering. She studies him, grazing her fingertips along his temple, then flops down next to me.

"Riley told him that if he elbowed her again, she'd put peanut butter on his elbow and he'd not be able to lick it off," I offer.

She bites her lip. Her eyes are cast down. "I should go get her." We can hear Riley's sobbing from her bedroom.

"Tell her it's not her fault," I say after Clarissa. "This is true," I say to her retreating figure. "It's not. It's not anyone's."

We're afraid to move him—to wake him—so Hubbard snoozes the rest of the afternoon on the couch. We keep coming in and checking on him, watching his chest rise and fall. Riley requests of her mother that they go for a walk and look at flowers in the neighborhood and that when they return, they watch *Barbie Dolphin Magic* together. Clarissa consents. She cancels a late afternoon class, muttering how her students probably don't care, anyway—if anything, they're relieved.

After they're back from their walk, I say I'm going to the store, even though the idea is, at most, we shop once a week, and I was just there two days ago. Mask on, hands sanitized, I buy four pints of ice cream: strawberry, pistachio, salted caramel, a local maple walnut. I buy whipped cream in a can, maraschino cherries, a jar of hot fudge. When I get back, Clarissa says, "This is what you went out for?" And I say I want us all to have ice cream for dinner.

Hubbard wakes up just as I'm scooping ice cream into bowls. Riley acquiesces to strawberry (I knew she would) and lots of whipped cream. Hubbard staggers in, sleep drenched. We all behold him, hunting for signs of distress, but he looks sweet again—eyes big and dark, even if they are crusted from so many tears. "Ice cream, Hubbard?" I show him the pints, explaining the flavors.

"Hot?" he asks. Ice cream is not *hot*, Riley says, but absent any temerity. "Boo-boo?" he tries again.

Clarissa sighs. I know she doesn't mean to. I tell him I'm fine and suggest he try the strawberry too. He shakes his head and points. Salted caramel it is, and hot fudge that ends up smeared on his cheeks and, somehow, his hair.

Later, after we've got them in bed, Clarissa says she saw the listserv postings and would like to say, pointedly, that those people are knuckleheads and dumb-dumbs, and I'm not to spare any more thought regarding their bullshit. I tell her what I wrote, and she's horrified. She reaches to her bedside table, grabbing her phone. "There's been no posting this evening. Write them back now and take it back."

"I don't take it back," I say. "They're sanctimonious shitheads. They should hear about it."

"Charles." She sets her phone back down. "It's ugly."

"So they get to be rude to me?"

"They're upset about larger things and taking it out on you. But others will understand that. Consider that the rest of the community will see what you wrote. We need to get along with people. We need to get along with our neighbors—even the sanctimonious ones."

"This is about your chances for tenure. This is about me embarrassing you before your peers."

"They're your peers too."

I bat down my pillow too hard, turn on my side. "Actually, I'm nothing more than a glorified tutor."

"Please don't blame me for what happened today. Maybe also don't blame me for getting this job in the first place, while we're at it."

"That's fair, Clarissa. I lose my job, and you start trying to make me feel guilty for being angry about it."

She puts her hand on my shoulder, but I won't look at her. "It's because you're angry you wrote that. In normal circumstances, you'd think through this differently."

"Well," I say. "We're not in normal circumstances, are we?"

She says, "What about Cappie, your love?" Trying to lighten the mood. And frankly, that's her best-played card. I don't want that elegant woman to think I'm some hothead, willing to rage in pointless ways about pointless things. I tell Clarissa this. I tell her I'm still not taking back what I wrote, and I pretend to sleep until I actually do drift off.

A deep dread, an anxiety tightening my chest, rouses me. Hubbard is standing alongside the bed, his face so close to mine our noses almost touch. The blinds are drawn, but the quality of light suggests it's just before dawn. "Darf," Hubbard whispers. He looks expectant, eyebrows raised. I rise, following him, expecting we will go to his bedroom, that I'll read him some books and see if I can't coax him to sleep at least another hour. Instead, he pads down the stairs and into the living room.

His sister, in her yellow footed pajamas, is at the glass door leading to the back porch. She has her hands pressed to the glass. She turns to me and gestures I come over. As I stand beside her, she raises her index finger to her lips: quiet. Hubbard stands alongside me, taking my hand. "Butternut," she breathes.

In our backyard, near the cedar compost bin we just acquired this spring because the state has newly mandated we not throw away food scraps, is a black bear. I think of a stagecoach sans horses. I think of a caravan, some old-fashioned carnival en route to nowhere, its procession gloomy, lonely. The bear is prowling about the bin—more of a big wooden box. In fact, the woman who sold it to us touted that it was bear resistant, which, at the time, I thought excessive marketing. The bear stands on two feet, leaning its front paws against the lid, and delicately gnaws a corner. Its snout is longer than I'd imagined, its ears bigger and more pointed. Its fur ripples as it drops back down again. It tests another side. This time, as it rises, it puts its paws down more aggressively on the lid, then starts trying to push the box back and forth. The box shivers. Riley inhales. The bear ceases its snuffling and shoving and looks up at us, we three in our sleepwear, noses pressed to the glass. Its eyes match its coat, and its gaze is neither aggressive nor shy, but flatly engaged. We exist, the bear's gaze says, but only as a disturbance in its day. We are a problem the bear is not willing to engage in.

It drops back to all fours and lopes off across the yard, all ambling bristle and strength. Well, the listserv people were right about one thing, anyway. They're not cute, these bears. They are wild.

The sun is rising, rosiness in the east warming the gray sky. I could still email the people who run the listserv and take back what I wrote yesterday in my heat and depression, in my anger at the world.

Then Hubbard suggests he would like some crackers, and Riley says she would like to go outside and talk with Butternut, and I tell her we can't, that bear was dangerous, and neither of them must ever, ever go outside if they again see a bear in the yard, and I'm thinking I should tell Clarissa we're going to need to put a childproof lock on the sliding glass door as soon as we can. Also, Hubbard needs his diaper changed, and I need to make Riley her smoothie. The day is new, but I take no new meaning from it. I just need to figure out how to get by.

Mountain Shade

SHE DID NOT BELIEVE in ghosts. She lived in mountain shade. A green mountain, part of the Vermont range, which much of the year was a blurred blue-gray, its edges made mild by time. She thought it might be growing larger. After thirty years in its presence, she thought she'd be in the position to judge.

Out West, on a recent vacation, she'd seen the world from eleven thousand feet: gray rock and yellowed moss, withered sage brush, and tiny, delicate profusions of edelweiss. Her eyes had watered in the thin air. All about her was wind and thick white sky and further off jagged peaks. Time had held still.

Her mountain did not freeze time. Instead, it offered up another existence—some space rough and strange and indifferent to longing.

Outside of time, maybe. She was always trying to puzzle this out. Rows of her deceased husband's philosophy books still lined his study, and she could've dipped into any of these and found some system of thinking that could illuminate, or at least categorize, her mind's preoccupations. But in that beautiful dark room, those built-in bookshelves on three sides, his old oak desk, his brass lamp, his yellow notepads for all his lectures written in longhand: they went untouched, they were memorial to him.

That trip to Colorado: she'd been shocked that roads could wind up entire mountains, that these roads were paved, that signs told you where you were and what your elevation was. Charming, stupid arrows pointing and telling you that California was a thousand miles due west, while you with your friends sat at a bench and commenced picnicking, sandwiches purchased earlier from a general store decked out in the hokum of cowboy hats and pictures of elk standing in riverbeds as fog wisped behind them. They ate baguettes with tuna and arugula, and from a thermos sipped cocoa. Wind had brushed the back of her neck. She couldn't believe someone had sculpted something human into this terrain, that there was an apex, that one could arrive to it so easily. This ease: something in it lingered for her as particular travesty.

She'd never been to her own mountain's top. She felt sure no one had. Her mountain was obscure, one of many in the four hundred thousand acres of forests the state had preserved. Its paths were crumbling—old logging trails that had fallen into disrepair and never were anything more than tracks of dirt. They started in the woods just behind her backyard. Over the years, she'd traced them, learning how they crisscrossed one another but in such broad gentle loops it took a long time to figure out you were moving in circles. The old pines and younger birch and maple provided a canopy and thus a vegetal twilight, a constant dusk. Not this no-time she thinks the mountain signals, but an entrance into it. Paths could always, too, change or disappear.

Small movements accompanied her: the crash and clatter of squirrels darting through bramble or up branches—tails sinuous and furred;

branched leaves rustling; or the crunch of them underfoot, their scent of decay. Eventually she was joined by the sound of her own breath, which was too loud and immediate. She didn't like being reminded of her body. In the woods, she was part of something larger and, in that sense, she became less corporeal, less bound by her own particular history.

Occasionally she had a hard time coming back. Not in the literal sense. She could always, if she did get turned around, eventually figure out which direction was west and get home, even if that meant stumbling into a neighbor's backyard and then walking down the street. It was shedding the rough enchantment. She'd emerge from the trees and cross her sculpted yard to the outdoor deck, low and open and wood stained, with Nathan's fancy grill and her rows of potted plants, her bird feeder set low in the nearby maple's bows. All of it too safe, too easy, too shockingly undefended against the real terrain out there. She'd stand in a kind of limbo. Behind her, the woods held something both there and not there, an experience that haunted her, but which she knew nothing about. She guessed it to be a forgetting, star filled but dark.

Sometimes, this haunting felt so palpable she would—just before she came back to the house and was forced to see it as silly and small—sit on a large granite rock, often sun warmed, and let her shoulders heave, her composure collapse, let snot fall onto her breast.

This when Nathan was still alive. So it wasn't something as simple as a death wish. Just this awareness she had to carry, a sense of being outside what was really there.

Thirty years ago, after Nathan had accepted his professorship, they left Manhattan for what they'd both jokingly referred to as "the hills." Their friends—she thinks they spoke of it over fondue—were horrified. But they too were intellectuals, young and hungry, so they understood: sometimes, to lead a life of the mind, you had to live somewhere without skyscrapers or taxis or takeout.

The first year, the college provided housing in town, the town being just a tiny row of brick businesses built near a crashing river. An old mill town where seedy Victorians lined the tree-shaded streets. There were at least sidewalks and a lovely little campus, all gray brick and marble. Then, suddenly, the Manhattanites needed land. Or, not suddenly. It was cocktail-party logic. As they sipped wine among the tenured, they saw their peers lived in houses with charming brooks dappling through their backyards, or lived adjacent to dairy farms: wet-eyed black-and-white lumbering creatures posing so everyone could crowd onto the porch and sigh over their rustic charm. Faculty were from everywhere—New York, Houston, San Francisco. She remembers holding a glass of white wine, discussing how teaching composition was going—a lectureship, a pittance tossed her way, faculty hires so often having spouses—and realizing she and Nathan were going to do this, too: live in the country and take for granted vast pastures, unremitting quiet, crickets, cows, clover, silos.

They termed their choice "cusp-of-woods" living. The house was open and dark inside, large windows letting in streaks of light passing through the treetops. A kind of wavering, as if they were underwater. Other houses were spread out along the street. On all sides the forest encroached. And farther off, the mountains, her mountain. About a mile's walk were a gas station, a church, and a post office.

The world had changed after Nathan's heart attack, and yet surely the only thing that had changed was her. Two other faculty wives— friends—had arranged the trip to Colorado to help her clear her head, but she spent too much of the time thinking she was a wisp of smoke that might twist off into the night air. One evening, they sat in a steak-house and she told them she couldn't escape the notion that had she not gone out to run errands, she could've saved him. The mildest of afternoons: she'd gone to her office to grab a stack of papers that needed grading, then to the co-op to get something for dinner. She'd lingered over tart cherries, finally deciding on them as a small treat. She'd chatted with an acquaintance in the checkout line. But had she not tarried? As she spoke, she moved blue cheese dressing about her plate. Low-hanging lamps shaded in red glass pulsed, brightening and fading, in time to her heart roaring in her ears.

"You shouldn't destroy yourself thinking that way, Hannah," Beth said. "You don't know that anything would've been different." She sipped too long from her wine, waiting for Hannah to nod or otherwise agree. Emma then said there was a difference between mourning—which was public—and grief, which was private, and she felt Hannah needed to mourn more. Run a 10K in Nathan's honor or erect a scholarship in the philosophy department in his name.

Later, as Hannah tried to fall asleep, she found herself turning over this distinction. Nathan would've termed it a dialectic and said that such easily drawn distinctions don't really adhere to the more amorphous shape of our thoughts. She imagined it—grief versus mourning—as a delicate bauble, an overpriced hand-blown Christmas decoration. The unexamined life was not worth living, Socrates said. Well, the examined life was like walking barefoot across a field of easily shattered Christmas ornaments. She drew the sheets about her in the hotel room's unfamiliar dark. Her thinking was both indulgence and impatient self-excoriation. Neither was the answer. Nothing was.

Nathan had been fifty-eight. They easily could've had another thirty years together in their dark woodsy house. Had she not gone out for tart cherries.

At the memorial, she spoke of Nathan being an avid reader—not just of philosophy but of fiction that posed moral questions. He loved Mann, Camus, and Vonnegut. She talked of students through the years always telling her he was a wonderful professor, both wry and exacting, and how much, in particular, they loved his intro to philosophy course. And wasn't that something, she said, in this fast-and-furious age.

A few in the audience offered attentive nods. She told them he was kind, that he liked British humor and being by the ocean—he loved the whorls on seashells and the salt in the wind. That he was still that kid who'd grown up in the Bronx and spent his summers working in a cardboard box factory, that he often referred to the manual labor as part of his first inquiries into existentialism, that he thought roasted chestnuts from street vendors were the world's most perfect food.

Afterward, as people murmured polite, appropriate condolences, she remembered—overwhelmingly and almost to the exclusion of what was happening around her—his giggling over John Cleese in *Fawlty Towers*, sitting before the TV with a bowl of popcorn, the low light flickering and Cleese shouting and running about. He'd laughed so much, half the popcorn hadn't even reached his mouth, white fluttering kernels all over his lap. He'd noticed her watching him and flung some popcorn her way, which got no further than the arm of his chair. And at that, he'd laughed even harder. She wished then that what she'd offered to those who attended had not been so careful and banal. Perhaps more honest would've been to just put on that show and hand out bowls of popcorn, let people giggle inappropriately.

He had come home from a typically long run—sweat dripping at his temples—and had put on his glasses to kiss her hello, which was also habitual, if lacking in logic. He said he was feeling a little lightheaded, that he was going to take a shower. He waved off her concerns—I'm fine, my electrolytes are probably a little imbalanced, I'll take some magnesium. He went into the bedroom, and she went out into her day.

When she came back, cloth tote full of groceries, satchel full of papers, and walked into the living room, it was as if electricity had shot through her—that quickly she knew something was wrong. She called his name and then went to look for him in the bedroom, sunshine coming in through the windows slow and wavering and soft on him in this gross rigidity lying on the bed wrapped in a towel. His shoulders were jagged, one high, the other caved, and as she came closer, she saw his lips were the color of blue chalk. The ambulance crew were professional and kind and moved about her as she stood in the way, shrieking at them, What took you so long? And: What happened, what happened, what happened?

Later she learned they'd taken fifteen minutes to arrive, siren wailing, tearing along the small roads. And, one of them gently informed her as she watched them wheel his body out to the ambulance, a sheet draped over him, making him an object, making him anonymous, that he had

had a heart attack and had already passed on before she'd come home. "Passed on" was what the ambulance driver said. He had a smoker's cough and light-blue eyes. Passed on.

They had matching armchairs both turned to the large western-facing window. Red and oversized and luscious for afternoon reading, the chairs were turned inward so she and Nathan could sit in afternoon light and be bathed both in contemplation but also each other's presence. That part of her life was over. It was one of her first thoughts. Why was it over? Because it was.

There was little in her life she'd undo, but she'd undo those twenty minutes. Over and over she has replayed them. First, she'd called the ambulance. She'd taken her phone from her pocket and said something has happened to my husband, please come. She then put her mouth to his mouth and tried to compel his heart, pressing and pressing on his chest. His lips were cool and he was stiff, and her adrenaline was such that the room appeared to be whirling about and only they were still. She tried until she didn't—until horror crept into her and she saw him as a corpse. There was no response in his touch, none, and this was as grotesque a thing she could think of. She'd erase it instantly if she could, this knowledge of his skin without heartbeat, body without brainwave. This absence. She could drown in her understanding of it. Days now, it might be all she thought about.

Today she was at the sink, running plates under the soapy lavender-scented water. The blue-gray heft out her window considered her as she studied it in return, its thread of dark branches still stark in early spring. She had to teach class at two. Then she should pick up groceries on the way home. In New York, they now had companies that would deliver the ingredients of meals to your door. This sounded lazy, but she wished for it because if she were in the co-op perusing the cheeses and outside tornadoes were swallowing homes and barns and whisking them away. Or if she were grinding coffee and a madman appeared on campus, raising his gun, ratty eyes alight with rage, and firing. People would crumple and no longer contain themselves. She'd emerge from the store to air electric with keening. It would all be her fault.

She could sell the house, leave behind its shifting, branching light, and return to the city. But she didn't know how to change the tempo of herself to match its current grit and entanglement. And she would miss the mountains and woods. It was more than that. She'd become a part of this landscape.

She wiped her damp hands on her jeans and turned the faucet off. The regular grocery store would suffice—she'd save the co-op for another day. If people knew her mind, what mixture of pity and alarm she might engender. But some too must carry hidden irrational grief. They couldn't all run 5Ks or see therapists or do volunteer work.

It was only eleven. She'd walk an hour, then have lunch before going to campus to leaf over lecture notes. She turned to grab her fleece, hanging by the door to the back porch, when she saw a coffee cup on the table. It was because she'd finished her coffee she'd first begun washing dishes. She picked it up, examining its rim for the faint imprint of her lips, then dropped it, a rolling thud into the leg of the kitchen table. She'd been trying to assess if it were Nathan's. Picking it up, she bowed her head. Her mountain was waiting, but first she put more soap to the sponge, more floral-noted aromatherapy. She put the errant cup, now clean, into the rack to dry.

The walk took her through her backyard and onto a thin path through light woods that then opened to a dirt road along which one pale-blue house stood. The family who lived there had already set out their patio furniture, although it was too early for such things—the night still dipping below freezing and the daytime in the mid 40s. Today there was a damp in the air, and gray, austere light. Across the way, the horses in the pasture raised their heads from some hay to watch as she passed. The road turned left at the end of the pasture, dwindling into a trail that was nothing more than trampled leaves and slick old grass. On either side, the trees brought her into their hush.

Where the path first forked, she veered left, up a small hill to where the pines were thicker and enshrouded more, and the dusk that wasn't dusk began to take over. Her heart rate rose, and she heard her breathing while wishing she didn't. And—sure sign of spring—in the distance a small stream was rushing and letting off the smell of damp earth, of copper.

At the second branch she went right, noting it so she could reverse course on the way home. A tattered sign tacked to a tree read No Hunting. Her mountain cast the walk in shadow and cooler air. Pockets of it drifted downward from where snow was still melting at the higher elevation.

This never was for Nathan, this negotiation through a rough quiet. He'd run for miles and miles but preferred to stay alongside roadways. He'd listened to podcasts these last few years. Before that, music on his iPod. He'd always been after her to bring her phone. She kept on her wristwatch, but she didn't need to be checking her email, listening to music, even stopping to take photos. Otherwise she could not be absorbed by what surrounded her. Even though she had not wanted him to worry. What luxury, she now thought, to know you could stir worry in another.

She skirted a large fallen pine bough and heard rustling—the beat of feathers, the skitter of claws on bark. Then footsteps rose above that and she turned. Just come from the woods, stepping around an old maple, was a man with dirty cheeks and beard, a red flannel and Carhartts, holding a cigarette. He nodded and she nodded back. "Nice day for a walk," he said.

She agreed and kept moving. It might have been that he'd been unclean and also that he hadn't been on a literal path. She knew not to judge, however, and shushed the alarmed flutter of her heart. Maybe he had an ATV nearby and had gotten off to smoke, or was checking sap buckets further in. She'd not recognize danger right now, anyway.

She crossed a stream where years ago someone had set out a small wood plank, now glistening with old rain and snow and edged in moss, and came into a clearing of birch. One had an exposed section of pink-beige where a woodpecker must've worried it. She picked at it herself, tearing the thin white skin, feeling ashamed and excited to add to the entropy. She was a half an hour in and should turn back. But she could eat a quick sandwich and didn't really need to leaf over her notes. Blue was breaking through the gray cloud, weak light playing through the stark branches. She stumbled—a rock—and steadied her palm against rough spruce bark. This was her life.

At the outset, there'd been the initial pleasure of the greenery, the maple trees artfully arranged on campus, the Adirondack chairs beneath their boughs, a church with a white steeple at the top of a green hill. It was idyllic, a storybook picturesque. But once their adrenaline had settled—They'd moved! To Vermont!—she knew the town bored her with its small stores selling beeswax candles and postcards of covered bridges, apple-scented hand soaps and maple candies, vivid watercolors of cows. Now, if she had to articulate her dislike, she'd say it was because she found it false—an idea of a place but not an actuality.

But back then she could only suggest—after their first two years had wrapped up—that Nathan apply to teach at Columbia or maybe NYU. "Before we're trapped here the rest of our lives," she'd said. She shouldn't have said it. They'd been on the living room couch, their legs on the table. She'd made them omelets with mushrooms, which they were having with beer. A metallic crackle across otherwise calm air. She was ignoring his happiness—small classes, bright students, nice department. Or she was suggesting his happiness wasn't specific to the occasion or place—he'd be just as content elsewhere. Or she was saying her happiness was more important than his. And doing so all without sufficient ability to articulate what she was feeling, or the cause.

He pushed his glasses higher onto the bridge of his nose. "Hannah." He gestured to the large windows, the shifting gray-shadowed black of outdoors, which made them feel they were in the belly of a ship. Then, they had cheap lantern-like lamps, which glowed yellow. She already understood—and resented understanding because the logic was not hers—but he said it anyway. "This is the dream. We have it. It's ours."

She still mistrusted this town proud of its sweetness and light—because, she thought, it refused ugliness and brutality and, therefore, real scope. She kicked a small stone. She also mistrusted this self who conjured such stupid thoughts. What great truth, to see a rotting raccoon infested with flies or a pile of ingested, then discarded bones? If they'd lived anywhere else, she'd probably have come up with similar qualms—some sort of refutation of what was there as not really meaningful or true. That might just be, at essence, her. Her philosopher husband probably understood this instinctively and was right not to give in all those years ago to her amorphous uneasiness.

She came to a tree that had recently gone down, its roots heavy with caked earth, small bugs whirring and wriggling within it. Her mountain, to her left, was purple-blue and close. She checked her watch, startled another thirty minutes had passed. She needed to turn back and moved through a stretch of mountain ash and alder, then couldn't remember whether she'd come from the right fork or the left. They'd likely twine, a very loose double helix, but one route might wind her in a circle, and at this point she didn't have the luxury of time. Of course, it was part of the woods' bewitchery that its landscape constantly shifted in minute ways, but she was confused by her own confusion. This was not alien terrain. How could she have no bearings?

Before her were so many moldering leaves, not fully decayed over the winter. She chose the uphill path to her right. Perhaps she'd lost track because the walking had been easy, because she'd been descending. So now she'd go up.

As she crested the ridge, she realized she would've noticed traversing this steep an incline (or decline)—and then three deer bounded across the ridgeline. Their flipped-up tails, the undersides of their bellies, were white. She felt the ground shift with their gallop and saw their terse, shifting flanks. Then they were gone, swallowed by woods and fractured sunlight.

To hell with it. She went straight down the ridge's other side, eschewing the path and just grabbing at small tree trunks to keep from sliding. The direction had to be essentially correct if her mountain remained to her right. Not only would it be unprofessional and embarrassing to arrive to class late, it would make her fraying manifest. Her husband had died and therefore she'd gotten lost. It made sense. It didn't.

At the bottom was a small, fast stream that she'd need to cross before climbing another hill. She couldn't scout any path, so she sloshed through the ice water—sneakers soaked, pants wet up to her shins. If she'd really poured two cups of coffee this morning and not noticed. If Nathan were a ghost watching her as she went to Colorado and didn't go to the co-op. If they were separated by tissue-thin reality—just into the blackness, this otherness, and she'd find him.

She zigzagged about trees, pushing herself to keep her pace brisk. Her heart was high in her ears. The trails, if nominal, at least often stayed on flatter terrain. She still couldn't find a path. Her mountain was just a wall of rough spruce and pine, bare-limbed snatches of deciduous trees, ugly and overcrowded. She had to crane her neck to see its top and while doing so got caught in some light branches, which stung her cheeks. Her feet were heavy, her socks soaked in cold.

Maybe she was too close if the actual cliffs and shelves of rock were visible. So as corrective she headed east. A bird called out—the throaty harsh sound of a blue jay—then swooped from one high branch to another. She had half an hour left. Years and years, and she'd never been this turned around. The sky was marbling over, losing its blue, returning to its initial gray.

Her stomach growled in protest, in reminder. At breakfast, she'd barely touched her toast. Her mornings so slow and queasy now because everyday she woke expecting to see Nathan with his near-sighted smile rubbing his bristling cheek—to hear him sigh sour breath and then rise to brush his teeth. She'd slip into her robe and make coffee. They were neither of them early risers. Sunlight and birdcall would be thick about them at all the windows, the striped shadow of branches and tree trunks. After he'd showered, she would. Then she'd comb back her hair, dress, and return to the kitchen so they could sit and linger over good bread with butter and coffee. His favorite white mug was from their New York years.

She found herself at the bottom of yet another hill, which she charged up, thinking she could be tired and sad later. Her breathing was so loud, so heavy: being lost was the opposite of losing yourself. All this time spent in self-preoccupation, aware of your limitations.

Then she saw again that goddamn fallen tree, its dirty tangle of roots spread in the air.

She hugged herself. Light broke above, some cloud shift. She turned to her mountain, then sat in the dirt and cried.

The light scratches on her face stung with salt, and with the back of her hand, she smeared away some mucus pooling at the indent above her lip. She wondered if this were grieving or mourning. She grabbed a handful of leaves and wiped at her wet face. Someone somewhere would find that horrifying and lecture her about dirt or bacteria or ticks.

She stood because she couldn't just sit. She turned to her mountain once more, convinced it had tricked her.

She climbed the first hill she'd gone up before running ridiculously down it. This time, she stayed at the top of the ridgeline and walked along its path, which lead her directly away—as she perceived it—from her mountain. She was sorrowful and sore. She felt outside of every existence: the ones she inhabited, the ones she conjured.

She stopped. There, in the distance: the soft rush of cars along pavement. She kept going in that direction and then the trail crumbled and before her was a steep dirt cliff. But she could also see out to a paved road and, beyond that, the steely distant Adirondacks. She let herself practically fall down the cliff, sliding in a crouch to go faster down. She spilled over into some blackberry bushes, the purple tangle all whip snap and thorns, and came out onto someone's farm. A barn across the field—a few trucks parked alongside. A trough off to the left and beside it a stack of old tires. Farms inevitably had old tires on their property. It was one of those ineluctable but nonsensical things. She was safe, she was not lost. She was still pretty lost.

A man came out from the barn in waders and a dirty, torn blue shirt. He was holding a sandwich in one hand. He regarded her. Then he took a bite of his sandwich.

"I got lost," she said. "On the trails."

He nodded. "Those old logging trails go back and back for miles."

"How far are we from town?" She must've driven past this property a million times. But she could only think how glad she was not to be within grasping distance of a tree trunk.

"Which town," he said, and took another bite, chewing. She wondered how terrible she looked and thought how kind—in a sense—of him to regard her with such indifference.

She told him where she lived, and he said she was maybe five miles south from where she started. She could just walk back along the road, he suggested, rather than go back into the woods. She had no intention of returning to the woods. Class had already begun. She thought to ask him to drive her home—to say she was so tired and that her husband had died and she'd maybe lost her mind and maybe the landscape had just shifted to keep her centered on herself and outside the otherness it contained—but what right did she have to burden him this way? To burden anyone? There were so many reasons to keep grief hidden.

"I was in there for hours," she said. "I got so turned around."

"It happens." He pointed north. "You head back that way, you'll get home safe." He walked back into the barn, and she went toward the road. What philosophy could get at loss, begin to even explain it. Her mountain watched her as she began again to move.

The Forest Tavern

IN THE STUDY, the skylight filters in pearlescent post-rain light. My desk looks out onto an empty field. On my desk, beside my laptop, is *These Ever Flowing Years: A History of the East Coventry Inn*, written by Harriet Schuppert in 1967. Its cover is the inn drawn in ink. My neighbor, well-meaning, foisted this book on me once she discovered I'm a writer. (I've written two novels no one has heard of.) I'm trying to write my third now, a process that's going splendidly awry. I think I'll read this book. Maybe it will somehow (obliquely) help. My novel has nothing to do with local history or nineteenth-century inns, but today my procrastination takes the form of desperate optimism.

In 1800, it begins, the Vermont legislature builds a road passing through the local mountain range. Epapharus Jones (impossibly named) believes many people will travel this route. Also, a glass factory is being built upon a lake the town over. East Coventry will receive many travelers and be a place of industry. So he builds the inn alongside the new road.

Harriet discusses if the inn is built in 1810, as it's generally agreed, or 1812. She discovered a note dated 1811 in a mason's ledger describing how Epapharus paid the mason (in cloth) to build a chimney. Her take: the inn already existed; the chimney must've been an addition. Or was the inn still being built?

I email Jess, my best pragmatic gal, the breadwinner, my consultant bride, and tell her about the lack of clarity surrounding the inn's beginnings. Jess terms it The Great Chimney Debate of 1811. She tells me I don't have to dwell on the book too long—just read enough to make our neighbor happy.

I return to reading. Here's something delightful: the inn's first name was The Forest Tavern. Laborers who make dress cloth and carding wool stay here. Travelers crossing the mountain gap stop here. They travel in stagecoaches!

But East Coventry never becomes the industrious hub Epapharus imagined. The mountain road is too expensive to maintain, so the state turns over this responsibility to individual towns who can't afford the upkeep. By 1850 the road is in ruinous shape: very few stagecoaches, almost no travelers. Also: "The glass factory exploded in 1817." (What?) Locals still use the inn as a watering hole; some laborers still stay there, but patronage is sparse. Epapharus decides to sell the inn. Harriet includes his advertisement, which runs in 1853 and claims the road running past the "commodious house" is still well traveled and that East Coventry is flourishing. The Forest Tavern commands "extensive patronage."

Harriet doesn't discuss these lies. She does suggest Epapharus's heavy financial burdens and notes he's seventy-eight. Years elapse, and poor Epapharus dies at eighty-four having not sold the inn.

I go sit on the porch. It's September and trees are beginning to shade gold. The morning's rain makes the air smell earthy. So the inn began with failure: borne from ideas that never came to fruition and became a burden on this man's heart.

That night, Jess laughs about the exploding glass factory but tries to take seriously Epapharus Jones's failures. However, she also suggests (nicely) I return to my writing.

The year after Epapharus Jones dies, Royal Farr (really, with these names) buys the inn. Harriet doesn't say from whom.

Royal had been a partner in a forge business (forging seems mysterious) but gives this up to run the newly renamed The Glen House. (What a step down from The Forest Tavern!) He and his wife, Mary, have five children: one daughter and four sons.

As Harriet discusses industry picking up in Vermont in the 1860s (once the state gets a railroad), I'm wishing for more information about actually running the inn. I want to know how Royal makes it work when Epapharus couldn't, but we're on to the Civil War. Royal and his son Henry become soldiers. Royal commands a company. Before leaving, he signs the inn's deed over to his wife—in case he or his son die fighting. These poor people. Harriet is saying the Civil War ends in 1865 but hasn't even said whether Henry and Royal survive.

Phew. I flip ahead and see Royal builds a ballroom. A ballroom! Also, he starts writing for *The Coventry Register*. Holy cow. This, dated July 18, 1866, discussing how he knows of no other place better than East Coventry: "Our citizens are of a working class. We are not overrun with a hoard of poor, half-starved pauper aristocracy whose lives are a mere blank."

What an existential headache; what a punch to my pauper-aristocracy gut.

I get more coffee. As the microwave warms it, I rehearse telling Jess, knowing she'll tell me not to worry over Royal Farr's judgy insults.

The microwave beeps. I'm back upstairs, industrious. My life is not a mere blank.

Another newspaper article—this one describing the inn's surrounding beauty. It gives me a better beat on Royal: he can turn a phrase. An ad man before his time.

It is situated at the entrance of one of the wildest and most grand glens. From the glen's deep, shady recesses, the waters of the small river issue in such dashing and foaming manner. One can be fanned by mountain breeze under the shadows of the rocky walls.

Harriet explains the tavern/boarding house of fifty years ago is now a social destination. Yes, because Farr knew how to entice.

And now, this ballroom. It was built "circa" 1867. (No more getting bogged down in timelines.) Royal had weekly dances, charging $1.50 for locals and $2 for "outsiders." (Ha!) They'd start at nine pm and go until one am, at which point the inn would serve a midnight supper of oysters, ham, and beef. Harriet is playing coy with her sources. "It has been noted that many farmers got back just in time to do the morning chores." *Who* noted this? I want to know everything about these dances. There's something impossibly beautiful about farmers leaving off eating oysters and returning home to, say, milk cows. In overalls and caps, tipsy and brimming with rich foods as they sit in their barns, champagne still sweet on their tongues, patting the flanks of Daisy and Maisy and describing their evenings of dance and shouted laughter.

"There was a BALLROOM!" I email Jess. "There were balls. Think *Anna Karenina* minus Vronsky plus farmers."

"Lol, you know I've not read *Anna Karenina*," she responds.

Harriet presses on, offering a strange anecdote. "There was an old timer who used to mark the close of the evening by sliding down the bannister and rushing out the front door. It became a very famous act." "Old timer" isn't her voice. And who found this act famous? I worry when her sentences display a lack of agency. My instinct is she's transcribed someone's account, but she's discussing the years just after the Civil War. This section's final sentence: "A bowling alley and a skating rink were offered for guests who did not wish to dance."

I imagine Harriet in the living room of some ancient farmer, a Dictaphone before him, as he tells the tall tales his grandfather told him about the inn. Later, Harriet, who has honey-colored hair, sits in a small sunlit study rife with books. She's smoking a cigarette, tapping ash into an ashtray, listening to her Dictaphone recording of this old man's rambles, and deciding how much credence to lend them when Harriet's daughter calls up she's hungry. Sure, Harriet's thinking as she makes a grilled cheese. A ballroom. Midnight oysters. A skating rink. Details exciting and romantic.

At breakfast, Jess says if I'm legitimately interested, I should ask the historical society for materials that could verify Harriet's accounts. "But I think you're overthinking it," she says.

"The ice-skating rink, the bowling alley?"

"Fact is stranger than fiction," she says happily. "The ice skating could've been out back."

But, I say, the inn closed on November 1 and reopened May 1. "I don't think the inn operated during the winter months."

"Perhaps they were heartier in the 1860s." She kisses my cheek. "You should return to your book, not worry over this."

But she knows my newest novel is going terribly. I am glum as she drives off into the fall morning.

I return to the study. In 1871, Mary Farr sells The Glen House to Ebenezer B. Jenny for $500. In 1882, Ebenezer B. sells the inn to Mary and Royal's youngest son, Frank.

Frank has Will Allen, his brother-in-law, become the proprietor. Dances, under Allen's tenure, grow more riotous, more alcoholic. On February 14, the inn holds a Washington Day ball, after which Will is arraigned for serving liquor. This is interesting: in Vermont, Prohibition began in 1853 but was only loosely enforced. Harriet mentions no fines, no jail time. Then Will is arraigned again the following July—this time for selling liquor during an Independence ball. The people of East Coventry send a petition to the state's attorney asking Will not be prosecuted, which is successful.

The Coventry Register writes of Will's son, Will Jr., also getting into trouble. "Young Will" and his friend George go into the wine cellar to drink wine. Will Sr. discovers them and a fight breaks out. George gets cut, "leaving a gash clear to his bone." And then young Will "fled with his pitcher of wine and his knife." (I like that he kept the pitcher.) George, very loyal, says the stabbing was an accident. A warrant is issued for young Will's arrest, but the newspaper says young Will is "a gentle young man, and much liked."

Harriet doesn't tell us the outcome. Although I admire her, she's not the best at tying up loose ends.

Another article. Some "bourbon ruffians" (a beautiful phrase) kidnap (!) Will Allen and drag him into the street and shave off his beard and make him declare he'll take down the Republican flag flying at The Glen House. He refuses, so the ruffians dunk him three times in the river and then tie him to a tree. But the article is a hoax! A college student wrote the article as a joke, not believing the newspaper would really publish it. The newspaper, not amused, says the student displays "a lightweight show of reason reminding one of an excited English sparrow."

The next chapter is titled "A Time of Rapid Change."

In 1902, Frank Farr sells the inn to Isaac Little. In 1903, Isaac sells it to Abbie and Henry Stone. And in 1905, the Stones sell it to Clinton W. Tisdale, who renames the inn The Green Mountain House (which is a snooze). Harriet believes the turnover has to do with Vermont's economic development but also says East Coventry still doesn't have a railroad depot despite, at this point, nearly half of Vermont towns having them. Also, the roads remain in terrible shape, with cars a rarity. Plus ça change.

Though people do seem quicker to realize they can't succeed running an inn no one can get to. So why the string of new buyers? Some echo of Epapharus, some misplaced hope.

Jess emails: "During the winter, the inn could've been holding balls but not having people stay overnight. That would explain the ice skating for those who didn't wish to dance."

She knows I'm glum. She's saying: husband mine, if you need to believe the perhaps existence of a nineteenth-century ice-skating rink matters, then it matters.

I tell her of the knife fight in the wine cellar, of the bourbon ruffians. I agree with her about the rink. I'm trying to reassure her back I'm not taking this too seriously.

Oh, the newest owner can't make it work either. Clinton W. advertises first-class service, hot and cold baths (hey!), steam heat, and gas lights, but finds himself about to be foreclosed on. Somehow, he comes up with the money, then sells the inn to Arthur Douglas in 1918.

In what first appears a non sequitur, Harriet starts discussing Milt Elmer, who moves to East Coventry in 1909, when he's "about" (?) eleven. He remembers Mr. Tisdale as a nice man and remembers the mail route that daily came down the mountain. "It was an old-top carriage, a three-seated rig." I feel the thrill of a specific voice. This book came out in 1967, which would make Milt just shy of seventy. We're finally in the realm of primary sources.

Milt remembers the dances. He discusses the midnight suppers, the flowing hard cider. We're in the 1920s, but I wonder if Milt were Harriet's source for the balls of half a century earlier. He told her what stories he'd heard. My Dictaphone scenario given more credence.

Milt remembers fights. "A man by the name of Milt Sanford got into a tangle and, by God, he threw the man he was fighting with right through the window!" The brawls are "just a little exercise." He describes a man hurling firewood down a staircase at another man. He refers to this as "a modern defense."

Although Harriet lets Milt go on for pages, the rest of his recollections are vague, even contradictory. What Milt remembers most vividly is another man named Milt throwing somebody through a window.

In 1928, Ernest and Elsie Dahlin buy the inn for $6,000. The Dahlins rename it The Glen Tavern. Ernest has a "valve defect in his heart." The source now is Ernest Dahlin Jr., whose parents buy the inn when he's five.

Ernest Jr.'s father tears down a barn likely used for horses and cows.

Blackberries grow on the property's southern border. An icehouse is on the hill east of the inn. A woodshed is beside the icehouse. The Dahlins turn a shed into a garage. Elsie does the washing there.

We move inside. A lighting fixture in the kitchen still uses gas. "It is believed the inn was the first public building in the area to be lighted with gas, which was manufactured on the grounds." Gas was manufactured here? "It is believed" the inn made its own gas? This is akin to the bowling alley.

If Harriet is alive, she surely lives around here. I could show up at her doorstep and ask if we could discuss her book. I'd sit and listen as she verifies sources, explains outlandish truths, smiles away my worries that her book is stuffed with hokum.

I'll not email Jess about manufacturing gas on the grounds. Although if I did, she'd probably write back with a fart joke and I'd feel better.

We're sticking with lights. Another one, near the entrance way on the building's eastern side, used to be hung above the bandstand. (The bandstand!) At that point, the light had blue glass. "Very pleasant," Ernest says of it. The glass likely came from the glass factory the town over, which had been known for its glass tinted blue.

This must be the exploding glass factory of 1817.

"In the basement was an old wood, coal, or steam furnace," Harriet writes, and I close the book for the day.

I recognize I'm sitting up—that middle-of-the-night discombobulation —only because Jess lifts her head from her pillow. "What's wrong?"

"Nothing."

"Why did you just jolt upright?"

"1853," I tell her. "1853 is the year Prohibition began in Vermont; it's also the year Epapharus Jones first tried to sell the inn. Prohibition must've been the tipping point for him—barely anyone coming to the tavern, and then he discovers it's going to be illegal to sell hard cider to those who do. He knew: his failures were clear to him."

"Pete." Jess sighs.

"I know," I say. "I tried to tell you it was nothing."

· · ·

This evening, I'm meeting Jess at the inn to have drinks. It's Friday. We're looking to do something mildly celebratory. I also think she wants to get me out of the house.

The morning begins with death. In 1934, Ernest Sr. dies and Ernest Jr. is just eleven, the poor child. That winter, twenty-five government workers, as part of a public works endeavor, stay at the inn while they hunt for gypsy moth nests in the nearby woods. Every day, Elsie provides them bag lunches and serves them dinner. Their presence helps her get by in a lean, sad Depression year.

She does a brisk business during the summers. People—they have cars, finally—come from New York and New Jersey. Ernest Jr. remembers two schoolteachers from Long Island. They stay several summers and give Elsie a diamond ring to remember them by. (A lovely detail, but suspect.) Guests often play croquet or read on the porch. I notice none of them bowl.

Ernest Jr.'s Sunday chores include making ice cream for the guests. Once, he puts too much salt in. On cold nights he sits before the wood-stove in the kitchen and pops corn. Ernest is a sweet child. Perhaps he goes to bed before the balls start. Or they're more tempered. Or no longer happening. His memories suggest no inkling of them.

Ernest Jr. leaves home at seventeen—first for school and then to enlist. His mother struggles. During WWII, people travel less; gasoline is restricted. Rooms sit empty, she writes to her son, who's about to go into combat. She asks whether she should keep the inn in case he wants to run it someday. Not knowing what his future holds, he tells her if she can get a good price, she should sell. She does: to Chester Way for $16,000 in 1944.

It surprises me Elsie could manage through the Depression, but not WWII. I suspect the problem was not financial but familial: she didn't want to run the inn alone.

Our new owner, Chester, is a lawyer and a businessman. In 1950, he runs unsuccessfully for Congress. He renames the place yet again: The East Coventry Inn. And it's this banal name that sticks. Having done this important work, Chester gets out after three years, selling to Mr. and Mrs. George Fisher. They're the first out-of-staters to buy the inn. (Jess and I have heard this phrase, uttered semi-politely in our direction, a thousand times since we've moved here.) The Fishers turn the inn into a four-season hotel. Harriet hasn't given a year, but we're somewhere in the late 1940s.

The next chapter is titled "Out-of-Staters Looking for the Good Life." The couple writes a brochure suggesting The East Coventry Inn is for "cultured people." The dances end. (I think they'd already ended.) They convert a woodshed into a cocktail lounge, which makes me laugh. Harriet provides menus: either veal chops with currant jelly or baked ham with raisin sauce costs $1.50. One of the sides is "jellied vegetable salad," which is deeply terrible. They own the inn only two years before selling to Mr. and Mrs. Percy Stelle.

The Stelles introduce a Sunday-night buffet. This seems to be their only contribution, and they're gone five years later. We're on to Harold Curtiss and Bob Kingsley, who—like most of the recent owners—seem determined to make the inn more boring. They convert the cocktail lounge (scandalous) into the Old Fashioned Room. I don't know what constitutes an Old Fashioned Room, only that it has a fireplace. Had they known anything of the inn's past, they'd not have named it such, since they're inadvertently hearkening back to chaos. (Milt Elmer, now middle-aged: Does he pine for the violent balls of his youth?)

Harold and Bob renovate. They're aiming for a "club-like atmosphere" and to cater to Coventry's "upper-crust." People come from Connecticut and New York. Harriet offers my favorite sentence so far: "They were city people with city ideas." It's now 1956.

The 1950s strike me as a turning point. The social striving, yes. But also the owners trying to create respectability by gesturing toward the past. Meanwhile, the inn's history (the sliver I understand) was rough-hewn and rife with failures.

The pages still have their absurdist, off-topic charm. Harold and Bob bow out. The reason: "They had run it as a very personal business and it just got to be too much." Bud and Betty Greene drive to Vermont and see the inn. Betty says, "Hey, Bud, why don't you buy me that?" Three weeks later, they buy the inn for $149,000. They're miffed, when they first get inside, to discover the kitchen only has six shrimp cocktail glasses.

My heart is not in this. I've got less than a decade to go before the conclusion of *These Ever Flowing Years*, but I head downstairs. I'm going for a walk.

The leaves are like stained glass, made more dimensional with sunshine. When the wind picks up, the smell is of pleasant must, of clean decay. The sky blazes a flat cerulean. If I were writing, I'd avoid describing anything as cerulean.

"An abundance of partridge," Harriet said would be one reason why huntsmen would visit Coventry. Sure, why not?

I walk through dappled light. Even if the book excludes basic facts and dwells long on irrelevant ones, even if much might be untrue, couldn't the writing overall hold a kind of aggregate truth?

If so, what is it?

The pub's entrance is on the inn's eastern side, which is where the bandstand light hung in Ernest Dahlin Jr.'s time. What does a bandstand light look like? The center light—a chandelier of antlers—has that generic if ostentatious rustic quality much of the inn has.

The barkeep, Laura, comes in from the back, placing a bowl of french fries before a woman. "Pete!" she says warmly. She gestures I sit at the copper-topped bar. She knows I'm waiting for Jess. "I've been reading *These Ever Flowing Years* by Harriet Schuppert," I tell her. Laura grew up in this neighborhood; maybe she'll know something about the author. I describe some of my favorite details: the exploding glass factory, the wine-cellar brawl.

"There were two glass factories," she says. "One by the lake and then another here on Main Street." I adamantly do not want there to have been two glass factories. "Mrs. Schuppert lived down where the lumber store is now. She cared a lot about gardening. I think my parents have a copy of that book. Mrs. Schuppert gave copies to everyone on the street—the old families, anyway."

Two men sit at the end of the bar and Laura goes to take their drink orders.

I'm imagining Harriet walking down the street, knocking on doors, handing out her book. Neighbors telling her how wonderful. And then, once they'd seen her off, they'd glanced through a few pages, then put the book in a drawer to gather dust.

Am I the only one who has read it? My neighbor said, "as a writer," I might find it interesting. I hadn't understood what she'd meant. I still don't.

Jess comes and sits down beside me, sighing but happy. She puts her hand on mine, resting on the bar. "Tell me something funny you read today."

I want to tell her about the 1950s shift toward false nostalgia, how the inn's history became a kind of fiction then. How maybe everything I've read is fiction, an act of trying to give shape to something resolutely amorphous.

Laura comes over, rescuing me from myself, and makes us drinks. A few sips, some neutral banter, and I calm. I tell them of Bud and Betty Greene, shocked to find only a half-dozen shrimp cocktail glasses. I discuss the Depression-era public works men searching for gypsy-moth nests in the woods. I ask if Laura thinks there could've ever been a bowling alley, and she says sure, maybe, back in the day. The inn used to be situated on twenty acres. Twenty acres! I cry. When did it get sold off?

She shakes her head. "I don't know. It's just something I've heard."

I raise my drink in toast. Jess touches her drink to mine. Laura raises an empty pint glass. "To The Forest Tavern," I say. I see it, surrounded by trees, its windowpanes gold in the shadows. It's far off, almost obscured, in the wooded dark.

Sylvia Who Dreams of Dactyls

SYLVIA WAKES THINKING of dactyls as if they'd been spilling out across her dreams. Washington, Dumbledore. She stretches, throws back her comforter, opens the curtains, and lets ashen light bathe her. Some subterranean part of her head engaging in pattern assessment. Bothersome: yes. Trigonometry: no.

In the kitchen she drinks coffee from a mug glazed cobalt—dusted sunshine about her shoulders—and looks out to her back fields. In the distance a slim streak of lake is silver blue, and the mountains are August lush and serene. Gesturing, cluster fuck. This abstract clutter, this part of herself not making sense to herself—pursuing its own avenues of nonsense inquiry. A nighttime devoted to syllabic count.

Soon, a late morning of tennis with her neighbor. Veritas, festering.

She makes a light breakfast: toast with butter and marmalade. Marmalade. If it would work, she'd shake her head like a swimmer clearing droplets of water from her ears. Mucinex, Bessemer. Hexagon. There's no languor in this kind of thinking.

Already it seems beyond her to lead a rational day. Joshua. She showers, steam and mist hotly fogging the room, and with various cleansers scents herself with orange blossom and sandalwood. Then to anoint herself with serum and slather herself with creams. Slavish, lavish these rituals of older middle age. Joshua. That must be it. Her head engaged in fractal logic, tiny shapes mimicking—at least in sonic apparition—the large one. The one that comes at her from these absurd, oblique angles.

Her wrist extended, racket out, she whacks the ball, a great return just over the net, but has to drop her racket because she's hurt her wrist. John comes to her. She's worried her mouth is open in a tiny o, a silly shape that does no justice to her pain.

"You're okay?" Even-keeled, concerned neighbor. They play occasionally as the weather holds. He's a veterinarian, and she always wonders what his days are like, what mix of joy and heartbreak comes his way as he engages in new pets, sick pets, happy families, sad ones. If he feels all happy families are alike, etc. He touches the underside of her wrist—less assessment and more reminder of his presence. "Let's get some ice on that," he says and trots off to the Harbor Club's dining room.

She walks off the court and sprawls in an Adirondack chair. He returns with a bag of frozen peas, which he foists on her. "Maybe a sprain," he says. "Ice now and certainly Advil later." He sits in the chair beside hers and pats her knee—perhaps as he'd pat the head of a golden retriever. "You weren't paying attention."

"I was," she huffs. She wasn't. Dactyls, fractals, Joshua. Thoughts that cling as lint on a dress. Beyond them is the lake, with its little shivers, shimmers, its lack of placidness. The air is thick with moisture. Her wrist throbs and gives off heat despite the cold wet plastic bag of peas. Questioning, darkening. John is chatting about some volunteer work he's doing tomorrow, registering crew teams for the Dragon Boat Festival. She knows of it vaguely. In Burlington, an annual event to raise money for cancer survivors. She presses the peas to her forehead just for the delectable thrill of coolness unmitigated by hurt. Poetry, escalate. She'd ice these dream remnants, dream logic, and turn them into snowflakes, which themselves contain fractals. It all makes sense. "Can I join you?" she asks.

"For lunch?" He spreads his arm to the club behind him. "I bet they can squeeze us in." This is him being wry. The Harbor Club is lake-resort chic, and vacationers come from God knows where in their salmon pants and seersucker jackets, looking forward to meals on white linen tablecloths and the constant, buoyant tranquility that comes from lakeside fun. He's a member. She used to be, when she still had a family surrounding her, Susan and Jack climbing all over to dig into the beach bags for towels, for graham crackers, for bug spray. The house just a few miles south, and Rusty thought it was the civilized thing to do. Susan, when she was a toddler, splashing in the harbor, shrieking with some unbridled joy. Her children inhabited this Eden, thinking it their own. They now live in New Haven and Westchester, respectively. They barely call.

"No, to the Dragon Boat Festival. Is Geoffrey joining you?"

"Geoffrey is giving a reading across the lake. So he'll be busy letting women ply him with cheap rosé," John says, a second stab at being wry. "Then they'll sit around gossiping. He loves it." John watches some vacationers take their place on the court, lithe and young, likely married. "I'd love it too. If you really want to come, I'm going to leave at seven."

"I'll be ready." Her wrist has gone numb, but beneath that numbness is a hum of pressure, pain wishing to come back if only she'd stop trying to dampen it. "I think it'd be great fun." Fun is the wrong word—she ought not describe an event devoted to surviving cancer as fun. What will it be? She has no idea. She's not actually sure why she wants to go.

The tock-thwack of the ball going back and forth between this young athletic couple. She wonders whether this woman loves this man. The woman, her ponytail bouncing, her skin fresh, her lips rosy. A happiness of being generally well received and having to do very little to earn it. Sylvia understands. She's spent the majority of her life getting by on her looks too. It's an unfair universe. As if high cheekbones and light eyes have anything to do with the her that's really her. But with age she's begun to match her insides. A kind of withering as she thinks of it.

"Would you like to go to lunch?" John stretches, perhaps restless for not getting to finish their game. "My treat."

"I'm sorry about the game," she says, by which she means she doesn't wish to have lunch. She does wish she hadn't spoiled something they were both looking forward to. She was not paying attention.

He nods and says he'll be in her driveway tomorrow, bright and early.

"Bright and early!" she chirps—fatly false chirp, night frog, not delicate bird. Genuine, she thinks. Escalate. Dactyls still everywhere, like light falling through the trees.

Her wrist is swollen, gives off heat, so she picks up Geoffrey's book gently. She goes to the back patio—so much green tapering off to wheat and sunlit bands of gold in the distance, as if she lived in an impressionist painting. An hour to Burlington and an hour back is a long time with John, and to be caught out in white lies is never fun for anyone involved. Geoffrey, who'd insisted for years he had a novel in him. A decade of staying up late and going sleep-deprived to his day job as an accountant. And now the book has been embraced by the book-club lot. She bought it. It's schlock. She read the first ten pages and then set it on the coffee table in case the men stopped by. She read the reviews so she could offer vague praise.

In her white wicker chair, in the shade, she feels the rich buzz of summer is such she could drown in it. Again she attempts the opening pages: an accountant uncovering a crime. Chicory. Joshua. Geoffrey had had the timid audacity to knock at her door—two years ago now. And even though she saw in his features some mix of shame and need, she invited him in. She served him Earl Gray. As if his eyes bulged, but only bad novelists such as Geoffrey would describe it so.

"Sylvia, John just read over some of my most recent pages." Geoffrey, the auteur, sporting his affectations. Pages. "And he pointed out to me the obvious: that one of my subplots bears resemblance to your life." He studied his tea as if it might provide solace. "If you can believe it, I didn't notice. I've spent so long working on the book—so long in my own head—I started borrowing from the lives I know." He took a sip, although it was still too hot, and blanched. "Subconsciously, of course."

"No," she said.

He nodded, but a part of him had drifted out of her dining room and into his study, where he sat at his laptop, reluctant to delete hours of work detailing her and Rusty's failings. Hours spent rendering her life, or what he imagined of it, because of course he knew nothing.

"Geoffrey," she said. "Look at me." Pudgy man, a nervous cerebral quality to him. He married up, landing John. "If you make me a subplot, I'll never speak to you or John again."

He babbled about knowing he was in the wrong, not knowing whatever possessed him to bring it up in the first place. All would be deleted immediately, forthwith, yesterday. He asked for forgiveness, and she pretended to offer it. It never came up again.

The conversation showed her she'd become part of the local mythos, a story to tell. Geoffrey was just more earnest in trying to write it down and then more clumsy in bringing it up.

She closes the book, cares more about the band of gold out there, the scent of late summer grass and goldenrod. Tomorrow, she'll just have to lie the color of snow, snowflakes. They already think she's quite good at lying. Perhaps, if she were more generous, she'd consider that Geoffrey had written about her infidelity because he was trying to make sense of it, because it was alien to him. More than anything—because she no longer trusts what she perceives of couples—Geoffrey's fictionalizing her life showed her he had no pain of his own to draw from. Which is to say: he is happy. Geoffrey and John are happily married.

Negligence, Chesterfield. Blunderbuss, edelweiss. Tragedy.

. . .

The afternoon is fat with somnolence, a whir of crickets, the dip and rise of the red-winged blackbird in and out of the grass. Gray-blue clouds are settling over the mountains in the west. She decides to pick blueberries.

The bushes are in the backyard, near the shed. From the kitchen she gets a mixing bowl and carries it out crooked between elbow and hip. She kneels to get at the lower branches first, spilling the dark berries into the silver bowl. They look unevenly dusted, some matte, some with a bruised sheen. She tastes one and finds it agreeably sweet.

The trees beyond will soon yield fruit—one plum, one apricot, and, later in the fall, a small row of Black Oxford trees will produce apples. Bless Rusty's strange great-aunt, who either planted these varietals or kept them up. Heirloom fruit, purple-black and tannic, quintessential New England. Sylvia has learned they're old: originally from Maine and thought to have existed since 1790, which means they predate the house by half a century. They make sense on this property, create a kind of unity of landscape. In the fall, bees swarm as the extra fruit drops and rots, a sweet ferment. The kids picked them into October and, when they thought she wasn't looking, would see who could throw one the farthest. She'd watch from the kitchen window: low arcs against a gray sky. Such a discovery that first fall to find sensuous fruit just appearing on the land. Black hearts hanging low in the branches. The temptation of it—Eve made more sense to her then.

She lets more blueberries fall from her palm into the bowl. Deer, crows, robins have stolen away some of the more easily available berries, pecked or nibbled when she wasn't around. Maybe their mutual love of this house and its land kept her and Rusty married for so long. That he handed it over, signed away in the divorce, and then hightailed it back to DC: the place signaled to him his pain, he'd told her—one of their final conversations. She wanted it? It was hers.

She thinks—but can never pinpoint when, where, how—a slide occurred from actual happiness to only the appearance thereof. Or it was never actual happiness—just happenstance, and they were too young to know the difference. She'd come from upper-crust Delaware.

But finding herself at a university reeking of genteel charm, she'd adapted quickly to bluegrass and bourbon parties, to springtime horse races where you stood in fields wearing pastel dresses and mixing shakers of juleps. The rules felt clear: be pretty, be witty, and wear charm as if armor. Her only rebellion was not going steady with anyone. She didn't care. She preferred being out in large groups to going out with dull boys who wanted to lecture or grope her. Forms of domination she'd not brook.

A sorority sister decided she needed someone older. They were young enough then to conflate older with worldliness and to think twenty-five was old. Enter Rusty, getting his masters in architecture. Their first date was at a low-lit bar with black-and-white floors, sipping gin and tonics. This preppy boy from DC with freckles and ears sticking out—a wonderful grin, a strong jaw—resembled a blend of Alfred E. Neuman and Kennedy. The lime fizzed acidic in her drink, and Rusty had an easy laugh along with a serious temperament. This was good. He listened when she talked. He understood that she was more than her features, her figure.

In the spring they would go for nighttime walks on campus—the grounds, the university insisted on calling them—and she admired his understanding of construction and space, of buildings' histories. Crabapple trees blossomed white and snowy. Everything was shadowed brick and white pillars and black branches against a dark-blue sky. Cicadas in the warm dark offered constant throaty calls.

Was it love? She preferred him because he was interesting. He knew how a spiral staircase was built. He understood its elegance. She could recite a bit of John Donne—"Busy old fool, unruly Sun"—and he found her interesting too. They both loved beauty and patterned things. Magnolias were in bloom. The nights were scented with flowers. Was it love? Was it love, was it love.

She moves to the second bush, twisting the berries off at their stems, only taking them if they yield easily, attentive to those—shrouded in shade—still with white-green underbellies. The sun is a diffuse heat, and over the mountains the clouds have darkened to slate. Maybe a storm will cross the lake, the patter of rainfall. The bowl is almost full, and she brings the berries inside. Her wrist is again a thrumming heat, even though she did all the picking with her left hand. Inside, the kitchen is cool. The whir of the overhead fan is minor wind. She rinses the berries and gets some in a smaller bowl with yogurt. They are still sun-warm and seem rich. The yogurt is from a dairy farm nearby, and its taste reminds her of the scent of clean hay.

Sometimes, lately, she thinks of herself as Eve alone in the garden. Everyone cast out except her. Except not being cast out is also —unequivocally—punishment.

She wearies of her own self-pity.

She returns to the back porch with a real book. She's reading Wallace Stevens because Susan, as she begins preparing for her oral exams in American Modernism, is reading him. Surreal and cerebral, this poet who worked at an insurance company in Connecticut. Susan has, as professor, a man whose great-aunt lived in the same Connecticut town and called her nephew when, years ago, Wallace Stevens passed away. "Did you know?" Susan says the old aunt asked her professor nephew, "that Wally Stevens was a poet?" There is something so entirely wonderful about a man who on the outside led a life of banality but on the inside was rich and inventive and strange.

She'd wished for more schooling, but then, the summer after Rusty finished his degree, they were married. And then his great-aunt passed away—the bohemian one who lived by her lonesome up north in a stone cottage on the western edge of Vermont. And she bequeathed him this house. They came up to look and were gobsmacked by the surrounding loveliness. Was it not providential, the timing? He got a job at an architectural firm in the college town half an hour away. To pay for renovations, they sold some of the adjacent acreage and thus ensured themselves neighbors: John and Geoffrey, so young then themselves. She became a first-rate gardener. She was pregnant with Jack before she could blink.

Happenstance, happenstance: her husband, her home. A sorority sister sets her up, a great-aunt dies, and thus her life takes shape. Just: it seemed an adventure, it seemed good fun. She'd invested in none of it deep thought. She'd been a cavalier girl. She liked Rusty, she liked Lake Champlain, she liked dirt roads, she liked babies who smelled like stale milk, she liked hard frosty winters and learning to use the wood-burning stove. She liked that Vermonters were polite but remote, which meant she could be remote too.

Susan and Jack—twenty-eight and thirty—aren't married. Jack has a new girlfriend, but he often has a new girlfriend, one every year or two, and likely won't settle until he finds someone bright enough to captivate him. Susan just went through a hard breakup, someone from her PhD class, but on the phone Susan chokes down her bitterness and mumbles banalities about things just not working out and needing to move on. In conversation with her mother, she refuses to be vulnerable in any way.

It's punishment. Jack does it too. The children will talk to her of their work, so she learns of venture capital and seed funding and business models. Or she learns of literary analysis. But neither will speak of love—or sadness or happiness or anything in between. They think she betrayed them so many years ago when they were teenagers, so they'll leave her with no more opportunities for betrayal. They're very firm in their polite outrage with her. Meanwhile, Joshua, whom she hasn't seen in nearly a decade, still haunts her dreams.

Children, she wishes she could say. It's more complicated than your mother being a harlot.

But she takes it. The fact is, her life rolled on easily and well for such a long, long time. And led to her children, who are her life's blood even if they hate her. And even now, it's as if her days are cloaked in richness and beauty—if a kind of fraught beauty, as if the whole landscape secretly wished it could undo itself.

Happenstance is not a dactyl but a cretic—that last syllable long. Bitterly, however, is.

· · ·

The pink-navy sky, the evening star one white point: she dozed off. This is terrible. She'll never get to bed at a decent hour now, and she'll not be rested for whatever tomorrow's Dragon Boat Festival will entail. She's lapsing into old-lady habits. Twilight, and the fields are abuzz with lament, cricket cry a shivery call. She goes in to get a glass of wine and returns with it to the wicker chair, sipping it slowly, liking the small warmth it gives to her limbs as the air cools. She raises her glass to the night, hoping tomorrow she'll be more rational, less indulgent, in her thinking. She resumes her reading: Key West and tigers in red weather.

Buckling her seatbelt, she considers the early ethereal prettiness: transparent high clouds over silver water. The circumspect glimmer seems to reflect her mind. She isn't rested, but likes the freshness, the unexpectedness of being out before she's usually awake. John, whom she suspects is a virtuous early riser, has coffee for them both. "How's your wrist?" he asks.

In the night it radiated wild heat—one of the reasons she slept badly—but Advil has since tamped that down. "Swollen," she says, not wishing to go on. Another's pain is so uninteresting. She offers him blueberries from a Tupperware dish, along with some scones, dense and portable. She wants to be a good travel companion, a good sport. Adventure and rationality: these are her hopes for the day. And that language not tumble about her head as if laundry in a dryer.

"Keep it elevated." John reaches for a scone. "As much as you can today."

She wants to ask what the volunteer work entails but bets he explained it yesterday during her extended bout of not paying attention. She'll figure it out. She sips her coffee, earthy and strong.

"Perhaps it's the early hour," John says, backing out of the driveway. "But I have a confession to make." She laughs lightly and looks out the window to the fields. She wants no confessions. "It's so much nicer to give advice to patients who understand you."

"Feeling misunderstood by the tail-wagging set?"

"I spend more time thinking about it than I should," he says.

"Like tending to sick infants, I'd imagine. Jack used to get these horrible ear infections and be up half the night screaming."

"It's the absence of cause and effect. When you're shoving a pill down a pup's throat, you can't very well say, 'it's an antibiotic.'" John is in his late sixties. He could retire. What she hears is fatigue—wishing things were other than they were. It's a fine tipping point over into the existential. He's always struck her as heartier than this.

"You heal them," she says. "Hopefully this mitigates your day-to-day qualms."

"We just had to put down an old girl—a lab I've been seeing since she was a puppy. The family cried and cried." He fusses with the rearview mirror and takes a long swallow of coffee. He's trying to keep from crying. John, she thinks. Poor John.

"I admire you." She wishes her words were less vague. She eats some berries, sweeter for being chilled. "Today, I'll be a topnotch patient. I'll ice and elevate and not once, for my troubles, will I ask for a treat in return. But I won't wag my tail. There are limits."

It works. He laughs. Among the things he's telling her—trying to communicate—is why he's volunteering today. He knows a slow slouch toward crisis still eventually reaches that crisis. And when that occurs you're no longer in control of your life. Altruism as means of self-rescue. Which makes it no less admirable.

"I was thinking we might listen to Geoffrey's audiobook." John presses some buttons on the radio console. "It's just come out, and he's very anxious about it—if the actor did a good job, etc. Do you mind?"

"That's a lovely idea." He can be a good husband and she can look out the window and think her own thoughts without appearing rude. The conversation has left her flustered. Or maybe weary.

A fanfare of slightly ominous music. *The Accounting*," a man says, "by Geoffrey Benson." And then the story begins, the actor doing his best to inject energy into the opening scene.

They're traveling north along Route 7, driving through farm-centric

Addison County toward the more suburban Chittenden County. There's almost no traffic. Gardener, miscreant. Something of yesterday's dactyl anxiety is reviving itself in her. She drinks more coffee to combat it. The accountant goes over the numbers again. Something does not add up.

She's wondered about Geoffrey's manuscript—what he initially wrote of her and Rusty. She guesses he went in for cliché. Rusty comes home (probably Geoffrey gave Rusty a briefcase) and opens the front door, calling hello and hearing a startled gasp from the upstairs bedroom. She'd be in expensive lingerie—or putting back on expensive lingerie?—her hair a bird's nest. She'd come downstairs tightening the waist of her silk kimono, looking ashamed. Or perhaps she'd be defiant. She'd shout at Rusty, agape in the foyer: Yes, she'd taken a lover! Their marriage was finis, kaput.

But even Geoffrey knows she'd not likely yell. Nor was Rusty ever stupid enough to stand around slack jawed when confronted with things he did not approve of. Perhaps Geoffrey described the woman as petite and blonde, the man as a lanky, wholesome, graying redhead. She'd be a bit cold, Rusty a bit impatient.

He'd write of Joshua—the contractor who'd begun working with Rusty's firm, who kept showing up as she and Rusty did renovations to the house—expanding the kitchen, adding the back porch. Perhaps when the schlock-Joshua showed up at the door, the schlock-her, wearing a low-cut blouse, invited him in for a drink. In fact, during his breaks, they talked lightly over coffee in the dining room. He was a great reader. They eventually started a book club of two.

She drums her fingers along the coffee cup. She doesn't even know where he lives now. A dinner near the college—Rusty and his colleagues, their spouses—and he was new to the area, next to her, without a wife. He barely looked her way except to speak with the perfunctory low-level charm needed to maintain a group conversation. Her impression: both pretty and burly—dark hair cropped close, a full beard, black eyes with thick eyelashes, something soft about his lips. At one point he'd said, "You're not from here," and she told him she grew up in Delaware.

"I would've guessed the South."

She glanced at Rusty, sipping a beer and talking shop with another partner. "We met at UVA. The joke—at least to the Delawareans—is that in the North you sound Southern, but in the South you sound Northern. The muddle of being from the middle." All practiced. All nothing—light chatter. He told her he'd moved from Upstate New York, from Ithaca. Then he joined Rusty in talking about the project du jour.

Banal, all of it. Because later that night, as she took off her earrings, she felt buoyant, borne aloft, and her instincts said it was him—just being near him. But this was ridiculous. She considered how boring their conversation had been, which helped her put aside her feelings as the vicissitudes of self. She kissed her husband, next to her in bed flipping through the *Economist*, and switched off her table lamp. Then she dreamt of waterfalls—a downpour and rush, water luminous and frothing and fast, and the air misted over in refracted light, her skin damp with coolness. She woke up ashamed, confused. She was forty-two.

She doesn't know how most affairs work. Theirs felt quiet, ineluctable. Afternoons in his bed, sex and books, languid light from the eastern window falling onto the sheets. Two years later, he said guilt consumed him and he'd decided this had to end, he had to move. She told him she loved him. She felt sure she did. He only shook his head, a gesture she's never been able to parse. Only that she found—still finds—thinking of it so painful a pulse begins at her temples. These are thoughts that should remain buried. But her own mind fights her, offers up dactyls, tries to trick her into remembering.

John presses pause, asks her what she thinks. She has no idea. "The actor reads well," she says.

"I've read years and years of drafts, and I still find myself surprised Geoffrey had this in him. It's remarkable."

She tells him the poet she's reading worked as an insurance executive in Connecticut—a poet who's considered one of the greats of the twentieth century. "After he won the Pulitzer, Harvard offered him a faculty position, but he turned it down, not wanting to leave his company."

"It's fascinating what people contain." She worried as she said it he might think she was making light of Geoffrey—who will certainly not go down as a major literary figure—but John is too proud to worry over the comparison. He's right, too. What we contain is endlessly interesting, if also sometimes frightening. To her relief, he resumes playing the audiobook.

The accountant has returned to his computer screen to show someone the proof he'd found of malfeasance, but when he again goes through the very complicated algorithm, the evidence is gone. Poof! As if it had never existed! And such is the accountant's confusion that he then questions its existence. Could he have dreamt the whole thing up?

They park a few blocks away from the waterfront and walk down to the park, where food vendors already line the walking path. Behind them—closer to the water—is a white tent, a registration sign above its entrance. The light clouds have dissipated. The mood is confident, the sky azure. Groups rove the park in matching T-shirts—bright orange, raspberry—munching bagels, chatting. Some have large drums set out on the grass. Others are stretching, a mixture of toe touching and tai chi. By the docks, red crew boats are at rest. Their bows rise into the faces of dragons with yellow horns and oversized green eyes. Magnificent, she thinks. Elegant monsters to begin the day.

As she and John walk into the tent, a woman with a puckered mouth smiles incandescently at them. John explains he's here to help with community team check-in—which sounds very official—and asks if Sylvia can join him as an impromptu volunteer. Sylvia's made some wrong decisions arriving in a summer dress, wearing mascara, and hopes not to be hated too much. The woman turns behind her to some large cardboard boxes and hands them each an orange T-shirt—one large, one less large. Sylvia puts the T-shirt over her dress, feeling silly. The woman points John toward a table, then tells Sylvia she's putting her outside. She lightly squints. "Are you wearing sunblock?" Sylvia nods. "Follow the path to the docks. Once there, tell the race officials you're assisting people in and out of boats. The first race is at 8:20, so scoot."

She'd not imagined they'd be split up, but this woman is being accommodating. She'll scoot. John, settling in at his table, raises his wrist—reiterating his advice—and then she's out of the tent's shadows and into the brilliant day. A troupe, all in hot-pink T-shirts, Elvis wigs, and Mardi Gras beads, passes her in a swarm of chatter.

She wishes the children could see her amid this hubbub, that Rusty could too. He'd find all this energy agreeable. Actually, Rusty would wish to be on a team. The boyish part of him would want to win. The financials would interest him too—how much money is being raised and what percentage goes to whom.

The habits of twenty-two years. To be understood by another is a tremendous thing, and she regrets—above all else—this loss.

She told Rusty of the affair only as it was ending. In the moment, she didn't even feel guilt over it—she was too absorbed in her heartbreak. They were at a restaurant, and he turned white beneath his freckles as if she'd poisoned him. He nodded quickly and returned to his menu and didn't speak another word to her that night—not for days, until he left a note for her on the bureau that said they'd have to agree on how to tell the children they were divorcing.

Memory is liquid. It washes away. She still can't fathom her love for Joshua, her cruelness to Rusty, or what she really, in the end, felt for either of them. She doesn't know if she changed as she grew older, or this was really her all along, or if everything that happened was just more happenstance—except not brilliant luck tossed her way but the possibility for loss she then stumbled into and heedlessly embraced. Beauty and pain: twining helix.

Like John, she tries to make sense of what will not make sense.

At the docks, she tells a man at a check-in table she's here to help people in and out of boats. He looks mildly surprised, and she wonders if that woman made up a job for her on the spot. He says to go down to the first dock, parallel to the boat, and as teams arrive she can offer them her hand for support. Delightful, she says. It's the wrong thing to say, the last few days an epidemic of wrong-thing-saying. She marches down the wooden dock, feeling its soft sway almost as if she has to breathe differently to stay balanced. Sunshine dapples the water, quicksilver gleams over dark silk. Behind her are the Adirondacks, monolithic guardians. Jack had told her that as a kid he believed they were there to keep the water from spilling out. She saw the immediate sense in it. Barriers, borders, distant containment. Parameters. She gets a gold medal in mind racing.

A horn sounds, and she turns to two teams putting on life preservers, clapping their hands together, throwing fists in the air—all in sunglasses, all laughing. One set is in green T-shirts with ladybugs printed on them, with some also wearing black-speckled red headbands. The other set is in red T-shirts with black stripes at the sleeves. Two people carry drums. The horn blows again, and they trot down the parallel docks. She has the ladybug team. The drummer is the coxswain. She offers her good hand as the woman steps into the boat. Another team member hands over the drum. It's such a fluster of good cheer and jabbering, as if they were all gulls or small gods: she can't decide which. She keeps offering her hand and the men tend not to take it, while the women do. She's not used to so much touch, so many warm palms. She's not sure she's of help. More that she's at the center of a dance. She's a maypole, and around her they swirl with ribbons. The sun is warm on her neck, on her eyelids. She reaches out her hand again and again until they've all settled and have their paddles at the ready.

People are gathered along the waterfront, attentive. Everyone stills. A woman with a carnation in her ponytail smiles up at Sylvia. The horn sounds again, and oars hitting the water rise and splash. The coxswains' drums beat as they shout encouragement. The crowd erupts. It's all sunlight and cheers. The boats pull away, strong arms in conjunction. Her heart is a rattle in her chest. She feels elation surge through her as if she were the one rowing, or if, perhaps, she were that dragon smoothly cutting through the lake.

The ladybug team wins, and they're back very quickly. They seem to accept her help in more sincere fashion as they rise to step onto the dock, more acquiescent to some steadying presence. Or they just recognize her now as part of the process. The men still resist, letting go as quickly as they can. Someone pats her on the back, perhaps a thank you.

Several more times this happens—these are qualifying heats to see who competes later in the day. One team she helps all wear light-pink hats, with breast cancer awareness ribbons pinned to their T-shirts. Some must be survivors themselves—those who row—but she can't discern those who've fallen ill and gotten better from those who haven't. They all seem so radiant to her. Running through her, however, is fear manifesting as a dopey anxiety over logistics. No chaos can enter: no one must spill into the water, slip on the docks—which have gotten damp. No one can have a summer's cough or sun poisoning. No one must need her help beyond the token gesture it actually is. They are all strong. She loves them for it.

There's a midmorning break, and the race official says to return at eleven for the flower ceremony. She nods as if she knows what that is and, famished, goes to buy a coffee and bagel. The woman ahead of her in line takes an extraordinarily long time ordering—poppy seed or plain, cream cheese or butter. Finally, it's Sylvia's turn and she quickly orders. The woman working the food cart says, "Thank you for your patience just now. You know how it can be—chemo freeze."

Sylvia says yes, she knows, and walks away, her appetite diminished. She has led a life of brutally good luck not to have encountered that concept before.

She sits beneath the shade of a tree, dappled sunlight at her toes, and watches this brightly colored circus. The crowd is large, everywhere, wonderful. She smells of lake water, a lightly mineral smell, and the heat of sunburn spreads across her cheekbones. She needs more Advil, that throb and well returning, but she also doesn't care.

People begin to gather at the beach and the docks. She realizes too some are getting back into the boats. They let the boats gently drift—not racing but arranging themselves so that the dragons—and those they carry—face the land. Monsters narrowly aligned. She rises from the shade, throwing out the remnants of her meal, and walks back to the dock, which is where she now feels she belongs, even if she sees quite clearly all these people managed without her palm to brace them.

In the water—some she recognizes from the morning races, some she doesn't think have yet raced. They all have sunflowers on their laps. Someone taps her shoulder and hands her a sunflower too. It has a thick stalk, yellow petals, and a heavy center. A sturdy flower, very much of late summer—she has some growing in the backyard. The flower ceremony.

A woman at a microphone begins to speak—is talking of those who did not make it, who have passed away from cancer. This is memorial to them. In the water, they've gathered their boats close, have their arms draped about one another. Those leading the tribute are those who have survived. A light breeze comes in off the water, a rippling that goes through the crowd. Her wrist takes off in a kind of frenzy of pain. Someone puts an arm about her, and she clutches the sunflower with her bad hand so she can also put her good arm about another.

Mannequin, ruffian. Promising, fortitude. Shattering. God forgive her, she's thinking of Joshua at her dining room table. She'd brought out a book she thought he'd like. She opened it and touched a page to show him a passage, and he brought his chair closer to look—the windows behind them offering a flood of pale April sky. A linen tablecloth, a bowl of grapes, his chair close. He'd put his hand over hers, clasped it warm. It was as if she'd leapt into dimension, as if the whole world had leapt into dimension with her. She ruined her life for that moment.

She thinks of a line from Wallace Stevens about pungent oranges and bright green wings seeming like things in a procession of the dead. People around her in beads and wigs and bright T-shirts: they cry for those they've lost, those they've loved, those who deserved much better.

The dragon-boat survivors are throwing into the water their sunflowers, which drift, sodden and bright. Those close to the water kneel to let their flowers float away too. Sylvia takes her arm from this stranger so she can go to the edge and let her sunflower fall from the dock. Her wrist hurts so much the edges of her vision blacken, but all about her is vividness: cobalt-and-violet water, green-blue mountains, and this carnival of sunlit people, devastated and celebrating.

Potions

THESE ERRATIC March days. The temperatures keep plunging—everything frigid, wind and ice—then spiking. We're in a no-man's-land of weather. Today it's in the low sixties. I should find this intoxicating, but it stirs in me confusion. The soft air, the bright-bright sky: they don't match the empty tree limbs, the dulled winter grass edged with dirty snow. The snow melt has meant mud season is a few weeks early, so Shelby is glad, anyway. My blonde cherubim with her rough-and-tumble streak. Her playtime has begun.

In our backyard, along the eastern fence line, there's a row of hemlocks. Before them lies an old raised-bed garden I never planted anything in. Shelby, since she was two, has been using the garden as a sandbox—a mudbox. Philip thought of it. I remember her toddling across the lawn, holding his hand. He carried a plastic shovel and bucket. When he picked her up and plopped her into the garden bed, I almost called out not to do that, that cleaning her off would be a bear, but she squealed at the magic of his digging dirt into the bucket, then dumping it out. Next up, her turn. They sat there for a beautiful, quiet hour.

All subsequent springs have been variations on this theme. She makes mud pies. She builds small sculptures and calls them castles, houses, villages. She squats and blows hair from her eyes. She murmurs to herself or imaginary friends. We've given her a watering can so she can make the earth muddier still. She has pie tins and Tupperware and yogurt containers. Shelby is six, which is so big compared to the soft toddlerhood of two. Six is coltish and alert and wishing she were more grown up—that steady blue gaze on me and Philip, on everything. It feels she's first examining the world.

This afternoon, she's brought out a drawing pad and some pens. I watch her from the kitchen as I put mint into a pitcher of iced tea. Earlier this week, Kate, my work friend, suggested we play hooky this afternoon, spend time catching up. I can't even remember the last time we saw each other. Working from home, raising a young child: time is a constant blur. Philip, with their writing group, has spent more time with her than I have. I set the pitcher on the patio table, and Shelby, face alight, points to a squirrel running along the fence, its tail a plume. I hope my nod conveys some returned happiness.

The doorbell rings. I tell Shelby I'll be right back. At the door, Kate kisses me on the cheek, crying, "It's so good to see you!" She looks pulled together, professional: pretty apricot makeup on her lids and cheeks, a jade sweater, a silver necklace delicate against her collar bone. I've applied mascara, but I'm in yoga pants and a fleece. I look like I've forgotten she's arriving—or couldn't quite get it together, even when I knew I was having company, which might be the truth.

"You look wonderful," I tell her. "Set your bag down anywhere," I say as we walk through the house. "I thought we'd sit outside, make the most of the weather."

She sets her tote beside the patio chair and waves to Shelby as I pour us iced tea. "Your daughter is so great. I wish I had so little compunction about making a mess."

We clink glasses, and she catches me up on some jostling for power among the project managers, discusses with disdain an article about Italian-sourced spelt. We work for a lifestyle magazine: food and wine, gardening and vacations, recipes. Kate is an editor; I do graphic design. I admire Kate for having the energy to be disgruntled. I find myself increasingly numb to sunset pictures of Big Sur, to photos of roasted cauliflower.

"How's the writing going?" I ask.

"Oh, writing." She swirls her glass, sets the ice rattling. "You know what might be fun? Add some bourbon and you've got a mint julep."

I take her glass. "Two cocktails coming up." I fret about Philip's coming home and finding me boozy, but it's not yet three. I have time to gather myself.

When I return with the drinks, Shelby is crouched, writing something in her drawing pad. She's mouthing words, sounding them out. "A potion," Kate tells me. "I asked what she was up to and she said she's figuring out a potion." She takes a long sip. "Cheers."

That dinner party six months back, friends from the magazine and their spouses: that's when I last saw Kate. She'd been explaining how she'd begun writing short stories and thought a writing group would help motivate her. While pursuing writing as art sounded wonderful, I thought privately this group sounded unappealing. People taking turns playing teacher, playing student: it seemed somber, self-serious. Philip, however, brightened. Surprising me, he said he'd been toying with writing some essays about his life—a way of making sense of things. Kate suggested he join: the more the merrier. They'd clinked glasses across the table. Philip has been shy to show me his essays, but I assume he's writing about his father, and I want to give him space. In his recountings, the writing group is amusing, a little eccentric. A sweet older woman, obsessed with her toy schnauzer, is writing novels wild with violence and crime.

Kate has finished her drink in what seems seconds, which is unusual for her. I ask if she wants another. She stands. "I can make them."

I rise too. "I've put away the bourbon. I'll show you where things are."

I call to Shelby we'll be out again in a jiffy, that I'm interested in this potion she's making. She looks up—interrupted in her work—and stares at me with unnerving stillness, as if being called back to herself is a task requiring real concentration. I wave and she waves back.

In the kitchen, at the sink, I spill out most of my drink so Kate can make us a fresh round. "Is writing not going well?"

"It's great." She's found a cutting board and taken a withered orange from the fruit bowl, quartering it with a steak knife. "Yesterday I had my first story accepted for publication. I was beyond elated."

"That's great!" Perhaps we're celebrating, then.

She squeezes orange juice into her glass. "One of our articles quoted someone from Kentucky saying the secret to a mint julep is to add clementine juice. Probably hogwash, but let's try a version of it anyway."

"That sad old orange might not add much."

She pours bourbon without measuring. "We're making do. We're displaying ingenuity and pluck." She hands me my drink.

"To your story!" I almost gasp at the drink's strength—essentially straight bourbon—then decide to hell with it and take another sip. Let the afternoon become floaty and strange. Kate brought in her tote bag and has left it by the kitchen island, which is weird. "Philip says a woman in your writing group is writing gruesome detective novels."

Kate laughs. "Probably she'll sell her books for a bazillion dollars."

"I hope Philip is a good presence. He doesn't have any real writing experience, but he seems to find attending meaningful."

Kate's cheeks turn scarlet. "Most of us aren't that experienced," she says evenly.

"Are you okay?"

She shakes her head and studies the floor. Our breathing becomes the kitchen's predominant sound. Through the window, I watch Shelby, who appears to be having a conversation with a willow tree, squinting up, waiting for its response.

"I'm botching this," she says. "I've been thinking about it for months. It's none of my business."

My heart roars in my ears. "I don't know what you're saying."

"Do you know what Philip is writing about?"

"His father dying?"

She bites her lip. It's such a young gesture—that of an anxious child. She finishes her too strong drink.

"I'm sorry," she says. "He's seeing someone—dating someone—and he's writing about the relationship. I feel like such a fucking jerk for telling you. But were it me, I'd not want this happening out in the world while I remained clueless."

"I don't think that's right," I say, my voice high and distant. "Maybe you're misinterpreting what he's writing. He's not a good writer. Words are not his thing. He could be emulating you and trying to write fiction."

Kate picks up some orange rind, messy with pulp and pith, and begins ripping it. A tiny spray from its skin is caught in the light, a waft of citrus. Philip has done something awful and then compounded it by insisting his transgressions have an audience. The extreme passive-aggressiveness of this. He's trapped Kate into either being forthright or complicit. I need to remember that, not be angry with her.

"What has he written?" Then I'm ashamed. This isn't for her to tell me. It's for him to tell me. I say that. Kate continues ripping orange rind. The bright scent is nauseating. I say that as well.

She sets the orange rind on the cutting board. "I should go. I Ubered over here." She raises her empty glass and aims for a smile. "In my head I had one version of this where I spoke to you sober and displayed rectitude and you cried and I hugged you and we both felt relieved." She takes her phone from her pocket. I can't decide whether I'm supposed to be telling her yes, she should go, or no, she shouldn't.

"Why did you bring your bag inside?"

She grabs it. "Force of habit."

"You brought his essays."

"I really wish I weren't fucking this up." With her tote over her shoulder, she looks absurd, in transit. "I thought in case you thought he was going to lie to you and you wanted the truth. But, honestly, Lynn, you don't need to read the essays. Just talk to him. He clearly wants to be caught. He wants to have a conversation."

"The essays," I say. "Please give them to me."

"Do you hate me?" She hands me two stapled documents.

"I admire you," I say. "And later I'll thank you. But right now, I need to fall apart."

She flings her arms about my shoulders, holds me in that hug she'd imagined. I am numb. She murmurs she'll go wait out front for her Uber. "What's your story about?" I ask into her shoulder.

She gives a half laugh. "Honestly, the plot is minimal. It's mostly a character's private vicissitudes."

I should respond, but I don't have a response. I'm in some fog of Philip. I wonder why I can't make sense of things and if this is the essential problem. Kate pats my shoulder as if I'm a wizened old lady and tells me to call her if I need to talk.

Outside, Shelby is dappled in hemlock shadow and bright March light. I'll tell her Kate had to leave early and Mommy is going to take a quick shower. Leaving my child alone is terrible parenting, but where we live is safe, and I need to cry. "Shelby," I call.

She has mud on her chin and in her hair. With an old soup spoon, she's smoothing mud into a casserole dish. She glances up. "Mommy, look!" Grabbing her drawing pad, she runs across the lawn, tiny and bright and beautiful. She shows me a page. It's titled "The Muck of Luck by Shelby." "Ingredens," it reads, followed by a series of downward pointing arrows.

— mud
— 1 drop of pee
— 1 hint of pink tiger
— 3 leaves
— 1 cup of water
— 1 pinch of pumpkin spice
— some more mud

"It's my potion!" she tells me. "You have to stir it up in this order and then say a wish. Then your wish will come true!"

"Shelby, this is wonderful. How did you come up with this?"

She does a pirouette and says she figured it out all on her own. I praise her for inventiveness. In all earnestness, I find it charming, but my throat is thick.

"Do we have pumpkin spice?" she asks. "I don't really have to add pee. Mommy? You look like you are crying."

"I feel sad Kate had to leave so soon. I was thinking I might take a shower to feel a little better."

She nods vigorously. Shelby's eyes shade toward lavender—a cornflower blue, a blue of fields of flowers in high summer. This drab landscape of gray tree trunks, browned grass, dark earth: her eyes are wondrously clear in contrast. She's studying me. "I don't like it when my playdates end early," she says.

The shower is clouds of steam and jasmine-scented bodywash that's overly perfumed. I'm not crying. I'm thinking of Philip after he got the call from his parents—first learned his father had pancreatic cancer. He sat on our bed. I stood in the doorframe. He'd smiled, something beatific in it, and his eyes, which are Shelby's eyes, displayed a sweetness —round and open—I couldn't fathom. "We're going to beat this!" He hit the bedcover with his open palm. "He's going to be okay!" And, God, how I felt for him. The quivering joy, the irrational surety all would be well: this is Philip. Of course, I've let this fantasy lull me when I needed it. After years of not getting pregnant—and fertility drugs, hormones shot into my ass, constant emptiness—I turned forty and came to the false epiphany I wasn't meant to have children. I cried to Philip, bawled, choked on phlegm. Philip held my head to his chest. "Baby," he said. "It will happen for us."

I'm frothing suds in my hair. The air is toxic with clean beauty. It broke Philip when his dad died. And if I'd just soothed him, lulled him with optimism—as he'd done for me—then maybe this wouldn't be happening. Although I sense this is wrong, even as I'm trying to construct it. The stronger, more overarching thought: I don't know how to set the impossibly wrong right.

— 1 cup of still-not-forthcoming tears
— 3 glugs of night-blooming jasmine bodywash, unhelpful froth
— 2 stapled essays, unread
— 1 gallon of courage
— 3 ounces of bourbon
— 1 desiccated orange
— Mud enough to submerge it all

Out of the shower, I put on a pair of old jeans, a T-shirt, and think all I've managed is to make myself reek of flowers. I check out the window. Shelby is crouched in a froglike pose, staring up at the bedroom window as if waiting for me to appear. I feel ashamed. I wave, a maniacally oversized gesture. She looks away.

The essays are on the bed. Before the shower I tried to read one, but the words dissolved. I try again. The first essay is titled "Freedom" and starts with Philip remembering being a teenager, riding his motorcycle, the joy he felt as the wind rushed past. This segues into finding that sensation again upon meeting Caroline. The words blur once more, grow strange. I set down the essay. Other people have read this. He has literally asked for feedback about the rendering of his affair. He's made hurting me a public act. Rage comes into my abdomen hot. Why was I trying to blame myself? Because I couldn't undo space and time to make Philip's father whole again?

"Mommy?" Shelby has opened the bedroom door. She's naked, her narrow shoulders, her just protruding belly. There's more dirt in her hair, on her forehead. "You're supposed to come downstairs."

"You're right. Did you leave your clothes down there?"

"Yes, so I'd not track mud into the house. Come downstairs and let's work on the potion."

"First, let's get you dressed again." I put the essays on the bureau, which is taller than she is, so she can't see them. The second is titled "Façade." Philip is an architect. That metaphor would be an easy reach for him. I follow my baby as she skips down the hall.

Shelby pulls a clean shirt from the drawer. I'm thinking about outward appearances, about how I don't know my husband. Shelby then flings the shirt at me, a soft jolt to my shoulder. "To work on the potion," she says sternly, "we first need to find a hint of pink tiger. That has to happen first. We need to search my room."

My inattentiveness is making her angry. I pick up the shirt and hand it to her, then look around her room, painted lavender and chockablock with stuffed animals, pastel bookshelves heaped with toys and books. A hint of pink tiger. She pulls on her shirt and underwear and pants, then jumps onto her bed. She reaches for a pink bunny named Bergeron, cradling it to her belly and smoothing its ears.

"The pink tiger?"

She shakes her head and hops off the bed, plopping before a bookshelf, taking out books and flipping through them. I start rifling through her closet, looking for pink clothes or anything with a tiger on it. I'm imagining Philip with a motorcycle helmet on, his mouth open with laughter.

"I have an idea," Shelby says. I turn: she has a botany book, marvelous drawings of plants, open in her lap. I come and sit by her. She points to a detailed drawing of a tiger lily, its petals spread and curled at their tips. The petals have dark spots on them. The stamen splay from the flower's center. It's a rich drawing, fecund.

"Beautiful choice," I tell her.

"It's not pink."

"But it is a tiger lily, which you remembered from when we've looked through this book. I find that impressive. And I'd argue it shades toward pink. Coral, you might call it."

"Coral," she says. She's testing its mouthfeel, maybe deciding if it suits her private symbology. "Okay." She nods. "Now we have to sing a song over the pink tiger to get a hint of it."

"How does the song go?"

"Pink tiger, tiger lily, coral tiger . . ." She touches a coral petal. "Mud, mud, mud!"

We sing it three times. She has to coach me since she's magically memorized the order of colors and flowers and animals, and I'm getting tripped up. She delights in this, pausing to see whether I can get it right without her. By the third try I can, and we sing it loudly into the afternoon's stillness.

In secret, I've sung the incantation over the essays on the bureau. I need their essence to be in the potion. Hint of betrayal essays. This is ludicrous but true.

From the closet, Shelby grabs her wizard's hat—part of last year's Halloween costume. Conical and navy, affixed with silver stars. She settles it on her head, self-serious, and regards me. "You need a hat too." Downstairs, I rummage through winter hats until I find the most ridiculous, deliberately oversized and slouchy, charcoal gray with a huge white poof. I put it on, and Shelby nods approvingly.

Next, it's to the kitchen, where I finish the half-melted mint julep on the counter. It's a rush and a sedative, which is what I want right now, even if I don't want it. From the spice cabinet, I take a small glass jar, an overpriced mix of cinnamon, clove, nutmeg, and cardamom. "You don't like this," I say, handing it to her. "Why did you choose it?" Some days, Philip sprinkles it into the coffee grounds before adding boiling water to the French press, and the smell is fragrant and warm. One morning, Shelby insisted that we add some to her oatmeal. After tasting it, she scrunched up her eyes and stuck her tongue delicately out. "Yuck-o," she said. "Oh, yuck!"

"Because it is mysterious," Shelby says, clutching the jar with both hands. She heads to the porch door, looking back over her shoulder, her smile coy. "Because," she says, "it is *aromatic.*"

She has me in her palm. Recently, we taught her that word. Not in conjunction with the pumpkin spice, but—what? Some other meal. My child is so goddamned delightful, so attentive.

Shelby also suggests I bring out the food coloring. A drop or two of the yellow, and we will have our pee.

We troop out, and I take her cue, kneeling over the raised bed, my knees immediately muddied and cold. The sky is clarion, loud peals of blue, but absent of bird call, of spring. The dirt still smells of winter. Shelby is consulting her potion. "We need three leaves." Those, from last fall, are easy to find along the fence line. She takes her time finding the driest she can—old brown maples—since she wants to crumble them into the potion.

In my back pocket, my phone vibrates. "Hey, called it an early day! En route now. See you home soon, xo." I feel this little thrill of vindication: Normalcy! This afternoon's sadness just misapprehension! Then that thrill curdles into dread. He's coming home soon with his notions of freedom and façades and fuck him a thousand times over. I could call Kate, but she's probably with Ben, prepping an early dinner, and her husband is saying, Baby, you tried. There was no good way to handle that conversation given that Philip's behavior is so unmoored. Poor Lynn, married so long to an idiot. Or: Poor Lynn, always a bit of a space cadet. Slow to catch on even when her husband was literally spelling out his affair. Or: Poor Philip, driven to such extremes to capture his wife's attention. He was always the nicer of the two. Aren't we glad it's them and not us in this quagmire, them and not us so hopelessly amess.

I examine the half-moons of dirt trapped beneath my nails. What if Kate has written about me and Philip? That story she's publishing is us imagined, conjured. Philip out riding his motorcycle and then knocking on Caroline's door. She greets him, laughing, enchanted he's still wearing his helmet. She takes his hand to bring him inside. Cut to me out in the dirt, puttering with Shelby, drifty and oblivious and delicately sad. Cut back to Philip in Caroline's bed. They're holding hands. She rests her head against his chest, puts her fingers to the pale blond hair there. He's thinking about me, how he wishes I'd be simpler and chipper and greet him at the door radiant with delight before I took him inside to fuck him. He'd be telling himself he's allowed to chase happiness—that happiness is out there just waiting for people with the heart to find it. Cut to me with my mud-daubed cheeks, staring morosely at the hemlocks.

Shelby holds a leaf to the sky, shading it this way and that to test its dryness. It gives off an amber translucence in the sunshine, then grows dull as she sets it back down. I'm being paranoid. Kate came here because she was worried. But then I just turned into a bewildered zombie and sent her off. Maybe my fears should be anticipatory: Kate had never planned to write about me and Philip, but she's doing so now. So rattled after this afternoon with its bourbon and emotional shock, she's at her laptop—imagining as a way of making order. She doesn't mean badly as she draws us, gives us our sad dimensions. Just as Philip doesn't mean badly as he pursues his affair and writes about it to understand himself. Just as I don't mean badly as I imagine them writing, imagine them taking my life—my life!—and turning it into fodder for their exercises on the page. I'd fling dirt at them, wet fistfuls, but I don't mean badly.

Shelby comes trotting back. Her wizard hat is crooked; she's holding the leaves fanned, shades of chestnut and ochre. Here is beauty and play and I am down in the metaphorical muck when the actual mire is sweet and clean.

— Hint of betrayal essays
— Real stories
— Unreal stories
— 1 cup of cloudy loneliness
— The love of my confused heart
— My hot rage
— Mud slung; mud heaved; mud flung

Shelby sets the three leaves, balanced atop one another, at my elbow. She's studying her array of containers. The casserole dish is already full. A red pail seems to me a good idea, but she shakes her head. The pie tins, the Tupperware: they're too small, too flat for her purposes. She asks if we could, just this once, use the cauldron.

"We don't own a cauldron!" I say. "But I like the spirit of the suggestion."

She shakes her head. "We do. For Halloween."

She's right: in the back reaches of the pantry is a large tin pot with an oversized arched handle, an open-mouthed kettle we picked up years ago at a lawn sale. Philip had immediately seen its potential, saying it would be perfect to hold candy Halloween night. He's always been better at imagining than I have. I'm so tired. I tell Shelby that's a wonderful idea.

Inside, I consider more bourbon, but I'm lightly drunk as is, and with more I'll just drift into some private space, untouchable, when I need to stay present. He's coming home soon.

As I come back out, I lift the tin pot in triumph. Shelby is at the garden hose spigot and is filling the watering can until it's too heavy for her. She wobbles back to the garden bed, almost dragging the watering can. She lifts the pot, examining its bottom and then its insides, letting her face get swallowed by it. She sets it down again, happy. "We need so much mud," she says, handing me a large yogurt container. With her hands, she begins to fill the red pail with dirt. Once she's filled it, she dumps it into the cauldron. She explains I should do the same.

The damp earth against my palms is so cold, I inhale. Shelby laughs. I plunge my hands into the earth, getting mud on my jeans, my shirt, all over my arms. We get the cauldron two-thirds full, and Shelby decides this is enough. She pours water from the watering can in, then looks about the yard. She trots over to a tiny copse of birch, finding a sturdy fallen branch, white bark with black whorls, and returns to stir the mud with it. She seems to have an innate sense of proportion because now we have mud proper, thick and heavy, slick, with a dirty shine.

She uses the remaining water from the watering can to clean out a small chipped mug from Philip's alma mater, then pours in an additional tiny amount. She asks I add one drop of yellow food coloring. The water stains yellow, shading toward orange. She gently tips the mug's contents into the cauldron, a tiny splash, then rests the mug against the picket fence.

"We need to sing the pink-tiger song again," she says. "We need to sit on either side of the cauldron and hold hands over it and sing."

I'm a bit shocked but also gladdened I remember the words. I sit cross-legged, never mind the dirt all over me now, and clutch Shelby's tiny hands. We watch each other over the cauldron's rim and chant, "Pink tiger, tiger lily, coral tiger, mud, mud, mud!" three times. Something very tight in my chest loosens.

The leaves are next. Shelby crumbles two, and I crumble one into the cauldron. They smell of must and are delicate, dusty. She stirs again with the birch stick. Next, I am to stir. I kneel and the slouchy winter hat falls forward, too low on my forehead. I push it back, realizing I've planted a muddy palm print on it. Shelby comes around to investigate. She then lightly places her hand to the cauldron's surface and touches her wizarding hat. "We match," she says. "That just made the potion better."

The pinch of pumpkin spice is, in fact, a sprinkling, the scent of cardamom strong and lovely. Already the light is slanting lower in the west, glowing stripes across the bare yard. It's become windy, and the eddying gusts are warm. Winter light, spring air. This no-man's-land now has magic brewing in it. Shelby usually reserves this playtime for herself. Does she intuit I need to be tethered to the afternoon, to stay present within it?

We make a final batch of mud—more water from the watering can and more scooped up earth mixed into the pail. We pour that into the cauldron. I'm hoping this doesn't end.

As Shelby gives the potion a final stir, I think how my own potions were too predetermined, too filled with objects and ideas already laden with meaning. Not potions, just a jumble of complaints and overly determined signifiers. The potion needs to be neutral to allow us space to find within it what we want, what we need, what we wish.

"Now," Shelby says. "We have to hold hands over the cauldron and say, 'Thank you, mud, please grant us our wish!' Then we have to close our eyes and make our wishes."

"Out loud?"

"No, I got that wrong. The wish needs to stay inside you. Also, before we say thank you, we have to take some mud and draw it across our cheeks." She dips her index finger into the mud and comes around to me.

I lower my face, and she brushes a line of cold mud against my cheekbone, then another line beneath it. She gathers more mud with her fingertip and draws parallel lines across my other cheek. I close my eyes as her fingertips graze my skin. Then I do this for her. Her cheeks are so soft, and she also closes her eyes—trusting in me, in this moment she's constructed. The air is blue and warm.

We clasp hands. Shelby says we must also say the final refrain three times.

"Thank you, mud, please grant us our wish!"

"Hold on." Shelby takes back one hand and wrinkles her nose, scratching her cheek. "It itches." She giggles. Then she looks to the patio. "Hi, Daddy!"

Philip is watching us. He looks strange, inscrutable, as if he's wearing a mask, some hyperneutrality not natural to him, and I glimpse how Shelby and I might appear. We're sitting in mud, covered in mud, holding hands over a large pot. Shelby's wizard hat, my slouchy winter hat. The black stripes beneath our eyes as if we were preparing for a day of rigorous sport. But the ridiculous way we look has nothing to do with the magic we have mustered, and which I will not let wither under his distant gaze.

Then I see he's holding the essays. I left them on the bureau. I wasn't thinking, I did not think, not even to give myself time to plan how this conversation would occur. Here it is upon us, the future, whatever that may be.

"We are doing a potion!" Shelby shouts, undeterred by Philip's silence. Or maybe because of it. She stretches out her hands to mine. I take them. Three times, Shelby tells me. We have to say it three times in a row to make it work.

I shut my eyes and chant. And even when Shelby's hands unclasp from mine, I keep my eyes closed. I wish. I wish.

I wish—

Monsters

NANA SAYS MONSTERS reside in the woods. Pish-posh, Nana, we say, although we eye each other overly long before resuming our game of checkers. Outside, it rains—a gray patter, the thick and glossy heave of summer leaves. This July and August, Ben and I are here for an extended visit as our parents debate whether they can remain married.

"You think I'm being cute," Nana says. "But I'm worried. Do not go out there at night. Spare me your shenanigans. Or just get in trouble in the living room where I can keep an eye on you."

Ben sighs. "Honestly, Nana."

"Honestly, yourself," Nana says. Nana is a professor emeritus of sociology. Before retiring two summers ago, she taught at the local college for approximately a thousand years. Of course, being smart doesn't preclude you from becoming senile, but Ben and I drove up from Boston this morning, and she's seemed sharp all day. Likely she's just anxious: as her daughter goes through gut-punch life changes, her grandchildren, before her, swallow all their emotions.

The Mighty Marty's claws skitter on the hardwood floors as the dog tumble flops into Ben's side. Ben scratches his ears, and his eyes are closed, blissful. The Mighty Marty is a frizzled little beast, gray and shaggy and vaguely resembling a terrier—also a woodchuck. He's always loved Ben best, one feral heart recognizing another.

"Nana, we promise we'll be reasonably good," I say.

"What about this little lovebug?" Ben leans down to smooch The Mighty Marty's head. "Is he allowed out at night?"

"Past dusk, we stay on the lawn. Nor do we ever enter the woods with, say, plans to drink cheap beer and smoke cigarettes."

Ben laughs. Last summer, Nana found his poorly hidden stash in the garage behind the garden hose. To her credit, Nana didn't call our parents. She just poured out the beer and broke all the cigarettes and lectured Ben about the horrors of lung cancer. Then she said she'd decided we were old enough to learn to drink in a civilized manner, no matter how the law or our parents came down on it. She was instituting a cocktail hour.

We were allowed one drink, which we helped prepare. Ben and I became proficient at pouring jiggers and assembling garnishes. Late afternoons, we might settle on making Bijous (gin, vermouth, chartreuse, orange bitters). Then, weather permitting, we'd lounge on lawn chairs and, as light streaked through the trees, sip our cocktails. If we were ambitious, we'd play croquet. The Mighty Marty would chase the balls rolling through the grass. We'd laugh and cheer him on.

"Could we make cocktails?" Ben asks. This is on his mind, too, then.

Nana looks at her watch. "We could. I was thinking lime rickeys."

In the kitchen, we juice limes. Nana tasks Ben to stir the cup of sugar into the cup of water on the stove to make the simple syrup.

Since the rain still falls, we return with our tumblers to the living room. We pull chairs up to the fireplace, and though it isn't cold, Nana starts a fire for the cheer of it. The Mighty Marty settles at Nana's feet and falls asleep.

"Snacks," Ben says, standing.

"There are almonds in the cupboard. Crackers too." Nana glances out to the gray sky, the glistening grass.

When Ben returns with a neat plate—a bowl of almonds at its center, crackers nestled against a wedge of cheese—his drink is nearly full again. And the rickey's cloudy pale yellow has turned clear.

Nana assesses his drink. "This is not the kind of summer we'll be having, Benjamin."

"You said we could get in trouble in the living room."

Nana takes the drink from him. As she pours it out in the kitchen, he broods and watches the fire.

"Ben," I say. "It's cool of her to allow us this. Don't push it."

He shakes his head. All spring, he's been getting sloshed—ever since he got accepted to Stanford. With his acceptance, our parents, already prone to icing each other out, started saying terrible things to each other at night after they thought Ben and I had fallen asleep. Our mother has called our father weak-willed, boring, an insufficient provider to his family, a poor father to his children. Our father has called our mother slovenly and irresponsible and a slutty cunt. One child off to college this year, the other off the next. With sudden force, they saw they had to decide whether they were staying together if no longer pretending to stay together for us. At Ben's ostensibly celebratory dinner, our mother asked our father if he was really going to continue ogling the waitress's ass all night, and in front of his children no less. Our father threw aside his napkin. He stood. His jaw had a pugnacious jut to it. "You're so awful," he said. He'd already had two drinks. "I don't know where you get the energy to be so endlessly awful." He came around the table and stuck out his hand to Ben, insisting he congratulate his son on all he'd managed to accomplish despite having such a shitty mother. Ben kept his eyes trained on his plate, his cheeks molten with heat. "Fuck it," my father said, and left. We had to take a Lyft home, my mother complaining the entire way about our father's failings, his moral shortcomings.

After that, Ben started regularly turning up to the breakfast table with red-rimmed eyes, sour breath, bad attitude. He's admitted he likes drugs better than drink, but says he'll cease self-medicating once in college. He says he's not sure how I haven't resorted to similar measures, but I don't need to ingest anything to turn numb. Our parents shouldn't be together. In each other's presence, they turn everything surrounding them ugly.

Nana returns with her MacBook. "You need to see my Critter Cam."

"Critter Cam," Ben murmurs. Not sorry about trying to sneak gin but also not going to continue to pout, which relieves me.

"I'll show you typical footage first, so you have some basis of comparison." We join her at the dining room table, and she clicks on a video of the woods surrounding her lawn. The trees appear the wall of an amphitheater. Pale grass recedes into murky blackness. Tangled branches, rough bark. And within that density, patches of pitch. You can watch the videos in time lapse, Nana explains, and slow to real time if any animals have stopped by.

Ben says, "Stopped by. Are you considering inviting them over for tea?"

"Are you worried about being out here without any neighbors nearby?" I ask.

"I was worried about my bird feeder. Something demolished the one I had out. An acquaintance told me the bear population has been particularly active this summer. She recommended this system."

"Why not just take down the bird feeder at night?"

"Because perhaps there's no need to." She reaches down to pet The Mighty Marty. "We just want to know what's out there."

"Fair," Ben says.

Nana looks to see whether he's mocking her, but his face is calm. Something in him responds to her logic. I'm the one who finds this silly.

The video captures small shifts in light, branches and grass wavering.

A fox trots from the woods, its ears sharp, its eyes a zombified white under the camera's gaze. Other clips reveal a waddling skunk, a troupe of raccoons with sagging bellies and bristling fur. A shambling black bear as large as a golf cart rears up onto two feet and swipes at the bird feeder, its paw arcing the air. It drops back onto all fours and lopes toward the house, outside the camera's view. I imagine it nosing about the porch, separated from The Mighty Marty only by glass doors.

"Aha!" Ben says. "So it was a bear."

"What did you just witness?" Nana says sharply.

"The bear attempting to get at the birdfeeder."

"Did it get the birdfeeder?"

"It did not, Professor Nana. But another bigger bear could've done the damage you described."

"That bear is awfully big, though," I say.

"In the last month, only one other bear has come through, and it was smaller than this one," Nana says. "Now watch this." We watch the night's micromovements. Then some violent lurch sets the trees quivering, a treequake. The woods eventually still. Two sets of eyes—reptilian gleams—blinker on. Something in their stare—hard, without dimension or depth. They blinker out. I exhale; I'd been holding my breath.

"Shit," Ben says.

Nana closes the computer. "I don't want you out there at night."

"Maybe large cats?" Ben says. "Catamounts or lynx?"

"Catamounts are extinct. Also, you saw how tall those creatures were. If cats, they're taller than us."

"Call Vermont Fish and Wildlife. Send them the footage."

"Then I'm just some old coot in the woods scared of her own shadow."

"Cats in trees," I say. "Cats can definitely climb trees."

"Can they?" Ben says. "What's the name of that lake monster everyone is so fond of believing in?"

"Champ," Nana says. West of here is a beautiful large lake. The lore is some Loch Ness creature lives in its depths, a story locals always cheerfully espouse.

"Champ came ashore." Ben gets the crackers, cheese, and almonds. "Rabid moose." He goes into the kitchen, calling. "I'm just getting some juice!"

Sotto voce, Nana says, "This summer, I need you to keep an eye on your brother."

I nod. Nana's hand on the closed MacBook has a light tremor; her bones rise through her thin skin. She is old. This shocks me more than the video. I've only ever thought of her as experienced, capable, an agile thinker. Someone who finds solutions. She will, I decide, find a solution for this. She's just momentarily thrown.

"Chupacabra." Ben sets his juice before Nana. "Just juice. Bigfoot."

Nana watches out the window the fog of rain. The Mighty Marty starts to snore, and it's so delicate and heartbreaking, I reach down and run my hand along his head.

A pleasant week goes by. Midmornings, we walk old logging trails. My first thought was to ask why, if the woods contain danger, Nana continues her rambles, but almost immediately, I feel the irrational truth of it: the woods are safe in daylight because they're safe. Dappled light, a canopy of thick green, bird call. Damp earth that smells of copper. We're noisy, crushing twigs underfoot, calling for The Mighty Marty, who's crashing into brush, pursuing squirrels. Generally, Marty's tail wags fast when he picks up a scent, but once it dropped tight to his behind. A furious focus, zigging and zagging. Then he stopped and looked back, ears low, eyes bewildered. He trotted to Nana's side and stayed close, although when we came to a branching path, he zipped ahead to choose one. It seemed he was moving us away from whatever olfactory information had disturbed him.

In the afternoons, Ben and I find mild adventures. In town, we get maple soft serve. We take books to campus and sit in Adirondack chairs set out for summer. Today, we're at the lake, a stretch of beach with pines along its ledges and a shore strewn with shale.

Ben is considering how best to hurl a piece of driftwood into the water. Nana has requested we return by four, bringing olives. We'll be making martinis. My mother texts: "Checking in." I answer: "All is well." This has been the extent of our communication. No details. Nobody wants any details.

Ben throws the driftwood as if it were a javelin, but it flips on its side and floats. "They found a whale skeleton around here. In 1849, some railway workers unearthed it. Twelve thousand years ago, this was all ocean, which might explain the Champ stories."

"Ancient whale sightings passed down thousands of years?"

"I mean, strange creatures live in oceans. Maybe some weird old monster fish has lived in this lake since forever." On his phone, he shows me a website with Champ sightings. Some are surprisingly convincing. Far out, a brontosaurus-like head. Beneath the surface, shadows suggesting a serpentine body.

In the mornings, we now watch Nana's Critter Cam, hunting for looming movement or those hard, glaring eyes. We've yet to see again anything unnerving. This should be reassuring.

Ben skips a rock: one, two, three delicate plinks before sinking. "Tonight, I'm going to meet up with someone." I also try to skip a rock, but it lands with a heavy splash. "Just a little pick-me-up. Two months is a long time to be wholesome." He gives me a side-glance. "In the woods."

"That's entirely stupid. Meet your dealer here tomorrow afternoon."

"Our parents are ruining us with their anger and shitty behavior. Meanwhile, we hide in our rooms with our earbuds, pretending things are okay."

"So you're taking a stand or something."

"Or something." He skips another rock. "Whatever was there hasn't been in weeks. Still, we could go out and scare ourselves and feel brave and in control of things for a hot second."

"I'm not coming."

"Facing down our monsters. Metaphor with a capital *M*. I thought you'd be into it."

"Nana asked us not to do this."

"She won't know." Ben stands. "I could teach you how to smoke cigarettes."

"What if you get hurt?" I'm in a staring contest with the mountains. Ben reaches out a hand to help me up. We need to go get olives, he says. I clasp his palm. My anger is acute in no small part because Ben is probably who loves me best in this world.

The stupid plan: Ben will head out at midnight. Nana will already be asleep. The Mighty Marty, who stays awake with us until we go to bed, might start yapping if Ben opens a door, so Ben will climb out his window, à la some eighties movie. His rendezvous spot is half a mile out, a dilapidated toolshed that once belonged to the land's previous owner. As children, we weren't allowed to play in it, so of course we've always imagined all the fun we might've had exploring its confines. Ben chose the toolshed to entice me to come along.

All evening he's in a good mood. As he washes dishes after dinner, handing me plates to dry, he discusses with Nana what classes he might take his first semester. Nana, at her laptop, is looking up Stanford's sociology faculty and telling Ben whose work she recognizes. By the backdoor, The Mighty Marty snoozes.

Later, after Nana has gone to bed and we're in the living room watching Netflix, I try once more, telling him the potential costs outweigh the potential benefits.

"How boring of you," he says.

I harrumph and say I'm going to bed. I say I hope he gets eaten by monsters.

I wake to Nana opening my bedroom door. She's backlit by hallway light, in her bathrobe, her cheeks inflamed with displeasure. "Where is your brother?"

Nana is too imperious for me to lie. "The woods."

"Jesus." She wraps her robe tighter about her. "You will stay here."

"He's out by that old toolshed. He has some dumb idea about facing down his fears. You don't need to go after him." On my bedside table, my phone says it's 2 am. He should be back. Maybe he blacked out, or he's running among the trees, lecturing the stars about ancient whale skeletons. I should've gone with him. I could've kept him in check.

"I don't know how we're going to get through the summer. He's so self-destructive right now."

"Our parents," I say. "Nana, you have to understand how awful they're being."

"I know. Or, I suspect. If I'm not back with him in the next hour, call the police." She shuts my door.

I try texting Ben, telling him he needs to get his shit together and come back, Nana is attempting to track him down. But cell phone reception out here is, at best, spotty, and the text doesn't send.

I go to the kitchen to make tea. The Mighty Marty is by the back door, watching the yard. Seeing me, he yaps, asking to be let out. I shake my head and find a mug, fill the kettle. Marty yaps again. He assesses me, I swear, with contempt.

An hour elapses and I don't call the police. Outside, the black sky fades to gray and birds start to chirp. At sunrise, the light is subtle, an absence of night.

The front door opens. The Mighty Marty and I run to the living room and there is Ben, his hair askew, his skin pale, the telltale rim of red at his eyes. "What," he says sullenly.

"Where is Nana?" I cry.

Ben demands to know if I ratted him out. I did *not*, I say, but this is no longer the point.

"Nana said to call the police if she didn't return," I say.

"First we have to look for her. Maybe she tripped and broke her ankle, and we just need to find her."

The rosy sky is clearing into blue as we go to the toolshed and peer into its musty confines. A few rusted shovels and a shelf lined with jars filled with screws and nails, dust furring every surface. Then we stick to the logging trails, looking for Hansel and Gretel crumbs, but don't see her footprints or flashlight or any other small possessions scattered about.

The air is cool and damp. After a mile, the trail first branches and we debate splitting up. Ben says we've seen that movie, so we try one branch and then backtrack to the other, but these paths are like spiderwebs, becoming tricky and intricate the further we pursue them, and we start to lose our sense of where we are. The old pines grow thicker, and at points trails just end at streams or seem to melt into the forest floor.

"We should go back," I say. "She could've returned home and now we're the lost ones."

Ben nods. It's only nine, but we've been out here for hours.

The Mighty Marty lifts his nose and then zooms off the path toward a meandering stream we've been paralleling.

Ben and I follow the dog, small and shaggy amid the sunshine falling through branches. Marty stops before the water. He sits as if compelled, his rump hitting the earth, and howls. My arms turn to gooseflesh. This lament: it's like smoke rising. Ben scoops up The Mighty Marty, who tries to fling himself free of Ben's grasp. He clamps his teeth into Ben's forearm and Ben gasps but doesn't drop the dog.

"This is ankle deep," Ben says. "She couldn't have drowned, couldn't have been carried by its currents." Ben strokes The Mighty Marty's head. The dog is trembling.

I begin hauling fallen pine branches, rocks to create a pile of natural detritus. I take pictures with my phone—to what end, I don't know. The woods, with its daytime tranquility and cheer, keeps its violence hidden.

The Mighty Marty bares his teeth as Ben stands. "We need to look at the Critter Cam," he says.

I fill The Mighty Marty's water bowl and call Nana's name but can feel she's not here. I have a headache. I guess Ben must feel borderline incoherent: hungover and pumping adrenaline at once.

Ben calls me into the living room. He's on the couch with Nana's laptop. "Look," he says. Rustling black leaves and mildly shifting clouds. Then two sets of cold eyes glowing in the dark. They seem to stare at the camera. I'm losing my mind. Is it possible they're laughing? The trees shake, quiver, and I imagine belly laughs, guffaws. The eyes wink out and the land stills. Ben hits pause. He massages his temples.

"I'll call the police," I say.

"We're unsupervised minors. They'll send us home."

"I'll call Mom and Dad."

Ben's laugh is shaky, a sigh. "God, that would be awful."

It would be: our mother shrieking we were irresponsible shits, my father wresting the phone from her to demand we return to Boston, them beginning to fight about whether we should go, whether they should come to us, whose fault this is. All their energy centered on accusation, on being vituperative and mean.

"The police," I say again. "If there are repercussions for us, so be it."

"She's not out there."

"She's *of course* out there."

Ben taps the laptop. "This footage is from 2:20 am. Nana woke you at two. She was out there when those creatures were."

"So were you."

He glances out to the bright day, and I know he is ashamed. "I was sitting by the toolshed. I'd done a bump and was looking at the stars. It was so quiet. I would've known if large animals were about, if they'd hurt Nana. I'd have heard her scream or cry out. But the warm dark, the clear night: it felt calm. I fell asleep."

"So you're saying whatever we saw on the video didn't drag Nana off."

Ben has begun to cry. "No. You told her I was at the shed. How could she have not found me? Something bad must've happened almost immediately. Something that doesn't make sense."

My heart starts going too fast, but his irrationality helps me tilt more toward the rational. "Ben, go sleep for a few hours. I'm going to call the police and then go back out to hunt for her."

He rises and stumbles to his bedroom.

...

I tell the police officer our parents have gone to Montreal; they're Luddites and don't carry cell phones, and while I've left a message with their hotel, I doubt they'll be back today. I reassure him Nana has her wits about her, even though now, privately, I'm no longer sure.

"Gabrielle Moss," I say. "She lives at 37 Munson Road."

"Professor Moss. With the little dog with the silly name. I like your grandmother. I'll round up who I can, and we'll walk the woods. That's the edge of the Green Mountain Forest back there. It's very easy to get turned around." He's typing at a keyboard, a light clicking. "What was your brother doing out there?"

"Nothing bad. He likes it out there at night, finds it calming."

"Bears have been especially active this summer. Tell your brother he should respect that nature isn't always gentle."

In the front closet, Nana keeps a rucksack, which I fill with a large water bottle, chalk to mark the trails, granola bars, dog treats, and a flashlight. I put on hiking boots, eat a peanut butter sandwich, spray myself with bug spray. I'm trying to be prepared, to think like Nana in order to find Nana.

The Mighty Marty is waiting by the back door, and he sprints across the lawn. Before we enter the woods, I stand at its edge, looking up at the camera. I follow what I think is its line of vision. A woodpecker rattles. Chickadees are sounding their two-note calls, a pleasant sighing. Nothing is amiss. The day is affrontingly beautiful.

We return to the stream. The Mighty Marty wants to stay along its bank, nose down, snuffing. I guess the police, at least initially, will keep their search wide, staying close to the house. We're going to trace this water straight out. I'm kicking up mud, squelching along, clambering over rocks. The Mighty Marty is more nimble.

Miles in, my knees become shaky. We walked hours this morning, and I only slept two hours last night. I lean against a large tree, getting the granola bars and water from the rucksack. I call The Mighty Marty, shaking the bag of dog treats, but he stays by the water, his ears pricked. I imagine the police finding Nana and leading her home, a blanket about her shoulders, as she tells them she's lived alongside these woods nearly thirty years and has never gotten lost before, how one of the ironies of her life is, as someone who studies societal values, she lives on the cusp of wilderness. She said that once to me and Ben at Christmas. We'd traveled up for the holidays, and the weather that night was terrible. She was rummaging the garage for kerosene lamps, preparing for the electricity to go out. When it did, the family was sitting around the roaring fireplace drinking cocoa. She'd dispersed the lamps about the living room. Outdoors was a blizzard, the chaos of cold and wind, but the pockets of even glow made me feel we were aboard an old-fashioned ship.

The Mighty Marty headbutts my ribcage. I'd drifted off. I shake off sleep and return with him to the stream. After a mile, the land rises and flattens to marshy ground. We've reached the stream's mouth. No cave, no earthen basin. No boulders, no gnarled trees. Where the fuck are the markers, the signs and symbols, the answers? Where the fuck is Nana?

The Mighty Marty wades into the water. He lies down, his belly creating a small splash, and blows bubbles with his submerged snout.

I tell him I'm sorry, I don't know what to do.

We return early evening. No police cars are parked outside, nor do I hear anyone in the woods. The Mighty Marty and I need baths; we need rest. He has burrs caught in his fur, his coat is matted with dirt. I'm also covered in mud. As I change out of my muddy clothes, my knees continue to shake.

I assume Ben is still asleep, but when I go to the kitchen, I find him at the sink, its basin full of sudsy water. He's gently dunking The Mighty Marty. "Did the police already give up?" I ask.

He turns. The scent of gin wafts off him. "I told them it was a misunderstanding, that she'd called while you were out. In the middle of the night, a friend had called her, needing her help. She'd driven to attend to her friend but would return in a few days. I said once you came back, I'd explain the situation. They were relieved. They really like Nana."

"What the fuck is wrong with you?"

"A lot," he says. "Admittedly." He daubs soap onto The Mighty Marty's belly.

"Nana says you're self-destructive. But that doesn't mean you also get to destroy those around you."

"I'm trying to preserve the police, actually. Whatever got Nana could get them too."

Oh, Ben! Oh, my brother. "Ben, please. That isn't rational. By that logic, you'd also be gone."

He's spraying Marty with water. The dog's hair is slicked to his body. He looks so small, so vulnerable. "It doesn't work like that."

"How does it work?"

"Not like that."

"You're drunk," I say. "This is such bullshit."

"And you're a helpless child. My only ally, and you're useless."

He sets the dog on the floor, drying him briskly with a tea towel. The Mighty Marty then shakes, spraying wetness everywhere, before leaning into Ben's leg, his eyes closed. A hug, if dogs could hug. He retreats to his dog bed. I spend hours out there with him, and he loves Ben more for a five-minute bath.

"And you're useful how? Because last time I checked, this is your fault. Fuck you and your irresponsibility."

Ben sits heavily at the kitchen table. He raises his palm, asking I cease. "Let's not be our parents." He's slurring. "Let's be better."

If only Nana would come in and explain this has been an extended test to see how we'd handle culpability and fear. We failed, she'd tell us, but it's over now. You're still children. We'll check in again in a few years.

I sit across from him. "Why are there no solutions to this?"

"I made you a sandwich." He rises to go to the refrigerator.

In the west, bronze and mauve clouds settle luxuriously above the trees. "You can't go out there. Not once the sun falls." I'm giving in to his logic, also Nana's logic.

"I went back out, you know. I searched as I imagined the police would've searched. I crisscrossed the woods for hours." He hands me a huge turkey sandwich laden with cheese, tomato. I take greedy bites, getting mayonnaise on my face, wiping it away with my palm. "Tonight, we'll both sleep, and in the morning, we'll come up with a new plan."

I'm trying to parse through what a new plan could be, why my brother displays sudden reasonableness. It strikes me as false. "Please don't go out there," I say again.

Ben drums his fingers on the table. "You know what I've been thinking for months? That if I had any courage at all, I would've deferred. Kept you company your senior year and kept our parents from making you collateral damage in their battles. Then we could've set off for college at the same time."

Fatigue settles in my limbs. My brother worries in ways I didn't imagine. "That would've involved a lot of self-sacrifice. Too much. It's okay you're getting out. I'll figure out how to get by."

He sighs. He says he wishes he were braver. He says I must never let the bastards get me down.

Later, as I crawl into bed, I set my phone's alarm for midnight. I love Ben but don't trust him not to go rushing out into the dark. I could follow the subtext of what he was saying. He was thinking how he's going to leave me behind.

The Mighty Marty is at the foot of the bed, yapping at me. Morning light is fleshy and full. I grab my phone. It's 9:30. I've been asleep for twelve hours. My alarm, somehow, didn't go off.

I'm letting Marty out to pee when I realize Ben isn't here. I can feel his absence, and my neck goes hot, creepy-crawly.

I find a note attached to the refrigerator.

Good Sister,
I need to go back out there. There are more things in heaven and earth than are dreamt of, etc. If I'm not back, grab TMM and flee to Boston. I don't know what you can tell the jerkfaces to

calm them, but try blaming everything on me. I deserve it. DO NOT GO INTO THE WOODS. PS: I dissolved one of Nana's sleeping tablets and mixed it in the mayo on your sandwich. I also turned off your phone's alarm. And I love you! So if you can't trust me, who can you trust? Answer: No one. Remember that. I think the world is even worse than we imagine it.

Ben

I crumple the note and throw it in the sink. Then I retrieve it and smooth it on the kitchen table. I feel submerged in lead. I have to move but cannot move. I have to think but cannot think. I put my head on the kitchen table, smelling my terrible morning breath. If I sit here long enough, maybe time will cease going forward, will puddle as light does across still water.

Not knowing where The Mighty Marty is: this is what rouses me, makes me wander the house. He's asleep in Nana's bed, the blankets and sheets still twisted from when she rose quickly two nights ago. He's curled in a ball, his chest rising and falling too fast, as if he's having bad dreams.

I need to be on the phone to the police to explain away my lies, Ben's lies, and get them to hunt. I need to call my parents and let them yell at me. Then they can drive up here and direct the local authorities to search further, better, with more thoroughness. I need others to act, to intercede, to problem solve.

Running counter these thoughts: that anything—everything—I might do is pointless.

In the living room, I study the Critter Cam. A flash of what appears to be torches lighting on fire. I go back, unsurprised, and play the footage in real time. Those eyes. They watch the camera as the blackness around them shifts in uneasy, impossible ways, as if their presence is a disturbance, a violent rattling of the air. They laugh. And though their laughter is silent, it reverberates in my temples. It's hollow and ecstatic. One eye winks at me. Then they're gone.

I brush my teeth. I fill The Mighty Marty's food and water bowls. I make myself oatmeal. Marty and I drive to a dirt road miles away. It runs along fields of wavering tall grass that glimmers pale in the light. This stroll at the edge of the sun-drenched moors: we're just giving ourselves a reprieve.

Shadows grow long and elegant across the yard. Reason's absence gnaws at me.

Nana went out to rescue Ben. Ben went out to rescue Nana. Or maybe he believed Nana was beyond rescuing but still felt compelled to battle. If so, was his battling a point of pride? More self-destruction? Am I to rescue Nana and Ben? Will they appear if I just go out? Or knock three times at a secret cave? Do they show up only if I best the monsters? How do I best the monsters: run a race, solve a riddle, stake them through their charred hearts?

Nana is a decent person. Of late, Ben has not been especially decent, but he's young and will improve. So will I, I hope. None of us are bad. At least, we're not especially bad—not in the grand scheme of things. We don't deserve death by monsters. We don't deserve to be laughed at by them, mocked and jeered, because we're fallible and afraid.

Or maybe we do.

Or maybe we deserve this no more or no less than anyone else. It's upon us anyway.

Going out there likely resolves nothing. But if it does? Then not trying would make me the monster.

I give thinking like Nana one last shot. In the garage, she keeps a stash of what she calls "self-preserving accoutrements": a first-aid kit, a survival knife, a bow saw, a heavy-duty flashlight. I can't see the need for the bow saw—I don't imagine myself felling small trees—but I take everything else, along with a fire starter and Bic lighter.

The Mighty Marty: I don't want him to get hurt. But if I leave him in the house and don't come back, then I doom him in some slower way. The truth: I'm scared and want the company. I settle on putting him on a leash. We'll be together—a literal tethering. I think this is safer. I don't really know.

As dusk turns the world violet, I make pasta for dinner. I serve Marty pasta too, with lots of butter. I sit at the table watching twilight rise, sipping a Manhattan. It's the world's loneliest cocktail hour.

I'd settled on waiting until midnight because that's when Ben went out. But by 9:30 I realize I can't wait. I have to go now.

I turn on every light in the house so if in the woods I get disoriented, I can sight its lamp-lit blaze and get back. I put the leash on The Mighty Marty. He's wary—a little too still, too calm. But he's been this way all day. Grief has put us in a daze.

The lawn is already wet with evening dew. Ahead, the trees are so dense, so dark. I pause at the Critter Cam, thinking I should get within its gaze in case anyone tries to put together what has happened. But then I decide its footage will not communicate anything that would help in the end.

A tense hush envelops us. I switch on the flashlight, casting about its beam. My heart murmurs and jumps, unsteady. It smells fresh and wild in here, pine and earth. It's still. The Mighty Marty stays at my side. He gazes about, sniffing the air.

"Ben?" I call. "Nana?" There could yet be rational explanations. Nana is half a mile east, her foot caught in some suctioning bog, cursing her grandchildren. Last night, Ben got scared, called his dealer, and is now three towns away in some seedy basement, high as a kite, trying to escape his shame.

We move slowly along the path. The Mighty Marty jerks forward so hard I trip on a rock, stumbling and then falling. I keep hold of the leash but wrench my arm, which turns hot at my shoulder. "Marty!" I cry. "Stop it!" He's gasping and whining, choking himself to try to get at whatever is out there. He starts to snarl. I've never heard him make such angry, guttural sounds. He's snapping his jaw, clicking his teeth together. My shoulder throbs, and I try to switch hands, to grip the leash with my unhurt arm. That instant of poor decision-making: Marty races forward. He's hollering, gibbering, foaming at the mouth. He's all racket and rage.

Then he's gone. The woods are silent. It's an obscene quiet. The flashlight's bar of ghost light illuminates a rotting log covered in moss. I reach for the flashlight and it clicks off. I stand, shaking it, trying to get it to turn on again, then hurl it into the shadows.

The air pressure becomes impossibly heavy, as if turning to glass. The moonlight seems dimmer. The sounds of crickets, of rustling leaves, cease.

"Marty!" I cry. "Marty, please!"

Ho ho ho, I hear. Except it's not external, it's within me: a low rumble. Ho ho ho. Oh, ho! Ho. Ho ho ho.

The woods start to shake. Everything trembles. The trunks of trees are vibrating. And a crashing, as if something is dragging itself through the brush.

I run. I sprint toward the house. We're barely a quarter mile out, but I can't find the lights; they're not there. Everything is rippling saturated navy shadow. And the booming echo of whatever is coming behind me.

I come to a branch where there shouldn't be a branch and stay right, which I think is closer to the house. Behind me continues the wild shifting movement, the sonic booms asynchronous with my wild heart.

The toolshed. It's not there and then it is, and I run inside and close the door, which is a misstep because now I've trapped myself. Or maybe they can't get me if I'm not technically outdoors, not in the woods. Poor man's logic. Beggar man's logic.

I wedge myself into a corner, below some shelving. Dust and dirt thickly fog the one window. My shoulder is howling its discord. I raise my knees to my chest, hug myself. Why did I think I could do anything for them? All I've made are missteps. One after another. My failures a noisy, bumptious parade leading me here.

I will my heart to steady. I will myself invisible.

The room shakes and dust falls in my hair, on my shoulders, my face.

A shower of mold and mildew. I don't brush it away. Ho ho ho, I hear from within my chest. Oh, ho ho. I bury my face in my knees, create for myself a safer darkness. I think of last summer, Ben and Nana playing Scrabble, happily debating whether Nana could play "brillig." Not unless you're a Jabberwock, Ben countered. I might be, she said. She raised pretend claws at him. Well, fair play to you then, Jabberwock, Ben said, giving her a mock bow. Just look out my vorpal blade doesn't go snicker-snack. We'd do well in a sword fight, Nana said. I think we could take some bad guys down. Are we on the same team? Ben cried, leaping up. Nana nodded and also rose. I set aside my book to watch them dance about the living room engaged in fanciful sword battles with imaginary ne'er-do-wells. They were laughing to the point of falling down, each trying to outdo the other with silly flourishes and cries of triumph.

The walls vibrate and the dust is a flurry. It tickles my eyelids, catches at my lips. Some gets up my nose, and I'm clutching at my mouth to stop the sneeze but there it is: my tiny achoo.

The walls cease. Through the window, one eye blinks on—a sidewise look, dead and cold. In profile, but just the eye. The rest of the creature is darkness, is night, is some void. Oh, ho ho.

Why? I think, but there is no point in wondering. The walls resume their stormy violence. I drag the rucksack off my back, my hands trembling. I find the fire starter package, ripping it open with my teeth, dumping it on the floor before me. The eye blinks but does not vanish. It blinks off and on, off and on, evil neon, as I flick the lighter over the starter. This small room of untreated wood: I bet I can get it to go up in a blaze in minutes. I bet I can raze it. I might kill myself in the process— or maybe a wall falls and I burst my way to safety, or I set these laughing demons on fire—but I will create this havoc. Is there solace in this? The fire twists purple and orange and starts licking across the floor. The smoke begins to waft up, the crackle and burn become brighter. The smoke is mildewed and acrid. I will be as good as my loved ones, I will be as bad. I will swallow my fear. I will battle monsters yet.

Self-Preservation

THE VP OF STUDENT AFFAIRS was asking whether anyone would like another glass of chenin blanc. Paul accepted, as did Lisette, even though later they needed to drive up the mountain to their new home.

"A decade ago, we came up from Philly," the VP said. "At first, I wanted to run screaming—all this quiet—but we've grown accustomed to the pace. Beth loves it."

"I'm never giving up my garden. I'm never giving up these views." Beth swept her hand to a darkened bay window. Lisette had seen the land in daylight: fields buffered by woods. Further west, across the lake, the Adirondacks were lavender and gold these September afternoons. "How're you settling in? You haven't gone through a winter yet."

Paul said, "I love the work. We met at the University of Michigan. It's been a while, but we'll get our winter bearings again."

"I grew up in Buffalo," Lisette said. "I'm actually looking forward to the cold."

Beth laughed. "Let's see how you feel in January. You live up the mountain?" They nodded. "A group of women have a book club there. I could put you in touch with my friend Eileen." Lisette said that sounded nice. Being part of a book club didn't particularly interest her, but Beth likely knew Lisette didn't have a job and was trying to help her meet people.

Beth said Lisette was such a pretty name. Was she French Canadian? No, just named after a great-aunt her mother had been fond of.

"Do you two have children? Ours are just entering middle school. I can give you the lay of the land, if you like, or recommend day care."

Lisette thanked Beth but said they had no children. She murmured to Paul she was going to the bathroom.

In the hall, light came from beneath the closed door. A woman with dark hair came out and smiled at Lisette. Just a matter of instinct, but Lisette could imagine being friends with her. She splashed her cheeks with cool water. Of course strangers were going to ask about children. Some quivering in her ribcage, as if her architecture had turned gelatinous, and then she steadied.

Back downstairs, she whispered to Paul she'd drive them home and he should drink all the chenin blanc he wished. A group was chatting about visas for international students. Lisette listened. She breathed and behaved like a normal person the rest of the night.

Later, she was navigating the mountain road—no streetlights, just pines to the heavens on one side and a steep drop off on the other. Paul was tipsy, his cheek against the window glass. "They're nice people. I think this will work."

A truck, which had been tailgating her, its headlights close and impatient, whooshed past. Her heart was high in her chest. The cracked windows let in air that smelled fresh and black and wild. "I want it to," she said.

. . .

In July, they'd rented a car at the airport, and the drive had revealed a world soaked in green, all rolling hills and pastures. Before meeting the realtor, they'd toured the campus, with its gray-stone buildings. A bronze plaque said the college had been founded in 1800, which seemed very East Coast. The realtor had suggested she'd drive so they didn't get lost. The mountain town east of here was a little rural, she'd said with a laugh.

She and Paul had murmured at the river running down the mountain, limpid among sand-colored rocks, and the ragged pines and their rough shade. At a country store, they'd turned onto a dirt road with just the occasional house tucked behind the trees. A jolt of insight: living here would be lonesome. But then the realtor had pulled into a gravel driveway, and the white farmhouse's postcard prettiness had robbed her of her instincts.

The house, built in 1870, had burnished pine floors and a pot-bellied stove in its living room. French doors led to an expansive back lawn. In the master bedroom, two oval windows looked out to the yard. Dusty light had slanted across the floor, almost pearlescent.

Her heart had hammered yes. Orange County, with its matching taupe homes and landscaped rock gardens, would become their past. Their pain over their lost child would become their past. Nothing that simple, of course; neither thought that way. But hope that newness might preserve them: on this, they agreed.

Lisette corresponded with old work colleagues, telling them Vermont was like a picture book. Inwardly, though, her thoughts were like sunlight-streaked shards of glass.

Because mailmen didn't travel up here, most days she walked to the country store, where they had PO boxes. One raw October morning, she entered its old-fashioned shadow and warmth. Another pot-bellied stove with two mismatched rocking chairs alongside it, a mounted deer head above shelves of maple syrup and honey. An older couple, Ben and Jane, ran the store. They'd moved up here in the 1970s, Lisette had learned from Jane, the chattier of the two. They had a white lab named Murray, hefty and doe-eyed, who slept by the stove.

Lisette went to say hello to Jane. "Lisette," Jane said, "give me your hands." Across the counter, she took Lisette's free hand, rubbing her knuckles. "You're not used to the cold." Her fingertips, Lisette realized, were violet. She wanted to say stop. She thought of her colleague squeezing her hand as she'd waited for the ambulance. Pain had dizzied her, her abdomen on fire. "You need gloves. Snow tires too. You have about three weeks." Jane took Lisette's other hand. "It's hokey, but the landscape can reveal things to you. When I first moved here, I was picking berries. A gorgeous, warm day. A neighbor came out to tell me rain was coming: he didn't want me caught out in it. He pointed to some clouds, saying they were coming in low. I thought this was ridiculous. The sky was a blue jay's wing, but I went in. Then the sky turned yellow and fat drops started hitting the windowpane. I thought he was a soothsayer." Jane was running her thumbs along Lisette's bones. "Ask Ben next time you're in. He'll tell you I've become pretty accurate predicting the shift in seasons."

"I believe you." Lisette couldn't think of more to say.

"Gloves. We can't have you going around with corpse hands."

Outside, Lisette's hands immediately looked raw again. About her, branches shifted copper.

Once home, she made herself tea. She thought of the emergency room doctor saying placental abruption and asking did she smoke, did she use cocaine, did she have high blood pressure, was she over thirty-five. The hospital's halogen lights had seemed a bright poison. The doctor had said maybe Lisette's age, but also, sometimes, inexplicable things happened.

At the kitchen table, Lisette cried. So much about the world was good, and yet she persisted in thinking about horrible things.

The next morning, Paul suggested she email the woman who'd gotten in touch about the book club. "Are you feeling all right?" He was buttering his toast. "You're looking pale."

Her transparency ashamed her. "I had a bad dream."

"Should we start looking into finding you work? I could talk to people in my office."

She nodded. At Irvine, she'd worked in advancement—fundraising, approaching wealthy donors. She'd been good at it. And she missed the order of a workday.

He finished his toast and rose, coming to kiss the top of her head. "We could commute together. Don't forget about the book club."

"Do you think it's just an excuse to drink bad chardonnay? Or do you think they all earnestly leaf through Thoreau?"

"It'd be funniest if it were both," he said. "I'm hoping it's both."

She went into the living room with her laptop. The day was overcast, and she was tired of herself. After she'd recuperated, she'd been unable to return to work. At the building's main entrance, her bones had crumbled; her heart had turned into a hummingbird's wings. Her boss had been so good about letting her Skype into meetings, deal with donors off campus, but the only decent thing to have done was resign. Paul had been the one to say, let's make it all new. He'd perused academic job boards. Vermont had started out as a lark, a way to improve their moods.

She found Eileen's email. Four women met once a month, alternating houses. This month they were meeting at Katie Pike's house. The book was by a Southern writer—a family traveling to pick up a father released from prison.

Lisette apologized for not writing sooner. If she read the book in the next few days, could she drop in?

"Sounds great!" Eileen responded, providing directions to Katie's house.

Lisette thought she saw a deer winding its way among the backyard's trees—some shift in movement. She wrote back she was delighted.

She had to get that book; she had to get gloves. First, though, a walk. Too early for mail, but she wanted exercise. She wanted to have respectable habits.

Her footsteps were quiet on the dirt road. The air smelled of decaying leaves and she wondered what Jane's neighbor could've told her about the landscape. Around a slow curve, a house was set back behind a copse of pines. Nearby, some tires were stacked against a rotting gazebo. Half a mile beyond was a pristine white farmhouse with green trim.

Up ahead, a woman was walking. She looked small surrounded by so much land, a wash of dark hair. She turned as if catching Lisette's stare in the wind and put up her hand in a wave.

Lisette caught up. The woman she'd seen in passing at the VP's party, but she didn't think they'd been introduced. "Hi," she said, feeling shy.

"Jennifer," the woman said, and Lisette introduced herself as well.

"Do you live up here?"

Jennifer nodded, gesturing east. "I grew up here, moved away, and then came back."

"My husband and I just moved here from Southern California." They began to walk together. "It's beautiful, such an interesting mix of people."

"This place is strange. Down the mountain, you're more bound to daily life. Up here is almost outside of time. But when I was away, I missed it." Her glance was sidelong and startlingly beautiful: her eyes were the glossy dark of polished wood. And she smiled as if she knew some secret. They approached a house with a small weathered barn. Before it, a white horse flicked its ears and then went back to nosing fallen apples.

"Do you work for the college?" Lisette wanted this woman to be her friend. She could tell Paul she'd made a friend.

Jennifer had worked in admissions and liked the kids. Lisette volunteered Paul also found the students nice. They came to a rustling field, pines in the distance. "I generally turn back here," Lisette said, although this wasn't true. She just wasn't sure how far they should travel together. "Maybe we could walk together again?"

"Let's." And then Jennifer was off, moving briskly. "See you!" she called over her shoulder.

Lisette wished they'd exchanged phone numbers, but in a place this small they were likely to see each other again. She was grateful Jennifer had called this place strange. It made her feel easier.

• • •

Katie Pike also lived in an old farmhouse. Hers was cozy and over-stuffed: bookshelves piled with books, throw rugs everywhere, a coffee table heaped with wine bottles and plates of cheese and crackers. A fire was crackling.

Katie brought in another bottle—a white, in case anyone wanted white. She was in her early sixties, Lisette guessed. She had a gray bob and wore a large sweater and jeans—an unusual mix of frumpy and chic. Earlier she'd said she was from Manhattan but had moved here in the eighties. She owned the tiny art gallery near the country store.

Eileen, who'd greeted her at the door, had lived up here since graduating from the college and now worked for an architectural firm down the mountain. She was perhaps in her early forties, as was Mary, who was insisting everyone try her pumpkin bread. Mary's husband was a chemistry professor, and she and Lisette discussed being the spouse carried along for the ride. Mary said when they'd moved, they hadn't realized how few professional opportunities Vermont had. She'd worked in marketing for a pharmaceutical. Now, she said vaguely, she did some freelance writing and volunteered. This alarmed Lisette, who, like Paul, had been thinking the college would swoop her up when she was ready.

The fourth woman had sharp cheekbones and an artfully disheveled ponytail. She'd moved up here with her husband to start a company that made goat-milk caramel. They owned ten acres and tended forty goats, she was saying as she offered Lisette a mug filled with candies in wax-paper twists. Lisette wanted to laugh, but the candy was mellow and beautiful. Abagail had a two-year-old named Fox—"a redhead like his father"—and she'd only recently given up breastfeeding.

The conversation veered toward children: Eileen had an eleven-year-old son; Mary had fraternal twins, just entered kindergarten. Katie had grown daughters in their early thirties.

"We don't have children." Lisette waited for someone to tell her children would come, but Katie started nattering about the blue cheese, which she'd gotten on sale at the co-op. The fire was bright, and Lisette leaned back into the sofa.

Eileen held up her book. "Yay or nay?" She turned to Lisette. "I picked this one, so I have some skin in the game."

"Of course we don't just vote yay or nay," Abagail said. "I thought the writing was fantastic, but I hated the mother."

"She's dreadful," Mary said. "Leaving her children to fend for themselves, the older boy taking care of the toddler. Her drug taking, her selfishness."

"At the end she took care of her dying mother," Eileen said.

"And then hit her son!" Abagail said. "Then she ran off with her deadbeat husband so they could do drugs."

Katie said, "Her brother was murdered. I think we're meant to understand she was in a perpetual state of mourning and rage over how he died."

"Her parents lost a child and they stayed decent," Mary said. "Everyone in that family suffered, but no one took it out on those they loved except her."

Katie was slicing pumpkin bread. "History is acting as pressure on them all. It's haunting them as the ghosts haunt them."

"I actually laughed when we got to the first chapter narrated by the ghost child. I liked that the author just went for it," Abagail said.

Mary poured more wine for herself and Lisette. "I did not care for the ghosts."

"Why?" Eileen asked. "They're not there for schlock value."

"I can appreciate the good writing, but *everything* went wrong for this family. Cancer, prison, murder, drugs, ugly parenting, police brutality. It was all violence, danger, and death. The sheer amount of it didn't feel believable to me. The ghosts pushed me over the edge. We could've dwelt on the real and that would've been more than enough despair."

"Except the ghosts are real," Abagail said. "Who else is narrating the child ghost's chapters?"

"Lisette, what do you think?" Eileen said.

Lisette swallowed too much wine. "I loved the ghosts. The child ghost: he's desperate for release and demanding his story be told. And he's greedy, looking for care because none had ever come his way in life." Her cheeks felt flushed. "Such a human ghost."

The room was quiet. She'd made them uncomfortable, letting them know she'd found despair electric and moving. Eileen leaned across the couch to clink her wine glass with Lisette's. "Cheers!" she cried. "It's a magnificent book. I'm so glad you think so too."

Abagail's phone dinged and she jumped up: Fox wouldn't fall asleep and was sitting in bed singing to himself. "Kind of like that ghost child sings to itself," she said. "Oh my God, now I'm giving myself the creeps. Let me just talk Tim through this." She went into the kitchen. Mary said she found Lisette's thinking a good counterpoint to her own. Lisette took another goat-milk caramel and felt a little bit of her rootlessness slipping away.

Lisette woke before sunrise. It had snowed and all was shadowy blue light. Out the window, a person receded into the woods—a blur, then stillness. Her breath caught, and then she remembered: deer season. If she were out, the book group had warned her, she had to wear orange. This even though most hunters stayed far from populated areas and only went out at dawn and dusk. Years ago, Katie had emerged from a trail onto a road to see a truck barreling toward her. Three men were in the truck bed, and one—if just for an instant—had aimed his rifle her way. The men had shouted their apologies, their laughter wafting behind them.

A position opened up—assistant director of annual giving—and Paul asked the VP to recommend Lisette. HR scheduled an interview and down the mountain she went. She'd wanted to practice walking to the building—an old Victorian mansion set back on a wide lawn—but if someone saw her, they'd think she were mad.

Her body held as she went in. As those interviewing her asked about her experiences working with donors, she kept her body language open and relied on the muscle memory of having been successful with strangers in the past. When they ushered her out, shaking her hand and smiling, she felt triumphant.

At a tiny bakery down the street, Lisette, over coffee, told Paul she'd managed. She could manage. He was so proud of her! Later, on campus, she watched the students, with their computer bags and books, in chatty bustle. At the spacious library, she checked out some novels. The institution as institution calmed her.

Two weeks later, HR sent her an email thanking her for her interest but telling her the position had been filled. The weather was dreary, a light icy rain. She put on her dumb orange gear and went out anyway.

From within its weathered barn, the white horse was watching her. Jennifer was just ahead. Lisette called hello and caught up. Jennifer wore a clear rain slicker with a hood. Her breath came out in smoke. "I'm glad I'm not the only one out in all this."

"I'm hoping it's clarifying—a little cold and wet. Later, I'll appreciate more being inside with a cup of tea."

Jennifer nodded to Lisette's neon attire. "Did someone scare you with a hunting story gone awry?"

"People told me this is what's safe."

Jennifer waved a dismissive hand. "I've never had a problem. Believing you can ward off catastrophe has always struck me as a kind of arrogance."

They walked alongside a thicket, bare branches and red berries glistening in the wet. "Extend that thinking, and we needn't bother with seatbelts; we'd drive with our lights off at night. To protect yourself—to attempt to preserve yourself—is not pointless."

"I'm sorry. That wasn't criticism. I can get trapped in my head, not realize how things will sound."

"I just found out I didn't get a job I wanted." She was too rankled: they were only discussing outerwear. "I'm out of sorts."

As they came to a branch in the dirt road, corridors bordered by woods, the stuff of poetic decisions, Jennifer pointed left. "Let's walk this way."

The trees dripped rain. Their trunks were spotted with moss, which, in the diffuse gray light, glowed mint. They approached an elementary school, a single-level building with two long wings. This was the new school, Jennifer explained, built in the late 1980s. Jennifer had been one of the last generations to start in a two-room schoolhouse. "Back in the sixties, fewer than two hundred people lived up here. My mother used to tell me how her family would get snowed in for a month!"

"Does that happen now? People can't get down the mountain?"

"Four-wheel drive and all that, better plows. If there's ice or heavy snowfall, it can get tricky, but people up here are capable. You'll learn this."

"I suppose I will." Her skin was ice and her hat was soaked through.

Jennifer pointed to a cemetery, mossed-over granite and marble headstones in a field, saying some of her family was buried there. Lisette only nodded since the conversation, in the abstract, wearied her. As they reached the main road, Ben emerged onto the general store's porch, his eyes distant—perhaps studying the rain. He waved, and they waved back. Her mood today was all wrong, but she did want to make some friends. "I'm going to head back, but could we plan on walking again?"

"Tomorrow?" Behind them, the mountains were a very dark blue.

"Yes," Lisette said, surprised. "Is ten good? I live on Chandler Hill Road."

"I know where you live."

"You do?"

"Of course." Jennifer wiped some beaded water from her raincoat. "We all know everything about one another up here."

Most weekdays, they walked. Lisette would meet Jennifer at the end of the driveway. Jennifer, considering the mountains, her parka's hood obscuring her face, had some quality of stillness to her.

The cold felt a test of temperament. Lisette wore a wool hat, a puffer coat with goose down, waterproof mittens with extra insulation. No corpse hands. Although she'd been seeing Jane less: Paul picked up the mail now on his way home from work.

On clear days, the sky gave off hard light. Often they walked in agreeable silence. Lisette had questions—if Jennifer had ever been married, what she did for money—but wanted to stay circumspect.

Jennifer would vary their routes, small forays down even smaller roads. Billings Farm Road was named after the Billings family, who went back four generations. Old Tavern Road had had on it the town's first tavern. Lisette talked blandly about their life in California, but California— with its malls and freeways—barely existed here, where all was tree bark and ridgelines and snow.

The rest of the day she would read, waste time on her computer, clean, and make dinner in their beautiful kitchen. No more jobs came along. She started to drive to town with less frequency. In the abstract, it seemed a monumental task: to traverse a mountain.

A Friday night, Paul suggested they spend Saturday in town. They had lunch at an Indian place. She picked up the next book for her book club. They got coffees from the bakery and visited the campus's art museum. She felt both satiated and overwhelmed, and understood Paul's point. Her days held too much emptiness.

The month before, Mary had chosen some political tome about the oil industry. Lisette had skimmed it, feeling guilty but bored. She hadn't been alone, apparently: a little polite discussion about fracking had given way to debate about a crime procedural on Netflix. Amid the couch lounging, the wine and dessert, the gossip about people she didn't know, Lisette had wished they could gather more frequently. Tonight, she'd ask whether any of them wanted to meet sometime for lunch—after they discussed the murder mystery, which she'd also struggled to pay attention to.

As she and Paul were eating dinner, the predicted storm began. Out the French doors, the snow was thick in its descent, and she wanted to ask Paul to drive her but knew she had to learn to handle this.

Coming down the driveway, she flipped on her high beams. Wet flakes pelted the windshield as snow poured through some gash in the sky. Along the road, white burdened the spruce and hemlocks. An oncoming truck was a cut of yellow beams in the gray murk, and she turned the wipers to a higher speed.

Lisette had memorized the route to Abagail's farm, the turns and the distances, since street signs were scarce. At the second turn, she fishtailed but remembered to turn into the skid. On the last stretch, she was reminding herself in California she'd driven the 405 daily when she saw tied to a tree a red balloon freighted with snow, listlessly trying to blow away. Abagail had put it out for her.

Something streaked across the road, eyes a silver-green flash, a dispassionate gleam, and Lisette wrenched the wheel. Her head flung back as her chest hit the seatbelt. She closed her eyes and thought of Paul holding their baby, wrinkled and still, and how he had wept.

The car tipped into the ditch, a failed nosedive. She got her door open. About her, the trees spun in slow circles and the sky glimmered with strange pewter light. A car pulled up, its beams making her squint. "Oh, Lisette!" Eileen ran up and hugged her. "This happens. These conditions are terrible."

"Something ran out. I swerved not to hit it." Lisette pointed to the road, rough with white, trackless. Her stomach boiled and she turned to the ditch, vomiting.

"A deer most likely." Eileen put an arm about her shoulder. "Or a moose. Or even a mountain cat." She smiled as you'd smile at a child. "Let me go get Tim. He can tow you out. And then we'll get you home."

"Don't leave me!" Lisette cried. "I can't be out here alone."

"Of course not," Eileen said, ushering Lisette into her car. "We'll go together."

The next day they went out on Peddler Bridge Road. The mountains looked coated in frost and the sky was radiant, pale. Lisette felt slumped, propped up only by the bracing air.

Last night, Tim, in his truck, had followed Eileen driving Lisette's car up the driveway. Paul had emerged onto the patio, shivering in his sweater. They'd called ahead to explain what had happened. While Eileen had parked, Tim had rolled down his window and started discussing goat farming with Paul.

Inside, Paul had poured them scotch. The drink had swelled her head, made her that balloon. There hadn't been any tracks, she'd continued to think. Her fear and woe still swirling in her like snow, she'd told him she was going to bed.

Today she wanted to assure him she was all right: she'd bake him a cake, buy him maple candy from the general store. Her options were limited since she had no intention of getting into the car.

"Let me guess," Lisette said. "Peddler Bridge Road is where all the peddlers sold their wares."

"Where all the peddlers sold their bridges. Back in the day they sold so many bridges."

"Really?"

"If you believe that, I have a bridge I want to sell you," Jennifer said.

"Oh, dear." Lisette sighed. "I'm slow today."

Jennifer moved briskly, a hint of color at her cheeks. Her parka hood was down and her pale-blue hat made her eyes look black. "The Peddler family lived here years ago. I don't know anything beyond that."

"Where I lived was so decoupled from history. I worked in an office complex on Innovation Way. It amazes me how alive the past is here."

"You miss California."

"Parts of it. I had routines, a job, a group of friends. I felt more tethered to things."

"Why did you move?"

"We were looking for a change." Not today, she thought. She was too weary for self-confession.

"Up here." Jennifer paused at an unmarked trailhead. Someone had tamped down the snow, a sinuous path that seemed to disappear as the trees grew dense. "I thought we could try trail walking today."

Lisette shook her head. "I want to stick to the roads. That's more than enough wilderness for me."

"It's beautiful in there. The trails go back miles. I know them really well. We won't get lost."

"No." Lisette imagined the canopy of trees swallowing her.

Jennifer resumed walking. Snow fell in a hushed whump from a pine, and the snow dust, cut with sunlight, glittered. Lisette listened to her own breathing. "Do you remember describing this place as outside of time? I still think about that."

"You carry this sadness," Jennifer said. "It's a little like you walk within a cloud." Lisette's heart picked up, that too quick patter from when she'd tried to return to work. "Maybe discussing it would help."

"No," Lisette said. No-no-no-no-no went her heart.

"My husband left me. To this day I don't forgive him. My anger is still quick under my skin. But my sadness: I always fought it, avoided it, and that became a big problem for me."

"I do not want to face my sadness," Lisette said. "To face it is to give in to it." Last night, when she'd climbed out of the car, it had been all dark, snow, and looming pines, and she was going to be trapped always in that instant: alone and not up to the challenges facing her.

"But I don't think it's bad the way you're thinking it is. I'm saying there can be a kind of clarity in facing it."

"Enough."

"I'm only trying to help. You seem adrift this morning."

"I'm going to head home." Lisette turned back down the hill.

"Lisette!" Jennifer ran to catch up and threw her arms about Lisette's shoulders, holding Lisette to her chest. "I've said the wrong thing. I'm sorry." Jennifer's parka was soft and gave off light heat. The world stopped expanding in its confusion and closed down into this moment. She nodded and they walked back together.

Having the holiday party in January meant the season's burdens were over, the VP was saying. No one was stressing about having to invite Aunt Hilda to Christmas. January was fresh, a new start, and so the night could be truly celebratory.

He raised his glass and, along with the others, Lisette raised hers. She smiled at Beth, who'd asked if she were enjoying the book club. She was! she said with weird, forced gaiety.

"Eileen has loved having you join them." Lisette wondered if Beth knew of Eileen coming upon Lisette standing in the road, her car in a ditch.

"Yes," Lisette said. "Excuse me a moment."

Upstairs, she splashed water on her face. Then she went to the living room. A red ceramic vase glinted near an open fireplace, the wood embers glowing. In the other room, people were singing "Auld Lang Syne." "Should old acquaintance be forgot and never brought to mind?" They were discussing a college hockey game, a terrible masseuse, where to get good cardamom buns.

"Lisette." Paul came in, carrying her champagne glass. "Come join the fun."

"I'd like to go home."

"We haven't been here an hour."

"I know," she said, "but I'm tired."

Lisette told people she feared she was coming down with something. This seemed such fun, such a nice night. She hoped to see everyone again soon.

"Feel better!" Beth said. "Let's have lunch sometime, yes?"

Lisette said she'd love to.

In the car, she resented how Paul looked at her gravely, as if she were tragic. "I think you should consider resuming therapy," he said.

In California, for a time, they'd gone. A woman with expensive hair had nodded and nodded as they'd tried to make sense of what would not make sense. One of the few things Lisette had grasped during that fog: her attempted sense-making would only lead to more self-recrimination. If she'd been more attentive, more virtuous, better, stronger, more capable—more something—they'd not have lost their child. Let go, the therapist had said, there were reasons this happened. We were all hard-wired for narrative; we all told ourselves stories in order to give our days shape. Of course, Lisette remembered thinking, to see certain events as meaningless was to give into the larger notion that everything about their lives was.

"In the spring, when the weather is easier, I'll find a therapist."

"I'll drive you. But this is to my point. You're letting small setbacks become large. You can't stop driving for months because you once went off the road."

"Fine. I'll practice driving."

"And I think you should find volunteer work. Or audit some classes at the college."

"I have the book club, and I go for walks." She knew this sounded weak.

"I fear you're brooding, giving in to your thoughts."

"I'm not giving in to my thoughts," she shouted. "I'm avoiding them!"

"But that is not a life." Paul turned off at the general store. "That's a kind of blankness."

That night she couldn't sleep and went downstairs to make tea, which she sipped while staring out the French doors to their yard. The woods were a shadowed creep, a tangle of branches. She thought they appeared closer. If the trees were a threshold, she wasn't sure what was gained in crossing into them. Paul was right. She felt increasingly as if she didn't exist.

Lisette practiced driving to the general store. As she walked in, Murray, snoring softly by the stove, raised his head, thumping his tail. "I see you've got good winter gear now," Jane said. "Good girl. Next, we'll get you cross-country skiing in the back woods!"

Lisette, inordinately pleased the world hadn't crumbled as she'd driven a mile in broad daylight, laughed and said maybe she would.

She also scheduled her first meeting with a therapist—for the week following—and planned to drive herself. And, from Mary, she learned of volunteer work: reading to children at local schools. Mary had been enthusiastic about Lisette joining her, and Lisette had understood, then, how taking one step toward self-betterment could branch into more. She told Paul this at dinner, before book club, and he opened a bottle of wine so they could clink glasses.

Her knees felt like jelly as she pulled into Mary's driveway, but she'd done it. Inside, the twins whirled about in footed pajamas, shrieking and giggling as their mother herded them upstairs for story time with their father. Mary blew a piece of hair from her cheek and said she was happy to see Lisette.

Katie was pouring wine. Abagail and Eileen were chatting about Fox, who'd just cusped into full sentences. "Hooray!" Abagail said as Lisette set down a plate of cookies. "We're glad you're back."

Lisette said she was glad, too, and excited to host the next meeting. The women gazed at her a beat too long, a smiling equanimity that masked something. But that was paranoid of her. She accepted a glass from Katie and joined them at the table.

Abagail tapped her book cover. "I was telling these guys I'd been assigned this book in college, but now I'm not sure I read it." She laughed. "It's brutal! You'd think I'd have remembered that. I just remember my professor saying the stories were almost *too* good."

"She used to live outside Burlington—near the lake, I think," Eileen said. "I heard she decided Vermont wasn't rural enough. That's why she moved to Wyoming."

These Wyoming stories: Lisette had found the writing tightly wound, dense. A fist rather than an open hand. She admired the work but at points, reading, her chest had felt constricted: so much violence and bleakness had made her feel small.

Katie reached for a cookie. "Outside Burlington isn't exactly roughing it. She could've moved up here."

Eileen held out a wine glass to Mary, who'd just come in. Mary took a dramatic swig. "My children will be the death of me." She sat down. "I have a confession. I put the book down after the first story."

"Mary!" Abagail exclaimed.

"That apocryphal story of the half-skinned steer wandering the plains, staring hatefully at the man who'd started skinning it, completely rattled me. And then when the old man goes off the road and sees the steer, too: my God."

Katie said, "The old man has a vision of death that echoes a horrible tale he heard long ago. It's really beautifully constructed."

"More than I could bear," Mary said. "Sorry."

"Hey." Abagail put her hand on Lisette's forearm, and Lisette almost jumped at the touch. "I'd forgotten this book begins with a car accident in a snowstorm. If I'd remembered, I might've chosen something else."

"Oh, I wasn't thinking about that at all." In fact, her pity for the old man had felt urgent—his repeated attempts to stay the course, to problem solve, even as he grew confused. And she'd continued to think about his seeing, under duress, that which was not there even if it represented a truth which was. "I thought of the end as a moment of lucidity. Someone I walk with was saying there could be clarity in facing sadness. Here, it's facing death, but the idea is similar." They were looking at her too solemnly. "I don't mean to sound dire."

"Who do you walk with?" Katie asked. "I've seen you out once or twice on your own."

"A woman named Jennifer. She lives up here."

"Jennifer who?" Mary, who'd been looking toward the ceiling, listening for her children to settle down, shifted her gaze to Lisette, which made Lisette feel she'd betrayed something she ought not have.

"I don't know her last name. Dark hair, pale skin. She grew up here. We walk in the mornings."

Abagail, drumming her fingers on the table, looked at Eileen. "Lisette, you're not being deliberately creepy, right? Some sort of joke?"

"Of course not." Her stomach knotted. Their collective disapproval was washing over her.

"Realtors are required to give out this information. You're really saying you don't know?" Mary's mouth was pinched. "You loved the ghosts. It's not funny. You're not being funny. I say this story upset me and you pile it on. I don't appreciate it."

Katie was swirling her wine, studying it as if it were tea leaves. "Mary, she doesn't know what you're talking about." She looked up. "Lisette, please don't cry."

"I'm not," Lisette said, but she was trying not to blink so the tears wouldn't run to her cheeks, but maybe this was more evidence of her being creepy and piling things on. She stood, bumping her hip against the table. "I should go."

"Sit please." Eileen sighed. "This is a misunderstanding. Sit, Lisette. You don't know who lived in the house before you?"

"No. Ask Paul. We don't know." Or did they? He'd taken care of everything, dealing with all the paperwork. "Paul would've kept from me anything unhappy. We'd just lost a baby." She didn't wish to tell them this! She wished to take it back. Who gave a fuck who'd lived in their house?

Abagail again put her hand on Lisette's arm and this time Lisette did flinch. "A woman named Jennifer lived in your house. She committed suicide. We don't know any details. It was just whispered across the community."

"Her husband left her," Katie said.

"That doesn't explain it—not fully," Mary said. "Lisette, I apologize. I had a bad moment—not enough sleep and the kids have taken up joint tantrums. This is clearly just a weird coincidence."

"Yes," Lisette said, but she was drowning in her not-sureness. They were unsure, too.

"We're so sorry about your child," Eileen said, and the rest nodded.

"I bet," Abagail said brightly, "it's someone who lives further up the mountain. In Hancock or Goshen, even."

But the cemetery, the two-room schoolhouse, the names of all these nameless backroads. Lisette was frightened of herself, of how little she knew herself.

"And it's not as if we know every single person who lives on the mountain!" Eileen said. More vigorous nodding. Their beliefs were shifting, had shifted, and now: surety, a blanket they'd draped around their shoulders to ward off a draft.

"Really, I'm so sorry." Mary squeezed Lisette's hand, and Lisette hated her for it, maybe hated them all for the ease with which they'd retreated into easy narratives.

• • •

Paul was getting ready to leave, setting his coffee mug in the sink and grabbing his coat from the closet. "Did you sleep badly?"

She nodded, sitting with her coffee, which was souring her stomach. Her skin felt too tight across her face. She hadn't slept at all. "Paul, did someone commit suicide in this house?"

He looked out the French doors, a rare tension around his eyes. "Behind the house. In the woods. The realtor told me privately; she said she wasn't required to disclose it but wanted to err on the side of decency. The woman's ex-husband owned the house, so I dealt with him. Your book group told you this?"

"They thought I knew."

"They just brought it up? Hey, Lisette, we were wondering: Is the ghost of the sad mentally disturbed lady who hanged herself in the woods haunting you? Things going bump in the night? What's wrong with them?"

She had the therapy appointment coming up. If she could just get through the week, maybe she could start to sort this out. "It was happenstance—nothing like you're suggesting. You should've told me."

He put his hands to her cheeks and kissed her. "I don't want this to infect your thinking. It's terrible but has nothing to do with us. Promise me."

"I promise."

"Let's go to dinner in town this week." He straightened his watch. "Okay?"

"Okay," she said.

After he left, she worried the kitchen might melt, turn loopy and strange, some psychedelic washing away of space and time. Above the kitchen window, icicles dripped in a blaze of sunlight. Her coffee had a creamy beige film. She pushed the mug aside.

A knocking at the French doors. Jennifer in her parka, lips full, eyes sullen. She put her palm to the glass and the flesh whitened, her fingertips spread. "Come out."

Lisette shook her head and studied her mug.

"Come out, Lisette, and let's go for a walk." Jennifer had on her dark-blue parka, the buttons done up. Her gloves were in her right-hand pocket. Her hair beneath her hat was glossy. Her breath was starting to steam the glass. She wiped away the condensation with her fist.

What was it to move beyond your beliefs? To accept the world wasn't as you understood it? Lisette, her heart whirring, rose and put on her boots, her coat, her hat, her mittens. She didn't know why she did this. She opened the French doors.

They walked down the gravel driveway and Jennifer headed east, toward Peddler Bridge Road. The day was bright—a harsh glare everywhere. "I don't believe you exist."

Jennifer laughed. "That's hardly nice."

"Do you exist?"

"I feel like we're in some bad undergraduate philosophy class. I'm sorry if I arrived early this morning."

"When you said you moved away and came back, where did you go?"

Jennifer shook her head lightly. "It's not worth discussing."

"I want to discuss it."

"I have things I don't wish to talk about either. You of all people should respect that."

They were ascending a road that seemed to wind up forever. Lisette had to squint against the light refracting off the snow, pinpricks of hot white like fireflies that were never directly there.

"Do you think of yourself as having given in to your unhappiness?" Lisette asked.

"I think 'given in' is the wrong way to think about it." Jennifer was watching a chickadee dart among the branches, the fluttering of its small gray wings. "The truth is I don't tell myself stories about myself at all."

"You don't try to make sense of your life?"

"To what end?" She paused before the same path she'd shown Lisette the month before, the faint tracks into the woods, the pines heavy with snow, the boughs bent and creating darkness even amidst all this sparkling brilliance. "Let's walk in the woods. I'm telling you, it's beautiful in there. So quiet."

Lisette again shook her head. She felt faint from lack of sleep, from pushing beyond what she could understand or acquiesce to. She blinked and the world dimmed, flickered into something colorless and muted. Jennifer was made of marble, her eyes were filled with smoke. She was extending her hand, palm up, fingers beckoning. Lisette blinked again and a cardinal flared red in a birch. Jennifer was straightening her hat. All around them an aquamarine sky, the creak of trees. And was this lucidity? Was any of it?

"Let's go in." Jennifer started walking along the path, winding through the trees. She turned and called, "Join me!"

Lisette went in, the twining branches overhead a kind of comfort or horror. Or something else. Or nothing at all.

Millstone Hill

FOR THE HOLIDAYS, they had gone to Karl's parents' house in Charlottesville, and his parents, gracious people, had given her snowshoes, lightweight and modern, because, they'd said, they knew how she liked her tromps through the wilderness. She'd told them the gift was delightful while wondering if Karl had mentioned that this pandemic year she'd been spending a lot of time outdoors.

Now they were home—a nearly twelve-hour drive—and were ill-tempered from being cooped up so long. They'd been reluctant to stop, since the maskless surely lurked at rest stops and restaurants. For her, there was an added discombobulation: as they'd driven north, she'd expected the season to become more fully itself—that they'd leave behind ceaselessly mild Virginia to return to a frigid Vermont. But scarcely more than a dusting covered the ground.

Karl got out of the car and grabbed luggage from the back seat. "I'm too tired to cook. Do you want to just order Chinese?"

She didn't. Her knees were stiff, her neck tense. She wanted, even though it was nine o'clock, to go for a walk. But he'd find that reckless. She couldn't just go wandering the fields at night. And probably she agreed. She inhaled the clean evening air, and they settled on chow fun and shrimp with garlic sauce as they went inside.

In the morning, Karl was putting dishes in the dishwasher. He looked out to the rust-shaded fields, then smiled at her, still at the table with her coffee. "I'm off to make the world safe for democracy," he said. An echo of his father (echoing Woodrow Wilson), who said that when leaving to teach; Karl said it when leaving for his practice. In either instance, a wry acknowledgment of small worldly contributions, although she thought Karl did make the world safer for those he counseled.

"I'll be here when you return," she said, she hoped, lightly.

The quiet after he left became more expansive and more hollow. She went to get her pastels and drawing pad, feeling ashamed that while visiting Karl's parents she'd been glad not to have to face her art each day. Today she'd begin fresh, a new composition based on a photo she'd taken of a local barn in a sun-dappled field. She blocked out the barn and started shading in the tall grass, but soon she'd overworked everything into a green-yellow muddle. No shape, no dimension, no force. She ripped the drawing from the pad and tore the thick, expensive paper into jagged strips, feeling wasteful, ashamed, glad, horrified—so angry at herself for failing. Her palms had started to sweat. Heat had risen to her cheeks. She was tired. They'd driven all day yesterday.

She needed some exercise. She changed into sneakers—no need for boots—and some winter gear, then went outside to turn on her car. She considered the milky air. If anything, it would rain. On her phone, she checked the weather: thirty-seven degrees, which was twenty degrees warmer than it should've been this time of year. The shapeless pandemic days giving way to shapeless seasons felt a doubling of purgatory.

As a kid cross-country skiing during the purest winter months, she'd found in the drifts of white a hard solace. Her lungs would ache to inhale the freezing air, blood would whoosh in her ears. She'd had the sense of being small in open land but moving forward forcefully. Back home, her skin glazed with sweat, she'd peel off her outerwear, then brew tea and sit beside the woodstove. Out the window, the land looked tranquil but it was more electric than that, requiring rough motion to withstand its elements. You could not be soft out in it. You had, in some sense, to battle.

Along Quarry Road, she passed old homes in unbecoming pastels, light blue and beige, then the general store, with its ice machine out front, a Coca-Cola sign above its front porch, before turning onto Barclay Road, likely named for some farmer three generations back, or maybe even a family who'd first quarried here in the 1790s. The road narrowed and turned to dirt. Houses fell away and there were only trees, their branches a high tangle. Where the road ended, she parked: a small semicircle beside a pile of enormous rocks. The granite came from the old quarries, even though the last quarry, at least where the woods stood, had ceased operations over a hundred years before. Now it was so many old-growth maples, spruce, fir, and birch. Brush and bramble that, if you got far enough in, could let you forget civilization was nearby.

Her heart thrummed a little faster. She'd grown up in a different part of the state—in a valley, beside a large lake. And she'd gone away for college, for grad school, to Boston and then Chicago, because the good art programs were there and because she'd wanted to prove to herself she wasn't a bumpkin, that she could exist within clamor and densely arranged space. But her core, her temperament, was rural. Some part of her—likely the best part—mapped an inner landscape of constant fields, of trees in rolling slopes down to the expanse of lake, the mountains blue in the distance.

She decided on a five-mile loop, walking a corridor of ashen and gray-brown tree trunks. Thistle sprouted spiky at the path's edge, as did milkweed, their pods gray husks bent at the stems. Something in her quieted. When she got back, she'd try again with the pastels. She'd take a more delicate approach, not let herself overwork anything or destroy her efforts, even if bad.

The scent was fresh and beautiful but unexpected—cut pine, a waft of Christmas. Swipes of blue appeared across trees—neon paint, slapdash—and then she could see a weird emptiness ahead. She stopped: a tree had fallen across the path—been sawed, actually; the sawdust was everywhere. As she climbed over it, her breath caught in her chest. Acres of tree stumps, branches everywhere. Tree limbs were heaped like bonfires. Across this expanse sat large-scale machines, a phalanx of tractors with large pincers—what they must use to drag felled trees. She started toward the machines, stumbling over the uneven dirt and small branches.

"Lady!" Some guy was climbing down from a tractor, holding a thermos, wearing a hardhat. "We can't have you here."

"What is this?" She felt foolish, her voice high and anxious.

"A town project." He wore a work vest orange with reflective trim, especially garish in the drab landscape. "Once we're done, we'll clean up. We've got signs at the Church Hill Road entrance telling people to walk the trails on the western side of the forest."

"I came in off of Quarry Road."

"You've been walking a while," he said, not unkindly. "I'll tell the boss we need signs at that entrance too."

"I still don't understand. Why are you destroying the woods?"

"We're not." Color rose on his cheeks, and she realized he was young. He began tossing his thermos lightly from one hand to the other. "This is sanctioned logging. We're harvesting timber in accordance with the town's forest management plan. We're making way for new-growth trees."

"You're clear-cutting." She gestured to the alien terrain.

He laughed. "You know the forest is over 380 acres? We're not clear-cutting. We're providing canopy openings."

She didn't know what to say. Her heart skittered. The town couldn't have possibly sanctioned this.

He looked back to the ugly tractors. "Our lunch break is about to finish. We can't have you here while we work."

"How long will you be logging?" She'd last walked here before they'd left for Charlottesville. In under two weeks they'd done all this.

"Through the spring. While the ground is frozen."

"The ground isn't frozen. It's thirty-seven degrees right now."

He smiled blankly. His hard hat read "Sheffield Pulpwood." And if she laughed at the name's silliness? Or wept. She turned back to the trail. Behind her, the motors started up, a clunking and whining that created vibrations traveling her feet and spine. Those machines dragging their bellies across the earth, those rough beasts slouching toward Bethlehem. Once in her car, she stared ahead, not seeing anything, just thinking about that expanse.

Feeling a pressing need to be productive, she drove to the grocery store, then stayed in her car to search her phone for articles about the logging. There were none. Next, she looked up Sheffield Pulpwood, which had no website, although Google showed her a picture of a gray building beside a storage facility. The address was a town east of here. And if she'd found a website? She'd have emailed them a stern note? She put her phone away.

The day's dim light turned the cars in the parking lot dull. Longing stirred in her to be in the museum, in her office, cool and neutrally lit, creating the graphics for a new exhibit. Then she'd visit the installations still up from last March to study how she'd arranged the art, constructed the viewing spaces for visitors. She'd remember she once accomplished things.

Inside, she drifted down the aisles, one among the masked. So many here on a Monday afternoon reassured her. Their jobs had also been put on pause, or they were escaping the tedium of remote work.

She was choosing a chicken to roast when she saw Marjorie clutching a package of steaks. Above her mask, Marjorie brightened about her eyes and wheeled her cart over, asking Carey how the holidays had been. Carey wished she could hug her.

They chatted about their respective Christmases. Marjorie liked staying home with her husband and kids—no pressure to travel since they certainly weren't getting on a plane to visit her or her husband's parent. "My in-laws live in Florida. I can't imagine how they feel safe ever stepping outside. We're lucky we're here." She lowered her voice. "People are more civil."

Carey said she agreed. For the last half year, she'd had this conversation often with acquaintances. Though their numbers had started to creep up around Thanksgiving, overall they'd stayed lower than anywhere else in the country. Had few gotten sick because they'd been taking precautionary measures? Or was this just rural luck and soon their numbers would be bad too? In Charlottesville, more restaurants and stores had been open, more had roamed maskless in the grocery store. In the Harris Teeter near campus, she'd felt ostracized and ostracizing, as if she were overly prim and deserved snide glances. But also: so many selfish and reckless! She'd given them wide berth. In the parking lot, still wearing their masks, they'd been putting groceries in the trunk when a woman in a floral dress had laughed as she'd passed by. "Yankees," she'd said. She must've seen the Vermont plates.

"There's this air of refusal," Carey had said on the drive back. "This need to insist that nothing bad is happening. And we're the problem for suggesting otherwise."

He'd glanced over. "To believe nothing is wrong is easier than feeling hopeless or afraid." Her psychologist husband: this would be how he'd consider it.

At dinner, they'd brought up their experience at the grocery store and Karl's father, a history professor at the university, had suggested people up north being active in protecting themselves was an instance of the Protestant work ethic: New Englanders thought they needed to work for what they had, to earn things—including their health. Maybe Karl's father's theory made sense, she'd thought. Maybe Karl's did too. Also Vermont was comprised of so many small towns: people were more likely to be concerned about their neighbors. But no explanation seemed sufficient to explain people's divergent responses to this diffuse, enormous problem. She pushed her cart aside so a man could get by. "I was just in the town woods this morning," she said.

"Did you see what's happening?"

"Yes! But what *is* happening? It's like a bomb went off. A logger I talked to said they have a contract with the town."

"That's what I've heard too. This is a timber harvest for the greater good, but Jess Sutton told me she literally got lost. She was walking and then, just, poof! No woods."

"It's so ugly," Carey said. "Just pointlessly awful. There must be a way to stop it, or at least curtail it."

"I think that ship has sailed—if the town has a contract, they can't back out." Marjorie gazed at her shopping car. "How's drawing going? You mentioned pastels last time we talked."

Terribly, Carey wanted to say. "I'm picking it up again. I'm out of practice."

"I envy you your focus." Marjorie ran operations and finance for the art museum and claimed she was the boring numbers cruncher among the creatives, but Carey was sure she had a good eye. "All I do is bake so much fucking bread."

They settled on going for a walk next week—out on a dirt road south of campus that wound past a horse farm, the walk they'd taken at lunch before they'd been furloughed and everything had been put on pause.

"There's an article here about the woods." Karl tapped his laptop. He rose to pour himself more coffee, and she came around to look: the local paper said many residents were dismayed by what they'd come upon during their walks. The town was timber harvesting and would receive $27,000 for the wood. The consulting forester who'd put together this plan said there was small economic incentive—they could plant trees that would be more valuable in the future. But mainly they were logging for the forest's health. The forest, almost all old-growth trees, would benefit from having more young forest.

Karl was hovering, reading over her shoulder. He wanted his seat back. "Those pictures don't do it justice," she said, returning to her chair. Two close-up photos showed the fresh stumps but didn't suggest the destruction's scope.

"This could be the difference between theory and practice. I can see the argument that this is being done for the forest's health. The article says they're keeping 80 percent old growth and want 20 percent to be new growth. The money can't be the thing—$27,000 is nothing in a town budget, even one as small as ours." He watched her with his professional gaze, which told her she was revealing how distasteful she found his reasonableness. "Which doesn't discount how terrible it might look in the moment." He glanced at his laptop. "Maybe the logging company is cutting more than it should. Or the forester who drafted this plan hasn't been supervising the project closely enough. But he will now that it's come to light people are unhappy."

"I want it to stop." She spooned yogurt into her mouth, embarrassed by how plaintive she sounded.

He laughed. "The pith of it. I applaud your emotional honesty." He came to kiss her cheek. "There's so much we'd like to have stop right now."

Before he left, he told her he was off to make the world safe for democracy. Before, she'd never minded this silly farewell.

In the pandemic's first six months, Karl had done his client sessions over Zoom, upstairs in the study. She'd stayed downstairs, trying not to make sense of his murmurings, as she was supposed to be focusing on her art, not being a small-town snoop. Then one afternoon he'd come down to tell her he wanted to meet a client in his office. If they stayed masked it could work, but he wanted to run it past her. She'd been surprised—he'd been so adamant about staying home, being distanced. This client had started to weep, he'd explained. He couldn't bear any more Zoom and was going to cancel his sessions until the pandemic ended. This way, the man wouldn't have to shutter his mental-health work just when he needed it the most.

She understood that and suggested he try it out.

It had gone well, and Karl had thought to offer this option to the rest of his clients. Out of twenty, nineteen had said yes—immediately yes. Everyone dying for the chance to get out of the house. She shouldn't begrudge Karl. And yet he got to feel more normal—maybe even more virtuous—while she remained at home without any sense of when she'd return to the museum.

But even worse: this fresh humiliation of discovering her sense of self—artist first, museum preparator second—was false. A decade had slipped by since she'd done her MFA. And she'd been happy. Her job was tactile and active and dealt with situational thinking, creating environments to highlight works. But she hadn't been prioritizing her drawing, always telling herself eventually there'd be more time.

Now her days stretched out in slow, uneasy hours. And everything she drew was terrible. But if she could just submerge herself in the daily practice, the payoff would be immense: the truest part of herself would emerge.

If it existed. So far, all she'd found within herself was this horrifying absence.

She rose to wash dishes and let weak sunlight through the kitchen window warm her cheeks. The citrus-scented suds frothed beneath the hot water, and the refrigerator's hum was its own quiet.

Once done cleaning, she sat again with her pastels. She flipped through print photos she kept on hand, settling on one of the lakes near where she'd grown up—early sunset, pale tangerine sky fading into slate, the water a liquid reflection, a small peninsula shadowed into blackness.

Her proportions were wrong. And the delicate shades had to be saturated yet faded, but she bungled even the basic hues. A vomitous salmon, the stuff of a nursing home's walls, and this cloying, sentimental blue. She ripped out the sheet, bringing it to the sink, running the water and watching the colors melt, this ugly blurring. She balled up the sodden mush and threw it in the trash, her hands slimy with navy and orange.

She wanted to read more about the logging anyway. She sat with her laptop: the reporter had linked to the town's forest management report. One hundred seventy-seven pages, a shocking length, with ten appendices and six maps. She'd read it straight through. She'd sit here all day until she understood what had gone wrong.

The writing was circuitous, repetitive. It stressed how good the forest was—its walking paths, its natural beauty, its habitat for bobcats and bears, for barred owls and otters—while discussing the town's partnership with the Vermont Land Trust to preserve the woods in perpetuity. Conservation was a key talking point. As was "selective timber harvests under a forester's supervision." The harvests would create that 80/20 balance Karl had pointed out, a mix of "mid–late successional forest" and "regenerating forest." The harvesting would maintain a continuous canopy. It would not disturb the trails. It would minimize the use of harvesting machinery near the trails. It would minimize woody debris and slash in these areas.

She took notes on the passages where the rules set out were not being adhered to, thinking she could bring this to the selectboard's attention. Then she read a "mixed forest habitat" would be good for songbirds: the hermit thrush, the wood thrush, the black-throated blue warbler, the yellow-bellied sapsucker, the winter wren. This beautiful list, so unrelated to the ruined land.

She rose to make tea, watching the kettle warm until steam poured from its spout and a warning cry rose from its belly. The tea was floral and too hot. She sipped it anyway, trying to collect her thoughts. The forester seemed well intended but overzealous, too focused on the abstract balance needed to create an ideal forest without considering the literal effects of achieving it. The selectboard, faced with reading this long, dense report, probably had only skimmed it and then deferred to the forester's expertise. The logging company, she suspected, was taking advantage of the geeky forester, the naïve selectboard, and taking more trees than agreed to. And using sloppy, cheap methods to harvest them, as those at Sheffield Pulpwood were betting, at least in the short term, they could get away with.

Guesses, hazy theories. But trying to understand why things were happening—wherefore people's actions and motivations—felt beside the point. Reasons didn't matter when the events themselves were so consistently unreasonable.

In the study, in a storage chest, she kept a pair of birding binoculars. Another of Karl's parents' gifts. She packed them in a backpack along with a hat, mittens, water bottle. And she set out for the woods.

Signs were now nailed to trees telling people the trails from this entrance were closed until April. She started out on her normal route but then veered west toward Millstone Hill. The elevation climbed as the path skirted a quarry lake—the striated cliffs of gray and black granite tiering down to bottle-green water. It was stark, surreal, even a little lurid. Past the abandoned quarry, the path wound around an immense pile of old mined granite. It was a hill of rocks, many mossed over, surrounded by birch. Putting on gloves with good grip, she began to climb. The hill was at least twice as tall as a house, and steep. Sweat dampened her neck, and she focused on finding stable footholds. The moss suggested long stillness but was also soft and slippery.

At the top, she faced southeast into a light wind. Just as she'd thought: in the distance, she could see the loggers in the denuded space they'd created. She watched with the binoculars. The graveyard of branches, the wide rutted tracks in the dirt. Tractors with pincers hauled tree trunks into a loose pyramid. Other machines pushed the left-behind branches into piles. Men in hard hats used chainsaws to strip branches from the freshly fallen trees. They piled those discarded branches onto a trailer attached to a tractor. In one area they were cutting. Those monster pincers would grip a trunk, then a saw would slice through at the bottom. The tractor would lift the tree and drive it to be shorn of its branches. The tops of pines shook.

As the afternoon waned, she climbed down, stiff and bruised and cold from hours sitting still. The light would fall fast and she didn't want to be on the trails in the dark.

· · ·

She returned the next day and the next to watch the clearing grow wider. Her back grew sore, her skin clammy and cool as she kept her vigil. A new machine had a dangling claw attachment that wavered in the air, the trunk it held rocking like a rough pendulum. The men climbed in and out of machines; with zeal, they waved their arms in large arcs to other men, who'd then clamber down for some huddled discussion, their arms folded. She'd waste her mornings, pretending she was going to draw and then spending less than a half an hour on it before giving up, anger darkening her heart at her limitations. Then she'd pack herself a lunch, a thermos of tea, a heated seat cushion and hot-water bottle, and set out. The walk took an hour. She'd be at the top of the granite heap as the loggers were finishing their lunch break. She stayed as long as the light held, giving herself a head start to return by twilight. Coming out of the woods, she felt she might be some wild creature, twigs in her matted fur, her eyes in a feral glaze. This process of returning to herself was slow. At home she'd shower, then carefully apply moisturizer, lip balm, and hand cream. She'd comb out her tangled hair, apply mascara and lipstick. She'd cook, simmering and dicing and stewing, inhabiting domesticity so when Karl came home he wouldn't sense her new wildness.

But probably she overestimated her ability to keep herself hidden from him. "You're looking a little pale," he said the third night. They were on the couch watching Netflix.

"I've been sleeping poorly." This was true. For the past few nights, she'd been dreaming of being pursued through the woods, chased as she flailed through dense foliage, unsure what she was running from or toward, everything tangled and immediate and dark.

He put his arm around her, and she rested her head against his chest. Calm flickered in her, and with it a whisper of perspective: she was being strange. She should stop giving in to the lure of witnessing the hole in the forest's heart grow.

· · ·

At breakfast, Karl mentioned another article about the logging. Some members of the community had started a petition. He turned his laptop to show her. "You could sign it."

"And then what?" She was buttering her toast. "They take the petition to the selectboard? Who will do nothing except explain the town has a contract with these loggers, that both the forester and the Vermont Land Trust have already vetted this project? That they appreciate our concern but are already committed to destroying the woods for the good of the fucking woods?"

He studied her, then looked away, moving his laptop back toward his coffee mug.

"I'm tired," she said. "I'm sorry. But this is a problem without a solution."

He started discussing a list he'd looked at online, the top twenty-five articles *The New Yorker* had published the last year. An interview with Fran Lebowitz, an article about some Iranian operative reshaping the Middle East. Not all about the pandemic, he said, which he found hopeful. The great world kept on spinning, etc.

She understood. He was contextualizing the logging as one issue among a whole world of news and happenings. He was also deciding how to coax her into describing her current frustrations and sorrows, to thereby help her make her feelings more manageable. He was being good to her when she really didn't deserve it.

Maybe, she said, she'd catch up on *The New Yorker* articles today. Also, she'd been thinking of making a cassoulet. This afternoon she'd pick up a bottle of his favorite cabernet to go with it. He brightened and kissed her forehead and murmured he hoped she had a good day.

She could manage him too, she thought after he left. He meant well, but she didn't feel like being persuaded to be rational.

She looked at the petition, seeing her thinking reaffirmed. The wide clearing, the destroyed paths, the strewn debris: the forest management report had clearly stated they shouldn't happen. "Our town is obliterating our beautiful forest for the cost of a new car," it said, and asked the selectboard to stop clearing any more trees. The man who'd started the petition had also begun a Reddit conversation, which had immediately turned rancorous. One commented on the "shortsighted handwringers" who understood nothing about forest conservation. Another said those signing the petition must also be in favor of declining biodiversity—because that's what happened in late-succession forests. Those signing must hate songbirds. One said she knew responsible logging and this was *not* responsible logging. It was a travesty what was happening as people stood passively by. And ridiculous that during a pandemic the town had signed off on something it clearly had no bandwidth to manage.

Carey pressed her index fingers to her temples and closed her eyes.

When she left for the woods, she was glad to discover a cold snap and dense low clouds. She checked her phone. Snow was predicted this evening. The walk felt more invigorating for the chill. Above her, pine boughs spread a feathery green and the mildewing leaves at her feet had turned more fragile and crisp. She was just passing the quarry lake when she came upon an older man walking with hiking sticks. He raised his hand more in acknowledgment than greeting. She said hello and then lingered by the granite, feeling silly because she didn't want to be caught doing whatever it was she was doing.

Once he'd disappeared, she climbed up and settled on a granite slab, her backpack beside her, her binoculars raised. The tremors of machines and trees: it was a constant quaking, a hum, if silent from this distance. A tractor with an attached trailer was hauling logs down a forested corridor. The land, pocked with stumps and ugly with slash, had to be at least ten acres. As had continued to happen, a stupor overtook her as she bore witness.

Two men were studying a map or blueprint, their hard hats tipped down. They looked east, and one gestured to a tractor, which rolled slowly toward them. The man driving it stepped down and conferred with the two men, then got back in and drove to the clearing's eastern edge. He started felling a tree, the pincers grabbing its trunk, then sawing close to its roots. After driving the tree to the felled pile, he returned and cut down another. And another. He was creating a path, she realized. Not eating outward at the edges as the rest were. They were preparing to log elsewhere. The forest management report had delineated the different areas, but at that point in her reading, she'd been skimming, overwhelmed by all the information. Wherever they were going, she'd not have the same view. She didn't know if they'd be near any trails or miles away, too far for her to trek in and out each day. Even with the cold, beads of sweat gathered at her upper lip.

The snow started falling early, right when she needed to think about leaving. The flakes were large and dry and crystalline, accumulating on her jacket, her mittens. They dissolved on her cheeks, a stinging cold. If she continued sitting here, the snow would bury her. She'd film over in ice and become one among these rocks. And that woke her. She stood and dusted herself off. She climbed down carefully since snow was blanketing the granite, making it difficult to determine where the ledges were, how thick the moss. She looked up: like fireflies, white movement there and gone. Her walk back, the pine boughs hung heavy and fairy-tale iced. Once in the car, she blasted the heat. She was shaking with adrenaline, with some surge to act. In the rearview mirror, she saw her cheeks were mottled, enflamed, and her hair was in matted dark clumps. She drove back in the deepening dusk.

At home, she had to plan. Karl would be home around 5:30. She dashed him off a note. A last-minute invite to have outdoor cocktails with Marjorie in Marjorie's backyard. There were leftovers in the fridge for dinner. She was sorry about the cassoulet and wine—they'd have it tomorrow instead.

She tapped the pen against the notepad. She needed to give herself more time. She and Marjorie might even have a masked movie night afterward. He couldn't object to that, although he'd think it strange, since she'd done nothing like this during the pandemic.

She took off her damp clothes and put on fresh jeans, a turtleneck, a sweater. She put on her snow pants and parka. She packed a dry hat and mittens in Karl's backpack. In the kitchen she wrapped a fancy butcher's knife, gleaming and sharp, in two tea towels, then poured sugar into large Tupperware bins, snapping down the lids. In the garage, she took their largest hammer and two wrenches. What else? She didn't know. This would have to do.

The snowshoes sat on an old side table. They looked like mini maroon canoes. She'd been planning to cross-country ski, but she'd try these out and almost laughed imagining telling Karl's parents how useful she found them. They went into the back seat, along with the backpack. The roads weren't clear, and the snowfall was thick, the opaque glow of streetlamps illuminating the heavy flakes, but the storm brought its own hush. Her tires cut the first tracks on Barclay Road, her windshield wipers' fast arcs letting her see just far enough ahead. She parked and turned off her headlights, and the world leapt into blackened dimension, the forest receding into stygian gloom but the nearby branches dusted white. She put on her snowshoes and lifted her parka's hood. She settled the backpack onto her shoulders and headed in.

The snowshoes were light and gave her balance atop the snow. Tree branches creaked as they shifted and her snow pants whispered as the synthetic material bunched and lengthened with her stride. The snow provided pearlescent light. She searched for movement—foxes or owls or voles—but only encountered stillness. She felt alone.

When she came into the clearing, she inhaled. From beneath the snow, the tree stumps jutted like gravestones. As if she were in a massive amphitheater of the dead.

As she'd assumed, the equipment remained. The tractors were parked in rows and covered in weighted tarps. The snow coming down fast on her, she crossed the clearing. She felt small and she felt mighty. She'd shed her torpor and now she'd act. This action would be clean. It'd not be muddled by hypotheticals and second-guesses and confusion and contrasting opinions and helplessness. She'd display a brutal composure in keeping with the woods itself.

Next to one tractor, she took off her snowshoes. From her backpack, she took the knife and throwing back her arm, she brought it down on a ridged tractor wheel. Her shoulder jolted, reverberated, and heat shot down her elbow. Dropping the knife, she clutched her arm, trying to will the pain to subside. Then she tried to wedge the knife into the rubber, to start a leak, but she couldn't even create a nick. She rummaged for the wrenches and climbed onto the machine's side, searching for bolts to loosen, but some she couldn't reach and those she could were all too big for the wrenches she'd brought.

She retrieved the Tupperware container, circling the machine, looking for the gas tank. A story her father had told her: when he was growing up, a farmer down the road had gotten so mad at another man who'd been hunting on his property without permission, the farmer had gone to the man's house in the night, pouring sugar into the gas tank of the man's tractor, thereby ruining it. She struggled to push aside the tarp and finally found the tank on the back, but some mechanism needed to spring open a small door for her to get to it. She climbed onto the stepping ledge to get into the main cabin, but the cabin was locked. She went down and grabbed the hammer. Back up, she banged on the cabin's plastic windows—too thick to warp or crack or bend even though she was wailing on them, slamming the hammer as hard as she could, when her grasp slipped and the hammer clunked down the machine's side, sinking into the snow. She was cursing, yelling. She pummeled the cabin door with her fists until she thought her fingers might break. Her knuckles were bloodying—the seeping heat and violent throbbing. Snow had gotten beneath her parka's hood, and the wet icy slide of it down her neck made her weep. She felt out of body. She was the snowfall and the rutted ground beneath, she was this ruin.

The snow—it was feathery on her cheeks. Her limbs returned. Her chest was in ragged rise and fall. She was crouched against the tractor wheel, huddled as if it would provide shelter.

What had she thought she'd accomplish? Why had she thought to try? Her fatigue was such bodily heaviness, and while of course she'd get back, return home, remember herself, her better self, her best—verdant and rich with light—these things all seemed so far off.

ACKNOWLEDGMENTS

THANK YOU TO Tony Marra for choosing this book and to the staff at the University of Iowa Press. I'm grateful, too, to Kiele Raymond, who has championed my work and read it with such attentiveness, and to Michelle Latiolais and Ron Carlson, whose advice I'm always carrying with me as I write.

Some of these stories first found homes at literary journals, and I'm really thankful to Mark Drew at the *Gettysburg Review*, Richard Hermes at *Grist*, Anthony Varallo at *Crazyhorse*, Bradford Morrow at *Conjunctions*, Michael Nye at *Story*, and Ronald Spatz at the *Alaska Quarterly Review*.

My talented, supportive friends have been so good to help me along the way. Thank you to Karin Gottshall, Greg November, Ernest McLeod, Hugh Coyle, Carey Bass, Miciah Bay Gault, and Jamie Figueroa.

My thanks to the East Middlebury Historical Society and the Ripton Historical Society.

I've had the support of the Bread Loaf Writers' Conference, and I'm especially grateful to Michael Collier for letting me become part of such a wonderful community.

I'm so glad for Presley and Hubbard, who have my heart. (Hi, guys! I love you!) And to my family, who have been unwavering in believing I could do this.

Christian Felt
The Lightning Jar
James Fetler
Impossible Appetites
Starkey Flythe Jr.
Lent: The Slow Fast
Kathleen Founds
*When Mystical Creatures
Attack!*
Sohrab Homi Fracis
*Ticket to Minto: Stories of
India and America*
H. E. Francis
The Itinerary of Beggars
Abby Frucht
Fruit of the Month
Tereze Glück
*May You Live in
Interesting Times*
Ivy Goodman
Heart Failure
Barbara Hamby
Lester Higata's 20th Century
Edward Hamlin
*Night in Erg Chebbi and
Other Stories*
Ann Harleman
Happiness
Elizabeth Harris
The Ant Generator
Ryan Harty
*Bring Me Your Saddest
Arizona*

Charles Haverty
Excommunicados
Mary Hedin
*Fly Away Home: Eighteen
Short Stories*
Beth Helms
American Wives
Jim Henry
*Thank You for Being
Concerned and Sensitive*
Allegra Hyde
Of This New World
Matthew Lansburgh
Outside Is the Ocean
Lisa Lenzo
Within the Lighted City
Kathryn Ma
*All That Work and Still
No Boys*
Renée Manfredi
Where Love Leaves Us
Susan Onthank Mates
The Good Doctor
John McNally
Troublemakers
Molly McNett
One Dog Happy
Tessa Mellas
Lungs Full of Noise
Kate Milliken
If I'd Known You Were Coming
Kevin Moffett
Permanent Visitors